I0764424

The Beach

Also by John Fraser and published by AESOP Modern Fiction:

Animal Tales
Behaving Well
Best Friends
Black Masks
Blue Light / Starting Over
The Case
Confessions
The Cure
Down from the Stars
The Ends of the Earth
Enterprising Women
Exploring the Clouds
Fake Fur
The Future's Coming Everywhere
Happy Always
Hard Places
An Illusion of Sun
The Magnificent Wurlitzer
Medusa
Military Roads
The Observatory
The Other Shore
People You Will Never Meet
The Red Bird
The Red Tank
Runners
'S'
Short Lives
Sisters
Soft Landing
The Storm
Strangers and Refugees
The Test
Thinking Scientifically
Thirty Years
Three Beauties
Tomorrow the Victory
Unsteady States, Vol. I
Wayfaring
Wisdom

The Beach

John Fraser

AESOP Modern Fiction
Oxford

AESOP Modern Fiction
An imprint of AESOP Publications
Martin Noble Editorial / AESOP
28a Abberbury Road, Oxford OX4 4ES, UK
www.aesopbooks.com

First edition published by AESOP Publications

www.johnfraserfiction.com

A catalogue record of this book is available from the British Library.

First edition 2023

ISBN: 978-1-914938-24-5

CONTENTS

The Beach

THE BEACH gets smaller, the waves higher. The tide urges. We two are alone, cut off – desperate, I turn to her – she's slight and terrified – the sea will hammer us against the rocks – 'I don't swim strong,' I say. Fearful and lucid, too aware of death.

'I can't carry you,' she says. 'You'll have to save me.'

The wind screams in our hair. The water covers us – I lift her high, over my head, the sea submerges me, pulls and twists – but here we are! Around the point – another beach, still dry. I land her, like an Aphrodite. A juicy sea-fruit on a shell ... cockle-shells, I think, and giggle.

A pretty maid and silver bells ... down among the dead men, the wrecks all in a row, the captains sleeping, the semi-precious *matelots*, unfathomable – pearl-fishers hooking out their eyes....

'What's the joke?' she asks, still in panic, angry too ... briefly saved from nature, that bitch inescapable....

'Relief,' I say. Who knows?

She's well-tended, a silvery belle, out of my league, even if she gives the fairy's kiss in gratitude. 'Tasha' her name, on a label round her neck, like a port.

We watch a screen in an arcade. There's no one else. 'Look!' she says. 'The money!'

It's true – the value's dropping, like sand dropping through the hourglass. No explanation's being given.... 'The cash!' she shouts, 'It's going! Where?'

'No one can tell, it seems. A panic,' I say. 'I don't have cash, but this means there will be no jobs.... It isn't sand; it's the future running out.'

She's been hit hard. There's no one round, she cries, quiet – 'The people,' she says. 'They've all been carted off, they all had that sickness we didn't know we had until they told us afterwards.'

'I used to be quite critical,' I say. 'Wanting novelty, a change. Now we hope in any way we'll carry on. Look at the sea....'

It's tall as houses, full of struggling things.

*

'Don't try making out with me,' she says. 'I'm wooing someone really old – it's very hard....'

'I don't think of it,' I say. 'I've given up. My friend was sleeping over, when she was with me, with all her exes. It's stupid, but when I found out, I was quite disturbed....'

'Yes,' she says. 'It's stupid. There's no sense in ranking people by their intimacy, or your sense of competition....'

'The guy you're striving for,' I ask, 'Was the money his or yours?'

'Oh,' she says. 'He's a magician. He can make it multiply on sight....'

'I saved your life,' I say. 'What is it worth to you?'

'Oh,' she says. 'I fly high, much higher than you can. You want a gift? Here, there's nothing we can buy. I'd sing, but I can't hold a note.'

'Let's just expose our deepest thoughts,' I say. 'Our convictions. We'll remember those.'

*

'It's evolutionary,' she says. 'Why are there so many people without much, without enough? It's because economies are based on games. Sport, especially, it's a competition. Not just white goods and houses – it's health, rockets to the moon, car races and songsters. Competition – at tennis, in orchestras, in vaccinations. In movies and in pop ditties. Even in millionaires. Things getting smaller, cheaper, more fashionable, robots to do the work and clean, intelligent bombs, new forests, cute animals saved and housed. It's countries again – this time, dressed for the races, who wins, who gets there first, so all the rest must run, compete to cross the same, the finish, line.

'There's handicaps – old relatives to carry on your back, bad coaches, rickety legs. There's threats, and no charm to pull you through and win – so, try tattoos and agents.... They won't work – so cheat and bribe. That often works. Go to war – but against someone, something, different. New sport, new skills, new drills. A civil war means you come in last ... wearing your basalt trainers.'

'This is a last stage, then,' I say. 'There's been late cap, now the universal games. There was no socialism, no stage we've somehow missed. Nationalise or privatise. Try what you hadn't tried before. Foreigners? Let the good runners in, the rest, unless they do the dirty work – you keep them out. It's countries that compete, and somehow they must be differentiated. The flag, the anthem....'

'You must go further,' she says. 'The world's a stadium. There's the runners and jumpers, the lifters and the wrestlers. We watch, participate, Mexican waves, derision, weeping and cheering. Sometimes we compete. I have the cash you need, to qualify, then there's the squad, the coaches, deals, publicity....

'Stadiums never disappear – the Greeks had them, you go see them still. They resist more than temples.... They're not about survival – they're about playing games, winning; losing with a crooked smile. Fixing and training, exchanging players, cutting out the dodgy passports and the druggies.... All's striving, up to a point until you go outside or under the curve, and see – there's beating and killing, and the great mass of the unticketed, trying to get in, to figure out what's happening from the cheers and sneers.... The champions – they can do anything – poison competitors, put grenades in their lockers, have them banned....'

'Those arenas,' I say. 'They use them as refuges too. Or, like the Vélodrome – as camps, for shipments, deportations. Like Chile.... Long ago, of course.'

*

'A whole chain of stone-gatherers,' I say. 'Drowned. Where we were. They gather stones to border flowerbeds. They have hods on their backs – those bore them down.'

'I didn't hear them,' says Tasha, unbelieving.

'They work quiet, their trade is quiet, they saw the bay fill with water, with no way out. Go quiet or noisy,' I say. 'It is much the same. The sea roars when it reaches its end, drowns you out.'

'While you were beneath the waves,' she asks, 'You wanted to see nothing, no one more to save.... Just me?'

'Sometimes a single wave comes ashore, absorbs a town....' I say. 'Thousands drown, without a hand to grasp.'

'What's a life worth?' she asks. 'Or a fortune? What do we owe, what do we pay?'

'I know,' I say. 'In each case – it's nothing. A life has value, but no price. Maybe for a quantity, there'd be a sum? You'd be paid for a book on the history of space, and nothing for a snap of sky.... The same with time. A history of duration fascinates – the last second was a bore. Money too – it gives you privileges, but no rights. You're on a pair of melting skates – what will disintegrate first, the ice, or you?'

'No doubt you're right,' she says. 'It looks like you waste your life thinking of such things, Olbek. But as it went, your saving me brings no return. If you had been a jolly tar – it would have been a laugh, a whirl. But as it is....

'What I can't swallow, is – my life, like spume ... wind-blown. Or better, you pick it up, out of these waves, flotsam.... I'm just a totem, like those things they put on ships for luck, and they survived when all the crew went down....'

'A figurehead,' I say.

'Yes, one of those. A useless bit of ship, that swims to shore, survives,' she says. 'All of the ship that's left. its luck, its token; past. The only useless bit, surviving, half a woman cast up. Wooden, damaged, among the kelp. The magic of a pair of tits. She is a survivors' tree, dead generations on each branch. Ancestors you never knew and never will.

'Women existed for millennia before there were men. They invented men for fantasy, to do the dirty jobs, to swear and fart, lift and dig; we made life easy for them – emotions stuck on outside like pricks, sex made simple – just masturbate, forget it. No sweat. And then, time passes, as it will, and here you are, people who lift you up, saving lives and wanting a reward, like dogs....'

'Well,' I say. 'I got nothing. And I'm wet.'

'You'll dry,' she says. 'The sun will see to that. It's big and hot, bigger, hotter than it's ever been. And you can bet – the deeper you think you get, you'll find it's been said since the start of everything, when there were just two rivers on the earth, the Amur and Euphrates, all the rest to come. Everything about us has been known since the first day – even if the first day took a billion years, like the holy writings say. It took its time. In fact, time was invented for the second day, and on – there'd been no need for time before, you did what must be done – no closing times, no lie-ins, and no lies. Time, death and lineage. Inventions ... suggesting there was change and solidarity and consciousness and conscience that grew from experience ... quite untrue. People! Androids are nothing, compared to those. Inventors, mass producers, self-improvers, up to their necks in fantasy.

'You rant about the rich, the poor – it's not correct. That's cash, not people. It circulates without an end or reason. Inequality of the tiniest degree determines who will rise and who will fall, who is inert, and who is prancing through the trees with scarlet ribbons in her hair....

'And so, Olbek, you lift me up and save me – and I owe you for it! The deeper that you think, the more banal it is; the longer that we last – the lighter that we get. The sea goes high and higher, I'm light as a gull, there's thousands on the cliffs, all saved, a million voices talking of deep things, all lighter than the air.'

*

'There's where they sell pistachio *granita*, Tasha. Or there might be whelks,' I say, pointing and gesturing.

'It's all closed up,' she says, despondently. 'Out of season. It's tempest time.'

'Anyway,' I say. 'I agree. Deep is banal. It's not about what life is worth, or why we have one. Only one. The question is "how are we here?" and since we all know that, we have the answer to everything.'

'Very smart,' she says. 'You're so smart, now I've lost all my money, I could wait till you get lots, and then take yours. Not all of it, of course.'

'You remind me of the movie, Boudu saved from drowning,' I say, '– the hobo who takes over, enslaves, the bourgeoisie who rescued him. I wonder – was that a warning not to save poor people you don't know? Completely, a French take on things....'

'It's simpler if we forget the movies, and say "we're all androids",' Tasha says. 'Actors play all those parts in movies and they don't look a bit like us, don't talk like us, have sex or eat like us. There's the proof if you need it. Actors are us, and they are androids. That's the clinch.'

'I'm with you there,' I say. 'All you say sounds true.'

'That's not a compliment,' she says. 'And what were you doing on the beach? Hoping you could save someone? Trying to drown yourself?'

'More or less,' I say.

'You don't seem to know much,' she says. 'You could be my pupil.'

'I don't think so, Tasha,' I say. 'You're too fey.'

'Fey. Fey,' she says, trying out the word, perhaps the sense.

'That might be my slant.'

'I think it is,' I say. 'I like to know where I'm going, before I get there.'

'But you didn't,' she says.

'Sometimes,' I say. 'I don't care. But I'm not uninterested in destinations.'

She laughs. 'That's genius,' she says. 'The best thing you will ever say.'

I understand her perfectly. Like her, I want to be the only person, maybe perfect, first and last in the world, making my stories, planning and accounting. If there's only one of you, though, it's hard to say you're perfect.

I'm not vain. I could have drowned – all I assert is conditional. There is no check, no brake. No procedure that slows you down.

'Let's go where there's people, Tasha, get a drink,' I say, and guide her, take her arm.

The drink tastes like codeine. We're very cold. Too much of anything will kill you. They're expensive, the drinks. Tasha doesn't touch hers.

I say, 'I'm not paranoid at all. Except – if you take things seriously, not just grumbling and sounding off, but being militant, front line – they'll kill you, jail you – maybe even worse, they'll frame you. If they don't cast you down for standing up for someone – they'll set you up. A sex charge, harassing ... or peeping.'

'They're almost always true,' she says. 'But of course, if it was you, Olbek, you're transparent. Anything against you – it would be a stitch-up. Only I'd believe you, though. I know your sort – you won't get far with being in the right. It upsets people, that approach. They'll get you down so they can kick you more effectively.'

'Yes, Tasha, that's exactly what I said,' I say.

I buy another round. Tasha pours her first drink on the ground, stares at the fresh one, morose.

'Saving me,' she says. 'Must have given you the taste. You want the quantity....'

'It's Pascal – when in doubt, spit for luck – you never know,' I say. 'It's not about the species in itself – it's that the person that you save may have a clue to everything you hadn't guessed. Letting them go, drop – it might screw history for years....'

'People in danger,' Tasha says, looking hurt, 'Are either moribund or want to play at football.'

'I've only thought of this, my life's work, in the last hour or so,' I say. 'It's the unknown. I want to cheat the certain end.

There is this guy, a metre from the execution yard, or hanging by a thumb. The end – is more than nigh. It's fully scripted, the curtain's poised, the diva's bouquet waiting in the wings. And – I intervene. I stop the show, turn the inevitable into the unknown. I transform the end.'

'That's good,' says Tasha. 'It's a little raw. Self-regarding – but it shows you're striving high.... You believe in a second chance. I watch the first flight – if it doesn't succeed, the goose is cooked, the chick smashes on the rocks.'

'You'll settle for the paradox, then, Tasha,' I ask her. 'You're saved. Your second chance. And I saved someone with no qualification. No consistency.'

'It's your new trade, your hobby. Salvation,' Tasha says, looking miserable, 'You must get used to disappointment.'

'You're right, Tasha,' I say, illuminated – 'Life runs along beside us – when we are lyrical, it's an ogre. When we are sombre, it's a clown. When we are comforted, it kills our dog. We laugh – it cries. It's pointless being disappointed – in anything at all. Life is there always, our twin, we exchange the masks continually – tragedy and comedy. And in the end – our shadow kills us. That's what the old civilisations said....'

'That's what civilisation is,' says Tasha. 'Our good and evil, the opposite of whatever we want to be. And then it's gone, over, and why not. It's not alive, it never was. Disappointment? It's always there, running along beside us, like the wolves and the sleigh. It makes no difference, if you fall off – disappointment comes foretold, included in the package tour. You'd be disappointed if there were no wolves.'

'You're unhappy I saved you. We could do it over – change roles,' I say. 'You save me, and there's an end to it.'

This, we do. Not in reality, in case it all goes wrong, both drowned – but if there's someone, something, watching, planned it all – it's done. It could even be Pascal up there, down there....

'I'm satisfied,' says Tasha. 'We know how things get done, the mechanism, to make it flow, keep the drama, all the twists.'

*

'Do you feel a weight, from what we've done?' I ask. 'It's what the stay-ropes holding a balloon must feel when it's about to rise. It feels like lightness, skies and air.'

'I don't feel what you say,' she says.

'It's doing the right things when there's no need to, and no visible effect,' I say.

'If that's not fey,' she says. 'I don't know what fey is.'

We leave it there.

*

Scratch the soil anywhere – there's magic revealed. Emptiness. When you blow on your hand, clenched on the hoe, the coloured flags appear, a string of them. Enough for a parade. Ensigns of empires. Priest-kings, their many arms holding the skull, the goat, the sceptre and the spliff ... warriors to defend the god-king's bloody family tree. Death the magician ... the conjurer.... The old religion, hidden a centimetre below the scene we all see, the landscape, the asphalt, the sand that blows, revealing other sand.... The real world we all stand on, it's a skin that covers up the magic....

Travel round – there's an army of people who hope you'll save them – no sand, no waves, no beach, just save them. Every moment there's a thousand people saved ... by working blind, taking a slice of time, a sack of something from a truck, planting a seed. Nonetheless – they still want to be saved, over and over ... not to mention those who've given up or never started. All hoping for salvation. It should be easy now – everyone is huddled up together, the space is sandy hot and urgent, the waves are nearer – much easier to save a person – everyone can save, be saved.

Tasha is the only person I have saved. It's my character – I'm too trusting, too generous – a life! Risked for someone I don't know, who might have wanted, believed, committed anything at all, in a life I knew nothing of, dark and intricate....

Tasha said, 'I was too trusting. You, Olbek, an unknown, entrusted with my life. I'm must have been quite crazy....'

She said, 'Not magic, Olbek. Mescalin. That's what you need to take you there, under the surface.'

Those are delicate thoughts, considering where I am right now.

*

'Decide, my friend!' the boatman shouts. 'Here!' I say. 'I'll get off here.'

'As you wish,' he says. 'We all must choose a side. This is a side, rivers only have two – but if you teach, you should get off where there's kids.'

'Oh no!' I say. 'I can't teach. Not the scoured-out empty pans. There's no understanding between the young and me. I'm an educational fixer. A mechanic, a doctor of last gasps. It's not just the young who have to learn. They know much more than me or you – but don't do anything. The older guys – they're the ones who do the stuff, and so – it seems they need the books, the people – like me – who can classify, can sort them out, can keep a jump ahead.... Teach them what they don't know exists, what no one knows. Or there'd be no point.'

The boatman grins. He poles me near the bank. I spot some shaven heads, some grey locks, spreading bellies – those look more like my charges....

'The children,' I tell the tar – 'They go to school, and learn what I have long forgot. These are my guys ... they need to be saved....'

*

The headman, Oskar, looks resentful and contrite. 'We asked for you,' he says. 'More as a kind of joke. You are a luxury.... We have a need, but not a space, for you....'

'Oh,' I say. 'To me, a hut is more than good. It's culture. I'm a sponge – I absorb, distil, and then ... think pulque and mescal.'

'It's true,' says Oskar. 'A hut would suit. But here, you'd need to draw a perfect circle freehand as a floor. On the circle stands the hut, the circle's insubstantial, no one can manage it, certainly not you.

'The mature learners here, they're all moderns. Moderns who've been confused, and fallen from a metaphor into paradox. They had designed the new, and hankered for tradition; chose the wrong side, expenditure instead of profit, open relationships and open mouths when all should be kept shut.... Or turn and turn about. Some are pirates who reformed. Some are preachers, turned to robbing banks.

'They tremble, Olbek. The fear, the shakes. No one draws the foundation so's you can build a hut. You can't bunk down with them – the teacher must live separate and chaste. They believe in hugger-muggering, each tries to convert the rest – and in my own view....' He bends down, lets out sweet breath – 'I believe their problem is their ignorance. They need to start again. They can't find ignorance enough to recommence. That's why you're here. Teach ignorance, my friend!

'They all landed here, beside this hydra-headed river, a vastness of a delta, an omega, a Volga or a Danube ... a river also that can disappear, an Amu-Darya. A chameleon, a

Colorado. Or a drain, a Madre de Dios. Water, Olbek,' he says, focussing his smoked-fish eyes, 'Water has no edge, no cut, no judgement – just a destination and a power. Your students have that quality, my friend. They cannot draw, they cannot hold the pointed stick. They flow. Each mind has body, like a snake, a *Geist*, the spirit of the age.... "The snake you see a-writhe in fires....'"

'Salamanders,' I interrupt.

'All different, all fluid and convinced, opinionated, stubborn....' he says. 'A penal colony for me. And every one of them thinks they have never been so free....'

I interrupt again. 'I could make do with that shack,' I say, and point. He shrugs.

'It's for a boat,' he says. 'The boatman has the only one that's authorized....'

I take my case, unpack it there. I should have asked – 'Oskar, is there a result? A progress you expect from me? Must each one think originally, or all agree on procedures, what colours are, how to pronounce their words? And what do we believe?'

*

I'm peripatetic, that's for sure. I wander up and down – there's men and women of a certain age, I'm sure that when they see me, they sidle behind a tree, or sneak down to the mangroves, and submerge.

They've tried dialectics, rhetoric too – those are spent candles. The other trick the ancients had – a symposium! Food as reward for listening. When do we eat? I ask myself. And where?

What is teaching for, I ask myself, over and over, feeling the question like a third hand forever nestled in my pocket, turning over my small change ... no one knows, but we all do it, try; the old ones know we have to wind our tails just so and so to stop us falling out of trees.... It may not work, but that is social life....

And knowledge! – aha! the faith, the discipline, the free for all, catch as catch can – the certainty? Or does the certainty lie in – doubt?

Teach ignorance, Oskar says. That is salvation. From what? Tasha's long gone, since we shared our destinies, both ignorant as stones.

Stones evolving from the sand and kelp. Or vice versa.

'I hear you muttering,' says a short man, Valentin. 'Oskar must have meant "profess ignorance", or "identify, describe, it". Not teach it.'

'You're making bread, my friend,' I say, off-balance. 'Throwing everything in the bowl.

'Teaching is all those things. And more. Think ping-pong – all players have the same rules, my shot to you's a function of your shot to me....'

'What we need,' says Valentin, 'Is peyote buffet. It will bring us all together, together we shall all forget.'

'And will our ignorance be all the same?' I ask, much disturbed. 'I think it won't. We'll each have different monsters in our head....'

'Some will be pedigreed,' says Valentin, 'Some we can roast, and some will lead us to the fairy grove.

'Oskar meant – create emptiness. A flat surface, then lay out on it ... you can imagine what....'

'Back to the future? Ignorance? That's what Oskar meant,' I say. 'Whatever brought you guys down here, despairing and sophisticate – I should instruct you in the opposite.'

Valentin laughs. I must not.

*

'See,' says Valentin, 'I've laid the table out. Those giant sea snails – they're delicious, immortal too, as no one's ever eaten them. It's a taboo....'

They're very very slow. They loose a trail. They're labelled too – justice, equality, dignity. The shells are crusty and green-streaked. They're larger than the nautilus – as big as Triton's double horn.... They wander without destination – when they reach the table edge, they very slowly turn around....

'I'll sit with you,' says Valentin. 'Direct the show. When a snail stops before an eager guest, we'll start the talk, and you can teach us what to do.'

'We're all marooned,' I say. 'But, surely, the boatman will return....'

'You must know,' says Valentin. 'He only comes to take the sick, the moribund, cadavers. We look to you for something different, in syntony with what you did, way back – you saved a life.... Salvation! That is our need. And materially....'

'What, Valentin...?' I ask.

'A boat, you idiot,' he shouts. 'We don't know how. Build big! We need a bigger boat, to take us out!'

'The snails,' I say. 'Slow, but as a motor, possibly.... You harness them with fronds....'

'No, no,' he shouts. 'The river! It will always draw us through, drive us. The snails stay here – they're ethics, metaphysics, the frustrating roundabout of our dilemmas ... they're past, not future.

'The sea! The sea! Alas, we have no raft; we cut down all the trees to burn.... It once was cold, but with no trees – it's torrid....'

'Are you sure?' I ask. 'When I got here, there was a forest, quite impenetrable. Just earlier today – with snakes and parrots.... Are you testing me?'

He hurries off. He flaps his hands – as if to say, 'Details and perceptions? Don't bother me.'

He knows nothing. He can be the teacher now.

Aren't those the trees all round? Or maybe immature bamboos?

SHOSHONA

'Don't let Valentin take the initiative,' says Shoshona. 'He fell into a puzzle trap, turned spidery himself. Now, he'll riddle you and wrap you up. I'm quite different, I'm in your class.'

We watch two snails manoeuvring round. 'It's evident,' she says. 'It's time to couple, but they don't know how. Or they forgot. Or want to improvise or speed things up.

'Valentin has always theorised that time has an ingredient – it changes things, forward or back, or to a mephisto waltz – one step forward, one step back.... These snails – "justice" and "freedom" on their shells – want to have sex ... but time has taught them nothing. No development.'

'Dear pushy Valentin,' I say, 'he wants to cut things short. If you can't find the start, he says, be sure you see the end. He's right, for us as well. We'll leave, abandon the symposium, the snails, the headman....'

'Oh Doctor Olbek!' Shoshona says, and laughs. 'We'll never leave, not us nor you. We have our destination here. We decided it. We can't intend to go on somewhere we don't know where....'

We watch the snails fumbling round each other. It does not arouse.

'How many pupils are there?' I ask her.

'Dozens,' she says. 'But Oskar schedules gym at awkward times. Timetables are a difficulty for many – the astronomers and archaeologists.... The full class may not ever show.... And we who see ourselves as the economists – we have to wait to see the trends, but there's no data, so – it's frustrating.... Often we take to bed for months....'

'These snails,' I say, 'I don't fancy eating them; though it might speed things up.'

'I'm sure it would,' she says. 'But what would be the point? If time went quicker here, what would we do with it? Would we miss out on boredom, sleep? Or maybe nothing, nothing at all, would change. Does time go fast? Or slow? It seems it does, but then we check. How would we know, if time is fast or slow? It's useless – we might ask – "is the earth too big, too small?" The universe too old? Or too elastic? There is no way of answering. Who decides how fast the time should pass?

'Maybe some teacher, ages past, has eaten snails, and so, time goes faster here than anywhere.'

*

I quite regret dear Tasha – her head would never fill with puzzles like is normal here, although a free imagination too, like hers – is irksome; like a flapping door, unbolted window, in a storm....

*

'Make something of this,' Shoshona says, holding both my arms. 'There was this library, long long ago, the house of wisdom, Bayt al-Hikma. It's obvious what I thought. Explore it! But – all the books were gone. What have I lost? Where is what counts as wisdom now? Where are the shelves, the catalogue? There's my dead end, you see....'

'It must remain unknown,' I say. 'Books are rewritten all the time. It's like the Amber Room.... It disappears – and here it is! The world you see – is full of tricks ... little windows, opening a second, then they close. Who opens them? Sheherazade? Who promises? King Croesus? What lies within those rooms? Is the whole universe a carpentered box of curiosities, with secret drawers, butlers popping up, or viziers with scimitars, extravagant beasts or nymphs and satyrs ... all waiting to caress our senses, show how our reality was poor, lacking in imagination.... Our telescopes had found a swirl of dust and sparkles, the real jokes lie still far far out there ... and one day we'll be shipped off to nothing ... but it's there, always has been. Plenitude, the whole. Universe. Shall we enjoy it, super-reality? It will be a crucial test.... You and Valentin – you're moons of Jupiter. You're there, material, but I can't reach you, can't stand up on you. I put out my hand – it's on the far side already.

'It won't end well,' I conclude, trying to clamp Shoshona down. 'It never does.'

'You're way too intricate,' Shoshona says. 'You want an explanation of the explanation. Suppose that in the start an explanation doesn't signify, convince. Wisdom is evanescent. The Bayt al-Hikma's always emptying out. We reach dead ends – and we are dead. We arrive because we left, and then we want to leave. A paradox. We always leave, so either we arrive, or we're not here. It can't be otherwise.'

'What do you want, Shoshona,' I ask, quite exasperated. 'Explain the past, the present, future – or all those? Will knowing make you more content than ignorance? Or still more ignorant? You learn, so you can leave – if I could build that boat, we'd all sail off, all, every one of us.'

*

'You see,' Shoshona says. 'There's trees.' She points. The forest's back, or could be mangroves. 'No mystery, no mirage.

And now, we have to eat. There's only fish, so here's your pole and pin. Sit on the bank, you'll get a bite.'

We laugh. There's black fly and mosquitoes here – they bite much quicker than the fish.

*

'I could fall,' Shoshona says, 'into the river – such a splash! And you could save me. It wouldn't look authentic, though. You can't save Oskar – he's the head-man. Already safe. Give everyone who asks – a grade. We'll leave, you'll never see us afterwards, but our lives go on, and thanks to you, we're qualified, passed the exam....'

'You make it seem quite farcical,' I say. 'It's true – I saved Tasha's life and since that day, I've never seen her. Probably – her life goes on. Sometimes she'll be glad it does, sometimes, she won't give a damn. I want to please you, satisfy you. Go if you want, or stay. Imagine – life is a plot. It may be that Raskolnikov reforms, and gets parole. The first day out, he stabs an apple-seller – gets the guillotine.... Proust's friends – resisters or collaborators, or a bit of both...?'

'I wanted to teach you something, but,' I say. 'You'd gone through everything already – or you read up your ancestors, in a book. All quests, all journeys. No one need stay where they are – it's irrelevant. If you can, you take the plane – if not, the soldiers or the flood, the drought, the famine – they will tell you when to run, and don't forget your documents, if you've been issued some....'

'You shouldn't have come here, Shoshona,' I say. 'It won't clarify; and there's no dinner.'

I've finished teaching. I know nothing, it's all been lived before.

I twist my body in a sheet, lie still, and here comes the boatman. I am moribund, he puts me in the canoe, and off I go. 'Only one today,' I hear him say.

I'm always wanted somewhere.

*

Chico sends us out – river and forest, deserts salt and bland.... Everyone wants teachers, so they can leave, go where they want and are not wanted. He fled the Amazon, now despatches us to where it starts to rock and swelter ... to teach whoever wants their future, or their past, explained.

'An agency sent me to you, Chico,' I say. 'Teachers save and renew the world, they say. I had to play dead to get away.'

'You should have stayed with her, the Comanche, Shoshona,' Chico says. 'She was fooling you. She could have founded you a hut. Indians can draw a perfect circle, and set the birch-bark lodge atop. An experience rare and rich, Olbek. Habitation at a finger-tip.

'Those moderns end up everywhere – ports and rivers especially; uprooted, on the move. They make a settlement, then want a trainer or an educator. Spin tales. You were gulled.

'Too much peyote. You've walked the line with death too much, cheating it, simulating it. Your contacts? They pointed a direction, but you couldn't see.'

*

'Seeing isn't easy, Olbek,' Chico says. 'You live in a white world; maybe mostly people go down mines, live in the dark, and women cook for them, alone up in the light. Then there's the forest, and the plants – outside the city. And there's the first people, millions of them, you never see them, maybe they sell you berries by the highway, give you their hat, sit in court on Mondays, waiting to pay the fine and go outside again.... Perhaps they're Ojibwe – all those Iroquois they killed! The Iroquois – how many Hurons killed? Millions? And the survivors still exist, winners, losers – as if inside a survivor there was a Hun encysted, a Scythian, a Parthian.... Distant peoples, assimilated in your head, your skin. We don't see those, not ever, even when we're taught. They're mute, intangible....

'Not living in your cities and villages, your houses, not wearing your clothes, not mumbling your language, but eating things you've never seen and animals, quicker, bigger than you have.... A history, where you've none, a nation you have never heard of, with leaders, treaties, trade and battles ... all new to you, but happening all along, and long ago. As if you're a group of Zambians settling in Berlin, making a city, making food and stuff, and dances, movies, weddings ... never knowing you're in Germany and there are Germans all around.... Maybe knowing and not seeing, wondering, not thinking. Knowing, not saying. Knowing, saying so you don't hear. Or Romans thinking how nice their villas are, and all round are Etruscans, carving roads and water-skiing. And you never know! They are invisible. You're Zambian, or Roman, or a miner, of any sex or colour – and you never know, never see – all these other people, who don't know you, don't speak your language, don't recognise your customs, your religion, politics and economics – they do it all that themselves quite differently. And only once in ages, a tiny number ends up in your courtroom, hung over, pays the fine, or goes to jail.... And you don't see them, never, their history, their presence – like they're in two dimensions, drawn on the wallpaper ... or you are ... and they come in the room, switch on the light and you can't see it, or them, it's dark but to them it's light....'

'Yes, Chico,' I say, amazed, impressed. 'You're right! In the forest, the fields, on the rivers. They were all there, all around, and I never saw them, not one, they never spoke....'

'You'd not have heard them,' says Chico. 'I lived there, and I never saw one. I read about them. They were there, like

Saxony and Pomerania are there, but not if you think you're in Zambia....' 'Thinking, seeing,' I say, running ahead. 'Those aren't the right terms. It's the light – it comes on, and you don't see it.'

'Of course,' says Chico, 'You can draw a line round them, plant some trees – and if they step over, there are big big problems, and a reprisal, and you show whose boss, even if you don't see them, never, not one, but you can squat there and mine and shoot the animals.... And even if the unseen people all decamp, you never see them when they're there, or when they go.'

*

'I'm ashamed,' I say. 'Not just for what I didn't see. My students, who had reached dead ends.... I was a teacher, always had more to say, yet, I deserted....'

'Don't confuse, Olbek,' Chico says. 'There's the people that you didn't see, and the students who you didn't help – you ran; they wanted to, and stayed.'

'Suppose they know about themselves?' I ask. 'There's nowhere they can go, however far they travel. We're in time's jaws – it never spits you out.'

'Aha!' says Chico. 'What can they do to you?'

'Well,' I say. 'At least I saved someone.'

'Is it about saving?' Chico asks. 'Or seeing?'

'Put it down to the peyote, Chico,' I say. 'Don't think I'm telling you the truth, exposing. This antique stuff! I can make a hundred people just like me. It takes a morning. Like making gingerbread couples ... to what end, I wonder.

'You know, what intrigues me is how the whole genre of cine-criticism, sci-fi, aliens, thought control, the pop cult-flickery of anti-cap and anti-fascism, has been exploded. What humans do has no need, no place, for aliens and their dirty businesses. Humans do it to themselves. And to other humans too, of course. You don't need special glasses to see it. Tote no illusions and expect no mysteries.'

'I don't see you as an aesthetician, Olbek,' Chico says, laughing. 'Critique of modes and manners – it's not you. You don't have manners – and it's good, not a put-down on my part. As for fashions – you wear, and think, what you were born with. The most you're capable of, is trying to perpetuate your slow-burn revelations, inflate your oddness, make doubt and estrangement fill the gaps that science leaves, the holes philosophy can't fill.'

'Touché, Chico,' I say, laughing too. 'A thousand cuts! How do you go on from that, find a space where you're not compromised? Your vision's sharp – beware! It slices you even when it's sheathed. Let's trek, Chico, away from the burning trees! Take me with you, possibly....'

'Oh,' he says, 'I don't seek space. I want a dense and crowded place. In the open, you must compromise – there's the extraneous – rain, jaguars, taboo groves. You have to go where every centimetre is taken and exploited; and there, you can be free.'

'Discipline, Chico,' I say. 'I love it, know it from my birth, feel it over, over – every day. Let me share it, share yours. Give me necessity, my allotted floor. I'll pack some party cards – will give us threat, legitimacy, and – if there's a proper party, with clowns and poppers, we'll get in for free!'

'You're right,' he says. 'We must survive, it's all that's left. Do as the greats do – excess, then apologise, massacre, repent. Feed the hungry – set them to work. No one is out to help us, Olbek. We have seen the ruins dynamited, forests burned, peoples eradicated – immortalised on tape and put in archives double-locked. This is our last, our decisive struggle. After us – there may be no one....'

And we laugh. It's true, and of course we don't believe it, don't act as if we do.

'You've been a person of action,' Chico says. 'Also some kind of intellectual. Those idealistic snails ... then, your criticism of materialism – no theory of communication, or cognition, so you got out. A clever tactic.... And yet – I don't see you as an admirable man, enlightened, or even sympathising with your similars. You've had a try at saving. You could save worlds – you back off, close your eyes. That way you tumble – but you don't care. Not seeing is enough. All saved – except yourself.'

'Well, Chico, who are you to judge?' I ask, amused.

'I do,' he says, 'I judge. I've every right, I've walked the world as long as you, lifted the flaps of yurts and chivvied ostriches ... I could say that, from the start, you're wanting. An instinctive improviser. An almost-ran.... But I have followed your account. I'm judicious. You're dissatisfied. You know you haven't come to terms with those you have encountered and have left.'

'No one does,' I say. 'We always plead our honest case to painted wooden heads.'

*

'What have you learned, Olbek?' Chico asks. 'Little. Your limits. Tasha and Shoshona – they learnt less. They let their skins do their thinking! Valentin was stupid. He wanted to take over from you, the fugitive!

'As for me – in Rio they would have shot me, elsewhere – in prison! What could I accomplish? Nothing. Inform people over and over what they should know, and what they don't care about....'

'Why should they?' I ask. 'They've ways of keeping safe. They won't want to think about you. You'd be good and quiet in a cell. They'll help keep you locked up, you and your enlightened bombast!'

'You're wrong, Olbek,' he says. 'Think! Innocents in the maelstrom. Wozzeck! That's drama! You idiot – you saved people from the rapids, left them ignorant as before, and smug too! There was a story, and you dropped it! You deferred to their apparent humanity. Unfelt sentiment!'

'Why me, Chico?' I ask, 'Why give me your time? I'm flattered, but....'

'You look strong,' he says. 'You can carry my bag.'

'It's empty, Chico,' I say.

'Just wait!' he says. 'You must realise, Olbek, that what the species thinks about most of its time, and fears, aspires to, wears like multicoloured suits of clothes or tunics, wraps, is love, death, sex, and character. Poverty and greed, deceit and vainglory, power, hatred and forgiveness.... All these are of no significance to me, and not to you – if you will pause for once, and think. These are ephemera. They are all inevitable, they come and go, you want them, pry into them – experience each one and its reverse. I don't make this a revelation – it's happenstance, banal repetition, the "empty form of time".

'We live in being human. You are the cow, there is your meadow. The grass is there for you eat, then you will shit on it.

'The demon – that is something else. All the rest dies in each one of us.'

*

'Before we start,' says Chico, 'I need to educate you, Olbek. We joked about peyote. Where I come from, where you were, among the mangroves, and in the contract you may have had to educate those moderns in the first, and last, experiences – peyote accompanied us day and night. This modern stuff – the powders and distillations, they're medicines. Fake. They kill the pain, and soon they kill you too. Imagination! Embrace it. Widening experience, not restricting, falsifying it.'

He shows me something like – a mossy grotto. A terrarium? 'Look!' he says.

'There's nothing, Chico. Ferns, humidity,' I say. 'Some greenish rocks, a lizard.'

'You have to look real hard,' he says.

There's little coloured stones, like children's plastic – anomalies. They move.

'Just touch the frogs,' he says. 'A caress, no more. See – there's orange, yellow, red. They like the feel, a finger....'

And indeed they do. They cluster, silent, quite passionate.

'Don't touch the blue one,' Chico says. 'That one will kill you. Quite involuntary, but not worth the risk.'

The enclosure's held in by Tiffany glass. 'No!' I say. 'Death is death. I don't believe in artifice.'

'It's absolutely natural,' he says. 'Everyone, over where you were, partakes, and there's no fuss. You're abstemious, nearly vegan, sex at a minimum, no hedonism, even – you're without a leaning to enjoyment. Pleasure for you has almost never rung its bell. For you – the storm, the tide. The sacrifices....'

'I never saw sacrifices, Chico,' I say. 'I had suspicions – not that I saw wars or battles, but that is what they are, it's true. The rituals of roasting, eating enemies – of course, it goes on all the time, so common no one bothers to record it, though in a way – people condemn it, but I repeat, I never saw....'

'Oh, you are an innocent,' says Chico, and he laughs. 'Throwing in the sea, the inquisitions, the suicides enforced after each banquet, clueless losers!.... Use some imagination, Olbek,' and he picks out a little purple frog and rubs it on my cheek.

'Don't be reticent, my friend,' he says. 'Here, there is no violence, no addictions, cartels and dealers. They say that nature was given us to be enjoyed. We screwed that up,' he laughs some more. 'But if these frogs have any purpose – unfolding some reality is it.'

There's a pause. It lasts and lasts. I find the process boring.

'Well,' he asks, 'How do the people seem?'

'There's crowds,' I say. 'The people seem so very small, flat, pliable. They smile, it's fixed, maybe their mouths are made like that – the frogs' are, after all.'

'That's it?' he asks, disappointed. 'Don't you go underground? The animals, don't they talk? There's scenes from childhood...? You don't hallucinate?'

'You mean, the priests dressed like jaguars, the Andean pipes, the jars and sounding caves?' I ask. 'I've read the books, but Chico – I was a poor kid. I didn't have a nursery, had no *pelouches*, no clockwork peacocks, stilts, no tree house – all that stuff.... Maybe I just never acquired the fantasy, the aptitude, the need to spice the humdrum....'

'And yet you see it all,' he says, marvelling.

'I know it all,' I say. 'And I appreciate the frogs, it's just it doesn't tell me anything I didn't have already in my head.'

'There should be revelation,' Chico says. 'The fable says – ingest the slime, then you will have a goal, a ceremonial, investiture.... Even if you go back to the start – there ought to be a story, connection – a movement that recomposes your life, erasing stretches of banality ... a tale that peoples them with sympathetic robots, like in a pop-up book....

'People expected so much in the past – the Soviet experiment, *pax aeterna,* power to the people, a pact with nature, every tree a-swarm with parakeets.... Hope, Olbek. Seems it's been a well without a bottom, without water too....'

'These people, Chico – they are slim as cards,' I say. 'The frogs bring them to me – millions of them, fitting on a memory-stick. Your little creatures – they are playing us, we are their game. It's a great trick – we thought we had invented poker – but the fall-guys, the fish, the gulls – are us!'

The frogs, the frogs! How they must laugh! *Ekekekex*! And who's behind their tricks, their game? More frogs? – or maybe, Chico, it is you.... Caution and prudence. Don't jump – each leap is bottomless....

We know there is no watchmaker – the universe is as it is, don't ask the wherefore....

So – who winds the watch? Who sends us scurrying and falling off the edge – who summons up high tides, casts brains that look the same but – each is different, defective, vanishes half-empty, unfulfilled, unread....

'You're precious, Olbek,' Chico says. 'You are a fountain. Of history. It all spews out – the slogans, the graffiti. Like when people thought to rebel against the ads, against working under capitalism – all that. Old stuff – but in its time, it was exciting. Now – we're all parched without publicity, we all want work on any terms....'

'I know,' I say. 'I'm in your hands. Show me what to do, and help me do it – I'm your servant, till you drop me. Free me, I mean.'

It's false, my submissiveness. For sure, he knows it. Neither of us bothers.

'Except....' Chico says, quite sadly, as we hear the laughter of he frogs roll round their little universe – all of them, even the deadly blue, uniformly crimson in their inside, as we see – their huge mouths open, their small pseduo-clitorides a-tremble in their throat, like the tines of tuning-forks, sounding the single note....

'It's too bad, Olbek,' after a pause, Chico resumed. 'Your sensibility is deep and wide, you ride reality as if it were a horse unbroken.... But – you resist my little friends, my frogs – at home on earth and water, sometimes fire ... remember, their merriment, their concupiscence, the excess, the giggling orgasms, the piling on, the scrums. Notoriously, they 'would a wooing go!' ... they draw the veils aside, my friend.... A stroke, a touch – it's lighting up a cave you thought was full of bones and bats, instead, there's frescoes, heaven, hell. The door, Olbek! To enter, you must find the door. The frogs can be the familiars of Culsu, goddess of the door.... You know the corridor, my friend, where you can pace and race, passages, unending transition, a stretch of non-arrival – and you'll never find the door. There is no key, you need the elusive pincers to draw back the pins, open the portals – and there ... is the immense reality you didn't want to recognise.

'What ignorant folks call illusory, a deviation, reached by a *farmakon*, hallucigens, is the folded wings of our whole edifice.... We know the halls of mirrors – but we long to see the Little Trianon, the pastoral. The clouds, the *trompe l'oeil*, the skies, the lightnings.... The scientists will marvel at the furnishings, the vistas, the creatures, pleasures, pains.... They assure you it's reality – but you prefer to think it fussy, dull and speculative. They fool you too – they number it, disguise it, translate it into unspoken tongues....

'The unknown, Olbek. You're afraid of it ... the whitecoats fool you.... They dress the deep reality as a hypothesis, report, a project funded....'

'It's drugs, Chico,' I interrupt. 'Inside your head. And science is everything that isn't us – the universe – a project uninhabited, useless, a dead white elephant, purposeless and deadly dead. It miniaturises us, it's a mockery of an imagined infinite extent. It's emptiness, toxicity, a pointless limitless expanse, impenetrable – and still, meanwhile, we die of age and coughs and jumping off the bridge....'

'Inside your head?' asks Chico. 'What that goes on is not? What doesn't end up there?'

'Oh, solipsism, Chico,' I say, and laugh. 'Bishop Berkeley! There's only one reality, that we live in, you, me, and whitecoats too! Then there's our party trick – imagination. Inventing what's not there....'

'Well,' Chico says. 'We'll thresh this out when we are waiting for the bus to come.'

'I agree,' I say, 'that in some very tiny things scientists have found – you could say that reality has turned to unreality – the scrawling life, the Koranic quotes that squirm inside each aubergine – it takes us to the edge and far beyond, a space-walk. You ought to drop, fall kilometers, perhaps you do, but there's nothing to land on, smash you up. It's a cheat!... But – is it more reality you want, Chico, or more unreality?'

'Just more!' he says. 'Much much more. Don't quibble with me, Olbek!'

'Many – the most advanced, perhaps – will find all this insulting, Chico,' I tell him. 'It's your story. It's for everyone, but you don't give your tributes to the species-world, your *semblables*.'

'Oh, they won't care,' he says. 'And why should I?'

'You won't,' I say, 'because your self-absorption is a skin. Like a frog's. You stroke yourself – all creation shudders out.'

'You've mixed with people, it's true,' he says. 'But never chosen. You had a poor life since no one can decide they'll be born rich. But being hard-up's meaningless. Unless you choose to live in hardship, it's the common lot. If you live among the rich, then your poverty is envy. And Envy gives intense pleasure, Olbek. Love and hate in the same piece of cake that you can't eat.'

'You're full of truths, Chico,' I say. 'And of what lies in between a truth and your intuition. But I ask myself – what's so special about truths? The whitecoats say – look down a microscope, up a telescope, and you can't avoid the truth. At sea, it's all around you – waves. Almost everything is true, and yet we feel we are deceived, defrauded ... excluded, shut out.'

'I wonder if you have it in you, Olbek,' Chico says, packing the frogs into a bosky box, labelled 'wanted on voyage, but left behind'. 'More excitement? I'm sure you want to meet up again with Tasha and Shoshona, but it's most improbable. People become unrecognisable very quick. If you take up with them again, it might be that they want your cash, or that you're back where you once were and hoped to leave. Of course – usually you meet again with a Valentin; a nobody, the replica of you yourself....'

'It's true,' I say. 'In prehistory and history ... we are all dead; the distance between us and ancestors is so great we can know nothing of them, of their carvings, burials.... Now, take the distance between the living and the living – some painted, tattooed, others smooth and brown like Chico – I can't imagine them all, their variety, their musics, dialects, passions and devices.

'What do they think, and want to be – after a life in electronics, management, logistics? Shamans I can understand – my fellows too, some who fly in rockets, some who live in packing cases underneath the bridge ... beyond our grasp, but within the imaginable. But – the guys who run the planet, soldiers, navigators, wholesalers, slavers – the ordinary ones, who gladly, with joy, climb into the barrel and – over the falls they go!

'They live, so you can't dig them up and analyse.... The living, Chico. How mysterious, how complex.... Those ancient hunters and artists ... such simplicity!'

'Oh come, Olbek,' says Chico, laughing. 'You have all the elements you need to place them all – there maybe is no mystery in what the living moderns are, but rather what will happen to them when it's time to bury them; how to lay them out and what to put in with them....

'Always future-oriented, those ancient deaths.... Another stage awaited. Where is their after-life? Is their destiny in journeying, in crossing deserts, finding the blue stones, killing the giant elk...?

'Those moderns, passed in the street – aren't they our enemies, alien in customs, thoughts...? Maybe they led us to disaster, and we should grind them small....'

'All the time,' I say. 'All of us – we are alive and dead....'

'Well,' he says. 'Take yourself, Olbek. You saved a life. Perhaps that's all – an instinct, as you'd save your own, and left no sign. Your knowledge? Quite thin – you're right to doubt if it's of use, and worth the troubling to pass it on.

'I could take you into Africa – show you militias fighting the soldiers of the state. Some bring death, and some bring life.... Or teachers, reclaiming outcast kids, the witch children, *enfants sorciers.* Suppose we go, and you decide – where do you stand? Which side? What fits with what you've done? Stand back? Leap in?

'Civilisations mean hecatombs. It is a commonplace. Maybe you don't belong in one, Olbek, the only civilisation current? Is it worth you finding out?

'You see, I have my plan made, just like I told it to you. You think you're an anthropologist – perhaps you're only an experiment?'

'I can't keep up with you, Chico,' I say. 'I'm at the start. You are a library, with no one left to read in you.'

He looks me over, arrogant and sad. 'You're the only one I found,' he says. 'My last hope.'

It's ominous. He doesn't allow that *I* might have a hope. He's probably right.

*

'You're a wall, Olbek,' Chico says. 'A dear sweet wall, the plants love you, the flowers open up on you and fade. What shall I do? Knock you down, climb over?'

'What do you expect is on the other side?' I ask, dismayed.

'Oh, nothing special,' Chico says. 'Just where I want to go, and may not arrive. And you – what's on your sides? Shoshona – be very careful. She can't ride a horse, and the braves don't let women back in who've been with us. She sees her life as an experiment, like all the moderns do. It isn't so. It's banal trial and error, then in the laboratory sink it goes. Go in the earth, and in millennia, they'll dig you up, if you're not ash, see how full of lead you are, irradiated, cancerous. Then – off to a drawer or, if they are inclined, back in the hole you go.

'Tasha? – you're old fashioned, Olbek, so you savour sex. She doesn't. She's ephemeral – it's good – for her, but not for you. She doesn't want to learn from you, and you will spend your years seeking what she knows.... It's water, my poor friend. She flows. Even – she might make a name, and then another one, and so.... And so and so. You'll run along.... Names, evocations – they don't make a person. They are a wisp of history we must be rid of – those huge old cities, tall, too tall, where squatters add another floor and perch another one a-top, made of plaster-board and crows. What if they fall on you, the heights! all hollowed out like bones cracked for the marrow?'

'I'm glad,' I say. 'Service before everything, of course. And sacrifice that may redress injustice from the past.'

'Ah yes,' says Chico. 'Your nod to the history you're ignorant of, that fits your stuffy head firm under the yoke. Crops, you think. Downgrading women. Tasha's patrimony. The glebe, the harvest, the chickens in the yard, the kids.... Too bad the hunting and the gathering turned sour.

'Maybe a Valentin's more worth collecting? The non-conforming conformist. I'll bet he joined a gang, religion, party, movement – got himself a file. The cops – they love a manifesto! He's ductile, they'll watch him till he dies, and then take credit for his impotence.... They'll take his job, tell tales ... he'll have sex only with the spies ... wherever he ends up, the treadmill is the same....'

'Yes, Chico, I'll submit. I'll take my chance with you,' I say. 'I need conclusions.... I trust you've an alternative as well ... a crossroads....'

'No, Olbek,' Chico says. 'I've no such thing. There's nothing like you maybe want – it just does not exist. It doesn't make me glad, nor sad. It's so, that's all.'

'With you,' I say. 'Anything I did that might be brave, or honest – is nullified, erased, derided even....'

'Yes,' Chico says. 'That's the first lesson....'

'*Your* lesson,' I say. 'For you, not me. It's true, my life is broken-backed. To be consistent, you must change perpetually, and probably you don't think too far because you couldn't do what reason tells you to – you modify, but don't reject, and in the end, there's been accomplished nothing, because you're not the wave, not even a rubber manikin, teetering on the crest.'

'Cut a rug!' says Chico, impatiently. 'Do something you haven't done, stop whining about being human! Dance with me!'

It's easy – his big paws throw me up, I turn and turn, a pancake from the frying-pan, then I drop – a ripped umbrella, all my legs are broken, and he bowls me – a cedar-cone, all reassembled, I careen on the bias, he hugs me and I feel his heart go quick quick slow, we sweat, two hot loaves baked through and through – 'Now fly!' he shouts – it's really hard, you have to concentrate, switch on those special muscles, watch the branches and the nests! and you are up! Up above the canopy, the air is slippery, and 'don't look up', he shouts – it's high, the sky, real high above you, you are a tyro, barely aloft, and you come down, bumping through the monkey paths and sausage-fruit...

'There,' says Chico. 'Two things you never did before.'

'I'm whole, it's true, Chico,' I say. 'I'm exhilarated. But – no live fire, please. No parachuting. No detention without parole.'

'You could disappear,' he says. 'For ever. Or for years. In a terra cotta bottle underground – arms and legs broken so you walk backwards, work a loom behind your back, recite Demosthenes to the front – but ... no light, no light! No room, no public! Vanity! The fix is in, the cartel, the gagging clause! Once the rules cut in – there's no escaping them, no one hears your appeal. Think! What have you done? What do you deserve? Who is to blame, why did you get caught?'

'I know,' I say. 'The eternal question. Is 'very small' the key to 'very big and very far'?'

*

We could get a crew together, go somewhere, float an artificial island buoyed by oil drums, sail it to make a liberation. Quarrel and mutiny, end bad and sink.

We could locate Shoshona, live with her in polyandry, while I loved the absent Tasha for eternity, her portrait encysted like a goitre on my hand....

'Yes, we could,' says Chico. 'But I've done all that. I'm not allowed to tell my tale. I signed a clause excluding all my memories, I can't repeat them, but they're free to air ... never trust what's free, my friend, and if you ever are, no one will believe you ever, nor say 'ciao' to you before you die....

'And so, what do you want, Olbek? What completeness, what completion? You, rooted in old-time, conventional and obsolete...? Pilgrimage or expedition? Friends or fellow cons – a vow to spend your life together in sickness, or execution and reprieve at dawn? The jailers jailed, the prisoners made ministers and warders, oiling the guillotines....'

*

'Let's get intimate,' Chico says. 'Family. Mine cherished me. I had a houseful of sisters, all actresses – not one got a part, each time they spoke, the words came out different. It oughtn't have been so. What does family mean, then? They were taken off – the war, presumably, they never fired a shot, but they were taken, sold, warriors bid for them, and some we never saw again. A fine baroque house we had – all our pets were stuffed when dead, I played spinets in the gardens – there were trees, flowers – stretching for miles, and little villages, camps, sawmills and sheds for extracting steam.... And you, Olbek? Men can't have children – it doesn't make sense to say "children can't have men", except you were a child, and, well, you had yourself, a man.'

'I wish I'd seen them, Chico,' I say. 'Each having a different take on you, and everything – like those spinning scenes – a diarama, is that it? Like how they discovered how a horse runs, what it does with each leg – the trot, the gallop, canter. I bet your family did dressage too, one step back, two steps forward – like those Lipsinger horses, some such name....'

'Oh no,' Chico laughs, 'Those are white, like Viennese cream, *echt Schlag.* We were multi-coloured. Family. What does it mean to you? Time – what does it mean to you? Come on, let's get intimate. Where do you think it's all going to end? Will they take us all away, auction us? What if there's no bidder...?'

'Oh yes,' I laugh, 'That's often happened to me. You go back in the box and wait. Sooner or later, more warriors come, and you work for them, or sometimes you're abandoned, or you disappear. Obviously – it never happened to me. That's what family and time mean – you never know who's going to select you, or who takes against you. Sometimes they spy on you, and every few years, you miss a throw, and go back some spaccs – it's the rules. The rules are written very small on the box-lid....'

'My!' Chico says, and chortles. 'My! You're so eloquent! And about such a little thing. No one reads those rules – they're changing all the time. It's painful and humiliating, of course – part of the beauty, the great panoply of life. Try at all costs to avoid it, be on the *qui vive.*'

'Sisters,' I say. 'They've always had a special attraction for me....'

'You've dropped an ambiguity,' says Chico. 'I see what you mean and didn't mean. Well done!'

That's all we exchanged about our families.

*

'The little that you've told me,' Chico says. 'Leads me to say – look at you, saving Tasha! Your mistake was to buy her drinks she didn't want. That was condescending. She should have paid. As for teaching in the settlement – you should have given an exam. It's expected. It's the norm.'

'I didn't teach anybody anything,' I say. 'It's the Socratic method. It's why, when we're born, we know nothing, and make mistakes all our existences.'

'If they knew nothing,' Chico says. 'They'd all have failed. It shows you were quite brilliant – you must have taught them ignorance.'

'I'm sure there's more than that,' I say. 'Many of us are not satisfied all our lives, with what we know and don't.'

'Come to the Institute,' he says. 'We have a meeting to find things out.'

'Institute of historical geography' it says.

'There was no room for more, not on the façade,' says Chico. 'We start from basics, could end up anywhere. In any discipline.'

We're late. There's men and women, all sorts, sat round a table.

'The place is, as you know, too dangerous to visit, and the dynasty that came after the one we know little of, is "very scantily recorded"', says the lady prof. 'What we have is images – "high resolution ... available through Google Earth". That's what they show – earth. All the buildings may have fallen or been knocked flat....'

There's little dissent at this. We take a vote. I join the majority, that says there's little to be seen above ground. Some dissent, say shadows could be low walls, or trenches, even.

'We settled that quite quick,' says Chico, satisfied. 'If ever we can't decide, they have to send the soldiers in. It's very dangerous, for sure. Even more drastic expeditions get proposed ... air power.'

I'm lost. 'Don't worry,' Chico says. 'They aren't experimenting over there. They don't have cash to buy our stuff. It's not the time to dig things up.'

'It sounds quite superficial, Chico, if you're serious,' I say.

'It's all political,' he says. 'That committee. They hate me, want to get me out. Jailed, possibly. Blackballed. Worse. We fooled them, though – we didn't disagree.'

'I know nothing, Chico. And we see there's nothing to be seen,' I say.

'They know I'm on the other side,' he says. 'I stand against them. I shan't bomb those shelters. Of course, they could be silos, who can tell? In any case, the people there are right to do what they can do. It isn't much. We're watching them. Sometimes, they do wrong.'

'I think you're right,' I say.

'I sympathise,' he says. 'I can't go there, so I can't be called a fellow traveller. I like to think I'm useful, even if it means I am an idiot.'

'I scc you striving, Chico,' I say. 'I'm following you. But – you suffer, and will suffer....'

'Oh, I'm resigned to that,' he says. 'You should be too.'

'If I see right,' I say. 'In the interests of archaeology, we shan't bomb those sites, but wait till there's no people round, and dig them up.'

'Is it about archaeology?' he asks. 'There's everything to know on that, some guesses always on TV. I know about forestry and asymmetrical warfare – I thought they asked us in for that.'

'You're going much too fast for me,' I say, quite bewildered.

'I can go much faster yet,' he says. 'And incidentally, people aren't interested in what you think and don't know, Olbek – they expect to have the lowdown on your sex life – that's what they believe is interesting.'

'A sore point, Chico,' I reply.

We laugh.

'You like experiment,' says Chico. 'That's your best aspect. Experiment won't work if you talk loud about it, how you're doing it. Poor Russians! When they tried out socialism, they didn't imagine how people hated equality. Everyone loves their freedom, will tolerate fraternity with people that they like. It's the equality that gets those armies at your door and rockets on your head. See this?' And he pulls out an object, like a badly made, a tiny, submarine.

'It's a plastic kazoo,' he says. 'In China they made trillions, but instead of kazoo bands, the threats came in. They had to drop equality. And the kazoos. Now everywhere there's fiddling with economies, unnoticed – but the big words on those French coins have all been emptied out.

'Of course, I have no ambitions – if pressed, however, I would lead. I have new plans. The vanguard party is a problem, though, and doing everything myself is, frankly, vanity. There is a difficulty, though. Lenin's model's still tried out. Maybe it's the only one there is, and yet – the command structure of the Party leads it to abuse.'

He pauses very briefly.

'How I envy Lenin!' he goes on. 'After all those wars, invasions and alarms, after just eighteen months, he said, 'the main difficulty confronting the Soviet government is the famine.' Ah, my dear Olbek – how much harder would my task be now! Just take the famines – how many are they, and how many will there be this year? And all the rest. Flights and invasions.... Leave it, I hear you think ... stay as you are, put up with it....'

'It's disappointing, Chico, given what you know, and how you can skim the troubled world,' I say. 'How already you are contemplating copping out. If you think others will study you and take your lead – you'd be in error. You're not a Party animal, for sure....'

'I'm an exile, refugee, displaced,' he says. 'My one admirer is you, Olbek – who doubted everything you've done, and rightly so. Now, I see that you doubt me. That's your profession, I'm afraid: left at the post! You seek excuses justifying failure. But – no alibi's required!'

'You disappoint me, Chico, on two counts,' I say. 'That you have ambitions unattainable and vain, and that you see they're vain and unattainable. And famine – a terrible miscalculation, or a fearful weapon – or at times an act of God. Set your imagination working....'

'Those aren't puzzles,' Chico says. 'They're facts.'

'Equality?' I say. 'It's strange to see you so antique.'

'It's fact,' he says. 'You don't make facts happen, they do it by themselves. There's shades, but those are all subsumed.

With equality, you may get justice – but I shan't be there by then.'

'I know you hate to overload your boat, Chico,' I say. 'But Tasha had a way of bringing back the cash that disappeared....'

'My blue bird,' he says, quite cross. 'Is not a boat. Doesn't even need a cage – it's tight inside my head. Tasha? – bring her on.'

*

'I'd forgotten you,' says Tasha. 'It's odd, if you're on mission, that you want to see me. Usually, busy people are just busy. Where are you off to? Around the coast, looking for narrow sands and cunning waves? It's stupid. If you want to save a quantity of folks, or watch them drown – I'm singular, an anomaly, an original. A distant target, almost obscured by dust.'

'Things in the universe are never singular,' I say. 'They're planted in relays, over and over, years apart, you'll never see them cheek to cheek, but for each acid lake, there are a thousand more, as if creation thought in all those years past and to come, supplies might dwindle, models change, spare parts run out....'

'I fell off my rock,' she says. 'That's all. I was stuck back on.'

'Tasha,' I say. 'You must renounce, renege on everything. A mission means leaving behind all you casually thought about the places where you felt good, knew what to do, where to live and die, the way to use your language, dress; object, consent, take for granted and rebel. All must change. That afternoon, you lost your life. It's mine. I saved your life, but not for you, for me.'

'Stop!' she says. 'I don't want this. You've learnt a trick, you are the wave, you're playing it. You didn't save my life, it's mine, it's all I have, I've always had it, only I. You stopped it being lost, that's all, you didn't take it, and it wasn't offered to you.'

'Not me,' I say, 'the sea....'

'The sea,' she says. 'A terrible place. A-swarm with prey. With fear. Your destiny is set, unchangeable, fixes where on the ladder you've been put. That's where they'll eat you. You disappear entirely. I'm sure your fear does not, it is inedible, it passes on, down the line. I have it every minute.

'Eaten, Olbek, not scooped up and gutted, frozen, quartered – just swallowed up. Turned into crap,' she says.

'That's what I said,' I say. 'The sea! Was after both of us. I carried you, saved both of us.'

'There's no salvation,' Tasha says.

Maybe there's savings, though.

It's been a bad idea, meeting up with someone I didn't know.

'The good thing about money is that people love yours, even if they don't love you,' says Tasha. 'And when you die – it doesn't. I'd finance your expedition, but you aren't going anywhere, and I'm temporarily without a source. I'd say 'go find me some', but expeditions bring back slaves and countries, and I don't want those.'

'All this is exact,' I say.

'If you took the initiative,' Tasha says. 'I'd be more aggressive. Less Voguish, more "amateur porn".'

'There's a contradiction there somehow,' I say. 'If we're both aggressive, there's a collision. Besides, I don't read *Vogue*, and all porn's amateur or else it's something else.'

'You're right,' she says. 'It *is* all something else. And, while we're discussing your tastes – when you were teaching, did you talk about saving lives?'

'I didn't think of it,' I say. 'It's a conventional starting place. My best pupil, Shoshona – came from the desert. Her name did, at least. No sea in sight. She stole her work....'

'That's why she was your best pupil,' Tasha says. 'But I know you, Olbek. Did you teach them something, or just show them you? You, teaching....'

'Oh, they wanted to leave,' I say. 'You can't teach them what they want to be, or where they'll go. As for where they are – they know. They don't want to know any more than what they know....'

'It can be problematic,' Tasha says. 'I quite see. Maybe that's the nub – how you pass it on, know what they catch, and how the two of you mature the what it is you know and make it something more. Useful for something? Wisdom? It could be anything – making a pie, for instance. Can you be wise about that?'

'Forget it, Tasha,' I say, losing patience. 'I knew you for an afternoon, but know you through and through.'

'Like a pie,' she says. 'Well done. We're back to seafood now. If you start to nibble, I'll sting you. You'll be paralysed.'

'The Socratic method emphasises food,' I say.

*

'Well?' Chico asks. 'Have you harvested, Olbek? Do we eat? Has Tasha borne fruit?'

'Ah, Chico,' Tasha says. 'Let me introduce my mother, Olbek. He gave me life, and bore me on his head.'

We laugh.

There's no money, that is clear.

'You aspire to lead us, Chico, I've been told,' says Tasha. 'You have imagination – *l'imagination au pouvoir* ... do we want to be led by your imagination? Your fancy?

Improvisation, probably. A shepherd leads the flock, but the flock is also driven....'

'Yes,' Chico says. 'The shepherd seems quite harmless, because all she has is knowledge. Knowledge is supposed to be good and incontrovertible.

'Mistrust it! Shepherds don't know much, and they run a tight ship, sheep-shape. It's the dogs that do the tough graft. Maybe you'd prefer being one of them, Tasha? They're trained – but if you're a sheep, your instinct remains intact, precious and irreplaceable.... Are you a *facho?* Red, or black? Maybe a yellow dog.

'Or do you just flock naturally? Ah! Nature! Gives us the dice, the board to roll them on – unless you're stroppy, throw it all away. Afraid of losing, probably. Then there's nothing but the corner for you, punishment eternal, and the pointed hat ... maybe bible study....

'And you're wrong, it's '*l'imaginaire au pouvoir*.' The imaginary is everywhere. More powerful, more destructive than your weak imagination. That's fitted into all the heads. Avoid it, absolutely.'

'I know,' says Tasha. 'It is very complicated. Being rated, tested, put to some work, or none. I find work a puzzle. Finding work's a puzzle too.'

'You're right,' says Chico, much taken with her. 'If you don't like puzzles, work is hell. Hell's a puzzle too, they say, there's no rehab in hell, but there's equality, and that's a virtue too.... At least, if you believe "you can be anything". What a prospect! Oh, the horror! Worlds full of those rough beasts, on the prowl....'

*

'Chico thinks I lack initiative,' says Tasha. 'I'll tell him, I'm on a list to be a colonist on Mars.'

'Why would you do that Tasha?' I ask. 'Isn't here good enough? You want to start another stupid empire where there's no one, just waiting to have stuff dug up and shipped away?'

'Maybe they won't take me,' Tasha says.

'Of course they won't,' I say. 'It would be punishment, and you couldn't do the sums and assays anyway. They give you a shovel and you'd dig.'

'You're closer to me than a family,' she says. 'You could have left me on the sand.'

'Don't try to prove something as a zombie,' I tell her, quite appalled. 'Leave the earth? – you can't send postcards. For us, "new life" is death. You get saved only if you are alive – it's a paradox, I know....'

'Saving me, Olbek,' Tasha says. 'In a perverse kind of way, has finished you. Payback – you've won, and I'm your prize ... this is your best lesson. I'm your graduate. I know nothing, and my brain's installed quite wrong. You're used to that – Shoshona'd lost everything except her name, and you'd not anything to give. You could have taught her method, but, look at yourself! – the method doesn't give you anything ... it's a way of starting somewhere else. Or just not being where you see you are.'

I struggle. How can I be so misunderstood?

'It's teaching, Tasha. We depend on it,' I say. 'Other sorts are born with what is necessary – making nests and eating crickets, burrowing and sloughing skins. We humans don't know anything. It's all in flux. "*Panta rhei*" – the *plongeurs* have it tattooed on them. It isn't give and take, openness to everything, it's desperation, Tasha. Look where we're at – and so you can't wait to rocket off somewhere.'

'You've hit a theme,' says Chico, listening in. 'You could cash in, Tasha. 'Find a producer and seduce her.'

He laughs at his coinage. 'Promise not self-help, but self-transcendence.'

'You're superficial, both of you,' I say, much disappointed.

'You saved me from the deep, remember?' Tasha says, and they laugh.

*

'Where we are,' says Chico, '"Earth" – unassuming, even gritty, dusty. We might see it as challenging as Mars. More so, since it's full of us, people like us, people like you and Tasha.

'I confess – I can't sustain relationships. When desire has been consumed, after the initial orgasm – I lose interest. Onward, I think. On to the next sweet nothing. Olbek is different, I suspect. Confuses sex with sentiment – no one can respond sufficiently with either – sex is overwhelming; sentiment ... well, you don't always feel like it, it's evanescent. As you age you want more and more sentiment – to feel you're valued, that your absence will leave something....'

'Yes,' I say. 'Another paradox. Your absence leaves a hole. Leaves nothing. That's what absence signifies.'

'You must have been disastrous, Olbek.' Tasha says. 'They made you a super-teacher, sent you off to that crap settlement – like in those movies where they have a bleak location and no plot, and have to make an eerie drama full of freaks and misfits.... They create profs and experts from the guys who can't teach two-times table to the tots. For, after all, the savants write down all they know. They just can't teach; like Olbek,' and she tweaks my cheek. 'Can't tell people what to do to get away! Yet – everybody leaves! Or else we'd all still be at school! Shoshona was an empty shell, but still our Olbek couldn't tell her how to grow her substance!'

They josh, they chuckle, they're my friends, I guess. They find me wanting, and it reassures. I say. 'Just look at a minor dinner menu – for Critias, perhaps: on justice, with protagonist a tyrant. It goes to the heart....'

'At school we studied it, the Crito,' Chico says. 'There wasn't much.... A poor school; each day we pooled our centavos to have a lesson in philosophy – and it turned out that all those dialogucs were lost. You get exactly what you pay for, Olbek....' and he and Tasha laugh.

'I'm not discussing lessons, Tasha,' I say, ignoring Chico, 'But the panoply of thought. When you're young, you study language and at night – write poetry. Then you do axioms, then you graduate and leave and don't concern yourself again with justice; or where thought comes from, where it goes, and what it chalks on walls while it is passing by.'

'It's names again,' says Tasha, much amused. 'And ages.'

'No, my dear,' I say. 'It's different people, thinking, doing, different things.'

'Now I recall,' says Chico. 'This oddity, the Socrates who wasn't, and the Plato who was he himself – they didn't seat the tyrants, didn't eat with them. Tyrants, autocrats – they were everywhere, like ants. When you were in the settlement, Olbek....'

'We didn't eat together, nor eat much at all,' I interrupt. 'We would have done the meal with many courses, there was a sitar hired to play all day and night, and we'd have gone through all the books – even the Republic – except....'

'There didn't seem much point,' says Tasha, finishing off for me. 'Shoshona will know all about the potlatch. Dinner and gifts. They have music too, but the whites felt there was a plot behind the gatherings....'

'Did they have potlatches down where Shoshona's name comes from?' asks Chico. 'They knew everything they had to know, but numbers count. They didn't have a chance, too fcw....'

'You guys mix up everything,' says Tasha. 'Your memories! Your argumenting! History, geography, it's all a bumble pie for you.'

‘There’s no intent to argue through the principles,’ I say. ‘I don’t remember them, it’s true, no doubt they’re still disputed. It was just the method – equality of views until anomalies spring out.’

‘Maybe the tyrants who did not get invites,’ Tasha says. ‘Were the biggest of anomalies. Although you’d say it was a classroom set-up, like they are, the teacher knowing how it ends, and everybody cast out ignorant to face the waves. Slaves? They were in the galleys anyway, rowing to the beat....’

‘You weren’t the centre, Tasha,’ Chico says. ‘When you were saved, those waves were happenstance, and Olbek acted out of instinct. If it had been principle, he’d have remembered it. With instinct there is nothing to remember.’

*

‘There’s an autocracy here,’ says Tasha. ‘We were wondering about Chico’s plan, not bothering about politics. Now it seems there’s a tyrant who’s installed himself. Perhaps it was us installed her.’

‘Critias ended bad,’ says Chico, unconcerned. ‘They all do; sooner or much much later.’

‘We must ask Shoshona about the potlatch,’ I say, to move us along. ‘It “established hierarchy through destructive consumption”. That’s the fashion now, all over.

‘I don’t remember that she had possessions, gifted, or to gift. Besides – even if the boatman takes her here, we wouldn’t get her in. It’s even harder now there’s tyranny.’

‘Entering as a slave’s impossible,’ Tasha says. ‘Unless you have an agent. Chico has no credibility now – he recruited teachers, but he’s a duffer about cognition. No one learned anything, certainly not about letting people in.’

'He had hopes,' I say. 'Philosopher-king. That's quite ambitious – French, even. The book may have said it.... But books are out, and so are kings. Philosophy has run its course. It's easy to be anything you want, but very hard to be something others seek.'

'The answer is,' says Tasha, 'Shoshona studied with dear Olbek here. She knows how to teach. Chico can bring her in to teach all that she knows. All Olbek knows, that is.'

'I had high hopes,' says Chico. 'Teachers are identical. If they know their job, that is. Their price tends downwards – they've nothing new to say, it's only method, and my ambition, as you say, Olbek, is emptied out. I am adrift.'

'She could waitress, then,' says Tasha. 'Ticket her thus. While we discuss new institutions and their laws, we'll need to eat and drink. "Who who?" That's the fact, not a question. And who are we, and who are who? Some direct, the rest bring drinks. I haven't changed since I was on the beach. I contemplated life and death. That day, I had them both to hand. No one asks me what I am, or was, or tells me what's to come ... but it's clear, all through history we have needed somebody to pour the wine and bring the food....'

'You haven't understood,' says Chico. 'Not a thing. Haven't studied, haven't listened. What can I do with you?'

*

I'm recruited to tutor Xavier. He's keen.

'Yes, I'm a trapper,' says Xavier, 'Everyone comes here because they've never been. They think it must be like all they've never seen. I can trap, but I'm selective – otherwise....' and he laughs, 'There'd be corpses filling the woods, skunks and beavers in the house ... so, what are you, Olbek.... Where from?'

'Oh,' I say. 'It would be confusing. Places change so quickly. Right to left, revolution to counter ... once a grey place with ersatz sausage, then full of beautiful poor people who spit at you. I've travelled, so everywhere's all stuck or slid. This place – only has you and me. Most places are like that, I guess, but I feel it's hugger-mugger, and you're not attractive, Xavier.'

That could end it, the tutoring, right there.

'I was the enlightened one, in a reservation, settlement. Former Indians – a kind of transit,' I say. 'We tried to resettle some, but, you know, immigration is a problem....'

It's plausible, it isn't true.

'Acts of heroism – they no longer give an edge,' I say, with regret. 'Then you're close to people with ambition, want to change the world, but they're not coherent, it's impossible, and if you get too close, they're afraid you are a terrorist. Or perhaps they are. Or you all could be.'

'There's Indians here,' Xavier says. 'But you never see them. Because you hide.'

'It's spacious,' I say, 'I don't think I'll stay long.'

There's a row of kazoos, different colours, on the floor.

'I was recommended to stay with you, Xavier,' I say. 'And teach you, then the locals. I'm interested in music, like you seem to be. In whether it signifies anything outside itself. What it signifies *inside* itself.'

'Whether or what anything does.' he says. 'I'm not interested in that. If you don't know the answers that you want, we'll never get to them.

'I could start a kazoo band – but there's no one else who plays. I don't have room here for anyone but myself – I guess if you know that, you could put up with the inconvenience, the crush.'

The country is immense – you can see valleys with lakes, piles of snow – like a white-painted roof of corrugate, dips and humps identical, jogging on, for ever. What would be underneath?

'This is too big and cold to be a country.' he says. 'It's very democratic – we never see each other. Respect!'

We laugh. I heard all this before.

'It says "rooms" outside,' I say.

'Your hat says New York Yankees, but I doubt you know the rules,' he says.

'This bothers me,' I say. 'I know Siberia. Life there is spaced out, it clings. Death is not written in. Each life counts. But – what will happen if you die here, Xavier, unannounced? Animal killer! Drowning I can handle – but here, there's bears, knives, garotting. Any moment – and you're gone....'

'It will have no significance but itself,' he says. 'You'll have to puzzle it out alone. No explanations, no scenario. Be the detective – there's no executioner, no killer with blood on his gloves. Everything is suspect. And just what it is.'

There's a pause. 'I can't stand this,' I say. 'You have no liking of yourself. You don't want anything or anyone to change.'

I must get out!

'Don't forget your little hat,' he says.

*

You're sent out to educate. Tasha told me how nature works, I don't think it bothered Xavier – in fact, he lives by knowing it. Everyone there lives, has lived, by setting traps. Dead animals, live humans – caught unawares.

'Not everyone sees it like we do,' Chico says. 'We have the eye, you and I, Olbek. One would have wanted to do it all differently, and arrive at somewhere quite unlike where we are. The grammar allows it – "would have"....'

‘Suppose,’ I say, ‘we have it wrong, Chico. Suppose we do not know our motives, where we come from, what we can do?’

‘Mistakes?’ asks Chico. ‘Ignorance? We’re all displaced, our memories erased, and then filled in by pasts invented, futures hypothesised.... I think we shan’t survive, never be purged of the poison of colonialism. On and on – the gun and flag are dropped and then picked up again, and flourished – the tune is different, now glum, and now a perky Yankee Doodle – the flourishes, the fanfares and fanfaronades! ... the flag a shroud for everyone, that gun shoved up our arse....’

‘Exactly so,’ says Tasha. ‘Chico’s from the Amazon, Shoshona – from who knows where ... Olbek from a bottle, me from waves.... We don’t know anything we ought to know and don’t know if it matters.... Then, there are horizons....’

‘No one sees those,’ says Chico. ‘And to each other, we are characters, mostly in a plotless slide ... waiting for decisive shifts, instead we are increasingly inert and ultimately, we disappear. Art is more artful than the life – there’s ends, developments, and anecdotes. Here, on the earth, we strive to live between euphoria and misery....’

‘We know, and what we know lets us act quite differently,’ says Tasha. ‘From time to time. The writer says – “first write, then philosophise”. Shoshona should have written – surely she didn’t need to know the difference between philosophy and science – she wanted to get away ... a boat.’

‘Of course,’ I say. ‘We talked about her brain. About intuition, logic, all that stuff – I told her all I know, and something of what I used to think. She was fixated on that boat. I think she hated me, because I had a plan she would have understood but didn’t think of on her own.’

‘Does that hold us up?’ she asks. ‘What you want and what you know – it all seems simple. On the beach....’

‘On the beach was a one-off, Tasha,’ I say, exasperated. ‘I was on hand. If I’d been a whale, I could have saved you easier, not even eating you – but you'd probably have drowned. There are some givens in emergency.... Whales look after whales, not you....'

'Wc could send a boat,' says Tasha. 'That way she needn't know anything at all.'

'Everyone will come back here,' I say. 'And no one will get in. It's like those puzzles where incompatibles must cross a stream, a boat's too small....'

'There'll be an answer to that too,' she says.

*

Solange and Nooshi – they have a boat, a pleasure boat, but it will do. 'Both are interested in brains,' says Chico, 'Professionally. Nooshi will sculpt yours, and Solange patrols the crossroads between science and philosophy.'

Nooshi is abundant, fleshy – 'She'll sit at the captain's table,' Tasha says. 'The law of the sea. That piping when you walk up the plank – it signs who will be eaten if they wreck. On board, they feed her up, she's first to be saved. That's why they put the kids and women first into the lifeboats. They're food. They're tender, there's even a kind of boat named after them ... the tender.'

'If we're looking for a civilisation, how long can the voyage take? Especially if it's new, unknown?' Chico asks. 'The higher civilisations ate their enemies and the more devoted. All the militants and warriors. In the forest, we ate almost everything, but not each other....'

'It takes ten minutes,' Tasha says. 'The trip. You see the mangroves, over there. There are storms, of course, but we'll be watched, so will the tornadoes be. They could drop stuff on us if we try to land again back here. We'll cancel all our privilege; if we survive, it's jail for ever.... But it's humanity that calls.... Maybe, somewhere, they'll let us land....'

'Maybe, but not so loud,' says Chico, backing off.

'Olbek is special,' Tasha says. 'He saves people – he will navigate.... He's officially a corpse – so, faces no more punishment. Ghosts float, don't immigrate. And I'm a victim, nearly drowned....'

'Oh, that won't save you, not at all,' says Solange. 'If you leave your brain to us, you might get leniency....'

'Oh well,' says Tasha, 'Maybe our friend Shoshona will be deterred. Being an economic refugee is pointless if you don't earn much, besides, the hours are long, elastic too....'

'It's a pleasure boat,' Solange interrupts. 'Our brains must be pepped up. Music, the *thé dansant* type. If we had an aircraft carrier, we could do the symphony of a thousand. A submarine – Coltrane playing dirty. As it is, it's the Webern symphony. Ten minutes, and we're at the mangroves....'

'Music aims at the absolute,' Nooshi says. 'So it should be absolutely inexpressive. No words, no message.'

'If you want expression and meaning,' Solange says, nodding wisely, 'The most expressive is when you have words clear – sex, death and hunger. No *virtuosismo*. Belt it out – torch songs, live fire. Light it up! The rest is ticking over, mathematics. "Shrimp boats..." would be the most expansive – make Shoshona perk up when she hears....'

'You're the captain, Solange,.' Tasha says. 'Brains – your bread and butter.... Our brains are set up for five-finger exercises – but I hate pianos, drums, all that pumping, thumping. Percussion – it's wardrums and cannons....'

'Your brain,' says Nooshi, palping Tasha's soft shoulders, 'Must be soft as mush. Yumyum – do let me peek....'

'Nothing invasive,' Tasha warns. 'Let's keep everything where all finishes and starts – up in our heads. No convoluted fingerings....'

‘I think I may try Chico’s frogs again,’ I say. ‘Nooshi, Solange and Tasha – that is crew enough. I’ll stay here – think of me as messenger, a bottle full of longing and good hope.’

And so it goes. Chico and I alone ... the others.... No, we don’t expect them back. There’s brains galore for Solange, the settlement’s replete with them. If there’s a squall, Tasha endangered once, is ready to be saved ... over and over....

*

We avoid the blue frog, and watch the boat. The waves pile high, and squirm and wreathe, the spray rises spiralling to join a cloud – Solange rears up, she bares her breasts to calm the waves.... ‘Oh no,’ shouts Chico, ‘The sea requires a sacrifice....’

‘A brain?’ I wonder, as the music peaks, mirrors the waves – ‘Orgasm! Chico,’ I shout.

‘No, he says. ‘Not yet, we have to watch the harmony.... The sacrifice? It could be Webern’s brain ... it’s all there in the music....’

And so it is. The music ends before the end.

It’s mightily expressive – as the boat founders, flounders near the mangroves....

‘It’s unfinished, and unfinishing,’ I say. ‘Its meaning is revealed ... the women – saved in extremis....’

There’s Oskar, Valentin, a shadow, maybe Shoshona.... Pulling our comrades, or their corpses, from the brine ... possibly ... it’s hard to see....

‘It’s a kind of resolution,’ Chico says. ‘Tasha, Nooshi and Solange. A survival, and two specialists in brains – it’s better than a Crusoe any day ... he shouted, didn’t sing or have a phonograph....’

‘I never asked Tasha what she could do,’ I say. ‘She was a lightning, like those flashes in the brain that could mean God or gut-ache, indigestion, stroke.... I must celebrate her, but she remains unknown....'

'Like the sky,' says Chico. 'What does that mean, the thunder and the flashes? Exactly! Only what it is....'

'I know you, Chico,' I say. 'You want to slip in *Geist* somehow. Where does the energy come from, you will ask? What is a song, a picture – that can spark a neuron in your head? A flash in the pudding? And Nooshi's replicas – artistic reproduction, doesn't signify. Inert, it copies the inert. It shows a stele, a monument of life, can't elucidate, explain.... It obfuscates, it's coloured glass that celebrates and hides the light. ... there's taste and fashion, craft, come in, and history ... those beguiling referents.... A shadow of a shadow, mica, smoked skin, just as music is a memory from no one in particular, with a standard time tagged on ... a tick and tock to make you dance and prance, a pseudo-heart to have you forget your individuality, hold on to people never seen, speaking a strange language you don't comprehend....'

'Oh be quiet, Olbek,' Chico shouts. 'There's drama there. Your Tasha....'

'She'll be saved,' I say. 'She was a vagabond, living on the beach, searching for her future in the waves ... brain waves.... They'll pull her out for sure – people with no past, they have no destiny, so they recur, those indivisibles, content and form....'

He doesn't hear. The storm, the tempest, roar....

Nothing. We know nothing....

'Vagabond. It's a loose term,' says Chico. 'On the beach, we all are, more or less.'

'Saved's a loose term too,' I say. 'It's "drowned" that's not. And shall we ever know dear Tasha's end?'

'Almost – I hear a note of sentiment,' he says. 'All encounters are by chance – with parents, like the rest. Who are you waiting for, Olbek? The warrior who has you guess her name?'

'It's all been a disappointment, Chico – especially you,' I say.

'Changing the world?' he says. 'Ho-hum. I tried, hypothesised. It brings the individual some lustre – but then, the experts start to pick the bones. It never stops. If I were an immortal – maybe I would try – but as it is ... I know the enlightened ones, how they dispute. Once dead, I'd never stand a chance.... But you, Olbek. You're simplicity, in a frame. And – to be quite frank, Nooshi and Solange – they worked through their obsessions as though they were two spavined horses. Brains. *Sautéd.* With butter – dreadful for *your* brain.'

We laugh.

'It's Tasha,' he goes on. 'I never spoke with her, but we had sympathy. Your indifference – I'd say you were quite horrible. A freak of unconcern. Tasha – is she alive or dead...?'

'If you don't know,' I say. 'What difference does it make?'

He ponders this. 'I guess you're right. It sounds quite logical. And yet....'

'Where's the frogs?' I ask. 'Left behind? Hallucinations – now's the time....'

'No,' he says. 'I flushed them. Ho ho,' he laughs, 'to see your silly face. You misbeliever....'

I'm dismayed. 'Well,' I say. 'They brought just froggy dreams and visions – orgies, the pile on, underwater weeds. You'd need a quintal of each coloured frog to get a decent buzz....'

'I kept the blue one,' Chico says. 'Mortality. She'll do what is required. It's all gone down in disillusion. Sending out teachers to the needy? I thought my savants brought enlightenment – instead, they were dumb rocks, thrown against stone walls. They can be missionaries – after my suicide, they'll get fired up, and spread my message, if it's simple, obvious. It's the pattern, Olbek. Those "elementary forms". Don't be difficult – people suspect trickery.

'If I can't change the world, my missionaries will do it for me ... bring love, despair and bigotry ... schism, mania, blasphemy and heresy – the works. Bring it all on....' He weeps. 'That shipwreck....'

'I'd no idea you were attached,' I say, 'to Tasha...? Don't think of self-harm, Chico, I don't believe in mouth-to-mouth.... If you are desperate, though – I'll save you! That is my destiny.'

'I don't want you, Olbek,' Chico says. 'You're a disaster in a disaster.'

'I'm cute and smart,' I say.

'Alone in the world, and persecuted,' Chico says, 'is bearable. Without a goal, and you, Olbek, on my back ... hope's lost.'

*

'Apes,' says Chico. 'They're in a bad way.'

'I agree,' I say. 'Badly led, I guess. They should choose the wisest, but instead – the garish and the glitzy had their day.... And now – they're all in open jails, and even worse....'

'It's a dilemma,' Chico says. 'Even wisdom's not much good. But I despair at being seen as canny, or as even smart. What's your response, Olbek?' He gazes at me, with interest, for the first time.

'Oh, I avoid sea voyages,' I say. 'And regrets. No attachments. It reduces suffering.'

He groans. 'And yet,' he says. 'Only in Mongolia are they far enough from seas. The Mongols were once vigourous – even to a fault. But, my friend – the mechanism stalled. It goes well for a time, and then ... the fiefdoms go opaque and shadowy, there's shaky deals and superfriends and warlords in the wings.... It gives me pause. My model, as you know, is Khan Chagatay – but even there, division and succession, the princesses ... it hurts my femininist commitments, but....'

'Say no more, Chico,' I say. 'They chased you from the forest; where are they now?'

'They are too many,' he says. 'Vengeance would be a massacre. A murder of the species, of its impulse, even – its destiny, its history. It would all point to me: my desecration, my disinheritance, my persecution ... my revenge.'

'That's so,' I say. 'I believe it. And yet – your inflated image ... it indicates another tyrant, a resurrected saviour, planting his dynamite under every shack along the street.'

'I'm not complicit, Olbek,' Chico says, with a trace of uncertainty.

'Of course you're not,' I say. 'You're guilty before the fact, a perpetrator, an autocrat. The answer to complicity is drastic, radical commitment. Pure and pitiless. Suffering to the end, if you don't win.

'I could have let Tasha drown. I could have guessed – she's made nothing of it, my gift to her of life prolonged. She doesn't realise, that what I risked my own life for ... is but a squib, a sheep's fart, a spasm – her living, in obscurity. They'd not have pinned her death on me....

'Solange and Nooshi – they take posthumous blame for theirs and Tasha's death – and if they live, they're stuck – powerless and friendless, no means of communicating, calling for help or celebrating their enforced monastic lives.... And we'll say nothing, Chico. You know, won't tell. And you'll keep schtum about vainglorious plans to jig and jog the species on to your gerrymandered tracks.'

'That's drastic commitment, Olbek.' Chico says. 'As for not plucking a kitten from the wave? A gesture without consequence, that you exaggerate. You're ridiculous.'

'And you, Chico,' I say. 'Rule the world? Shape it into your convictions? You might as well try saving it – join one of those groups that wants to stop the plunder.... You can ignore, like them, without a hesitation – the universal, natural impulse to profit and destroy. You think they'll let you climb up on their backs and spout your self-satisfaction...? All in the name of Chico? I'll applaud, I'd be sincere. I love the outré, the pretentious, the fantasists. So, you're still ridiculous.'

There's varnished planks, convenient at our feet. We lunge at one another, each selecting a prickly board – heavy and splintered, too cumbersome to do the damage we hanker after ... less and less.

'The boat!' says Chico. 'Theirs! These planks....'

We would weep, except it's too collective – neither liked Solange; too much like us, an eagle eye. For us, the boat was Tasha's destiny. Nooshi can find her own fan base, somehow. When dead you – they – keep attracting curiosity, being dead's both dull and odd, you're a closed book, although no one really dies in books....

*

'Save me, save me!' Tasha shouts, her voice rising, unappreciated, far above the pentagram – inaudible except to chandeliers, champagne cups, glass slippers.... 'I have this terrible fear of death, not knowing where I'm at, with no address.... Having no future – doesn't hurt at all. It's *now* – not being here, and knowing that you aren't. We're all in the same splintering boat....'

Cling to the present, seeing yesterday's people still here today, opening their little shops, revving their put-puts, spurring their mules ... the present calms you.

'Help me!' she repeats, more shrill....

'Of course!' Shoshona says. 'I know you, Tasha, know your fears. Here, take my hand. Your little dinghy saves us both – I'll just pull it to the bank, and – move! – I'll sit here beside you, start the outboard, and at last I'm off! You're saved, and I've escaped!'

'Maybe we should think of Nooshi and Solange,' says Tasha, as they leave the mangrove bank behind them, and the little boat speeds on.

'All in the same boat'? they change their crafts and zoom around – like dodgem cars – don't try to count or track them....

'Oh, they'll be floating somewhere,' Shoshona says, quite offhand. 'They'll be taken to the settlement. You know, those guys are quite obsessed with death. They give up study, and the dinners, just to think of rites ... of burial mounds – *kurgans* they're called, or maybe they will even live in them, like desert peoples made the cities, pueblos – a whole people living in or on a blob, a termite-heap....

'The problem was – the dinners, where we didn't eat. Valentin would host us, serving that awful resinated wine until we puked, and talking about philosophy. And if we'd finished, and he'd had his way, resolved what was, was not, or stayed unanswered for another time – what then? It isn't about food, Tasha, and not about the drink. It's the inconclusiveness. The universe, you see, it has no end, but everything within it – does. That is the paradox – everything is mortal, all is relative – except it's not. We all die and if we do not disappear completely – we look like all the other skeletons or ashes in an urn....

'Some things go on – our helmets, bracelets, all that stuff – but really, it's unusable, quite out of fashion, smart one day, but obsolete.... Yet on and on, coining new scholars, experts in contradiction, inventing and transcending, living on negations turning into syntheses ... stuff, bling, accoutrements, and their interpreters – ever and ever, things quite indifferent, without an ear, a tympanum, a voice, a mind, a brain....'

'I see all that,' says Tasha. 'That Valentin. What a bore, for sure. Those dialogues between himself! No salvation foreseen in his programming. And all of you, floating in the universe, wondering why *you* will conclude, but there's no conclusion to the dinners, to the thoughts, the space, the time. How could you trust what justice is, is not, when infinite examples will exist, unresolved, not unresolvable, but unknown to you, and you unknown to everyone who thinks to put a drink stall upon your *kurgan*, sell granitas, pomegranate juice, and maybe wonder where their freedom lies.... Wonder and wonder – or not think of it at all....'

'Yes, yes, exactly so,' says Shoshona, navigating, wondering if there's land or something terrible to come, the burning ghats, oil spills, a sinkhole in the sea. 'We're quite a classic case, my dear,' she says. 'Escape by boat's a perfect subterfuge for us, the persecuted and discriminated – no one can track us – horses, motorcars – they leave a trace.... These little boats....'

'You imagine things,' says Tasha. 'No one will follow us, or love us, care if we are saved or drown.... Philosophy has made you think you have a value, even abstractly, reducing to a cypher. It isn't so. You drown – what's your value then? Who'll try to save you? Someone may, many will not. Forget those dinners. Remember genocide – the people giving you your name, maybe they remembered, roundaboutly.... Consider Chico, who you don't know, perhaps you never will, and Olbek who saved you; they don't value you, feel no impulse to save the millions whose lives are now precarious, not even one, a little one, who'd wait on table for you....'

'Oh Tasha, that's enough,' Shoshona says, and laughs. 'I'm not cut out for waitressing, if that is what you think, enslaving me, taking a cut, selling me on, deflowering me, putting my documents in your purse....'

Shoshona thinks how Tasha is improvident – walking along thc beach, not looking at the tide, ordinary, confused, without an interest, poor schooling, bad flaking skin, not beautiful, not well-arranged or manicured ... maybe we could do a boutique together, nothing more.... And Tasha thinks that Shoshona has her head filled with infinities and burial mounds and men manipulative and weird, an uninventive life, spent waiting in a hut for shipwrecks when she could have walked and found a bus....

'I'm not sure that we suit,' Shoshona says to Tasha, who does not respond.

Tasha thinks – 'A *shop*? Like you stand all day, like waiting for a tram, and if there's none, you starve and die? And she knows nothing – but, of her I know still less. And she of me. When there's a rescue or a wreck – the character involved starts off anew. You were a tycoon, then save someone and you're a philanthropist. You throw acid in some guy's face, then find a lost animal – you're honey-sweet!

'Life twists like a dog's leg – get wise! If you don't suspect already, your partners are all ruffians and rogues and steal your virtues and your name.'

She says – 'Leave Chico, and leave Olbek. They know where they want to go, and when they get there, find they don't. We can sail for ever – on the sea there's fuel indefinite: the fish. I have the book–' She waves it: *Your Life with the Stars.* 'Some stars are gas and some are flesh,' she says. 'They're all up there – they tell us where we are, we don't need land, not ever....'

It's perfection. After a day, they start to quarrel. Mostly, it's the fish. They taste of oil, and other things. Tasha and Shoshona – both are sushi fans – the old kind, that tastes of fish.

'We have to land,' Shoshona says. 'We need some cash. There's pirates on the sea.... Think of our pensions, Tasha, and protecting them.'

'Land ho! What country?' Tasha asks. 'There's lots against each one. And they don't make it easy, none of them, for you to land – only if you find a beach, deserted ... hop ashore ... like I once did....'

And she shudders, sicks up her lunch again.... 'The beach...!' she thinks. 'Some stranger, lurking there to pick you up....'

*

'Have you no fear of death, Shoshona?' Tasha asks. 'The tempests and tornados ... the fear; it pricks, it's like the vernissage, brightens the colour, gives lustre to the ordinary....'

'I feared the dinners, and Valentin, the afterwards....' Shoshona says. Then she recalls. 'No, not fear – loathing. We lived on top of death. It was our floor. Not fear, no, not at all. Anger. Asking people's help to get away from them – a stupidity, humiliation.'

'Play dumb,' says Tasha. 'That's the answer to most things. Is this the fever coast? Or Gaza, over there?'

'It's not just landing, Tasha, it's living there as well,' Shoshona warns. 'If we don't sink, we must avoid a rescue.'

'Don't you remember, Shoshona,' Tasha asks, 'About 'freedom'. You want to be free, don't you? We're free here, now....'

'I'm not sure,' Shoshona says. 'If we land – shall we be free? They were all casuists there, in the settlement, casuists like you. They were persuasive. Professionals. We're free here in this dinghy, we chose each other, making our own rules.

'Individuals have rights', they say, and we have no state, only you or I can violate the other's shell....'

'Well, are you going to try?' asks Tasha, shaping up.

'All we have here is freedom,' Shoshona says. 'It's the only right we have, but it's quite cramped.'

'You know what will happen,' Tasha says. 'We'll land, there'll be a state, we'll have many more rights – hypothetical – and spend our lives defending them.'

'That's what Valentin said life was about,' Shoshona says. 'And getting more like that. Rights. You go on and on, more rights appear, you're cramped and there's more threats and you must join with others who have threatened rights, maybe not yours – remember, the rights of each are the rights of all. On your own, you're full of rights – land on a shore – they're almost gone at once....'

'I know,' says Tasha. 'I had a right to life, and Olbek picked me up. He did his duty – what a pain he is....'

'It doesn't matter, Tasha,' says Shoshona, 'Remember "required non-forcing" – you had no right that Olbek took the risk. Rights are rights, and duties quite another thing. If he had a duty – and sometimes he felt did – do you owe him something? A kiss? Sex?'

'No, not sex,' says Tasha. 'A kiss, maybe.'

'We might be a moral community now,' Shoshona says. 'But were you then, on the beach – you two, responsible for his right to life, when you climbed aboard?'

'I remember,' Tasha says, changing registers, '"We often chose peace over justice" – they're not the same, of course, but we've no arbiter. When it comes to who's choice it is, for where we land – I'd choose peace, accept your choice. But maybe our situation is unfair from the beginning. You're qualified, I'm not.... If our relationship's unfair....'

'Yes, Tasha, you're a goose,' Shoshona says. 'I'm a high earner, potentially, and bright. But I used fornication to make my career zoom off.

'True, I'm conventionally beautiful, and you are droll and have bad skin – but is it unjust to say that our equality is artificial, false? Is it unjust that we pretend you've qualities you really lack – down to history and genes, those fatty foods, the spots ... we must close our eyes to that, you're stuck with those, my dear, from choice or ignorance, or lack of cash....'

'Is this how your dinners went, Shoshona?' Tasha asks. 'You make a nonsense, with your talk....'

'Oh,' Shoshona says. 'The talk is crucial – *sprachliche Verständigung*. And as for where we land, think of the need for forced attentiveness. Don't look at shapely bathers, the casino, or the naval exercises off the shore. Consider, if you can, the documents we need – your granny's birth certificate, for one. Some places they deport you if you're an indigene they class as an invader....'

'A warlike past,' says Tasha nastily, 'Atrocities, all that – it's been a weight on you, I'm sure....'

'My name reflects my father's ideology, his past, not mine,' Shoshona says, in a huff.

'Anyway, in those dinners, there was a big helping of phenomenology. Yum-yum! You weren't allowed to notice it, of course.'

'We could resolve this,' Tasha says. 'Instead of a free space – this dinghy is a prison, a space you can't evade.... There is no mediation. It's the end of time – that is, there's only time. And waves, like there are in space, that break on inhospitable shores – landings on non-substances, you can't stand up on them, your spacecraft – so misnamed! – breaks through a ring of gas on to a ring of dust, and on and on, the heat ... a meltdown, the distances you measure in lifetimes.... Until, Shoshona – one of us dies. The other inherits, the will determines. The game is changed, goes on. It's simple in the boat. you are yourself, then in a little while, you find you're wrong, you stay yourself, but you are becoming nothing, a not-you, negation – you're dying. I turn to you, or you to me – "help me" one of us says. There's nothing to be done, maybe a broad bird, white, pink legs, pink beak – hovers over you – "what luck!" you think. "At least it isn't black...." A mistake – the black ones don't come out this far. He stares at you – flies on. He doesn't land or eat, never! – that's why his parts are pink. They never land, they can't – it's years since they touched earth, they won't eat you, nibble you – they know, that's all. "Your time is up," they call, like for the rowboats on the pond.'

'It's easy, then?' Shoshona says. 'I always thought with death there was a wrench, a scene, a setting.'

'No,' Tasha says. 'You're right to fear, but wrong to dramatise. It would solve everything for us both – quick death, Shoshona. We could draw lots, like sailors do – though that's for who eats who. Think prisoners of war – you can die, but they can't kill you – the prisoners are held like we are here. Nature will kill you – no food, the sun, boils, and skin peeled off....

'In prison, they will let you die. Put you in the ground, don't care about your belief, your nationality, your name. Nothing – it's very easy for them, and for you. It's quick and unexciting. Outside, in peace and war – you can be killed in any way at all – casually, in camps, in trenches, from the air, by night patrols ... except, you're not a prisoner, so, in that sense, you're free. The dinghy is our prison, I suppose, except there are no guards, the war – perhaps, a metaphor....'

'The one who's left – they would feel truly free,' Shoshona says. 'So, quick? Death? I'd not thought about in that way.'

*

The breeze pushes them towards the shore. They do not speak, their eyes fill up with tears.

*

The beach is narrow. The city – looks as if the bombers have just passed, flown very low, looked in each room ... tossed in dry bombs, mostly, not incendiaries.

'Unless you've cash,' says Shoshona. 'It seems you live here according to belief. If you've cash, you don't live here at all....'

'Oh,' says Tasha, 'I know about that. Cash. It's part of life, like pee. The value runs away, like when your sample bottle comes unstoppered in your bag.'

*

'I think we're in the wrong place,' says Tasha.

'It's like the settlement without the thinking,' Shoshona says.

'You didn't do much thinking in the dinghy,' Tasha says. 'Fear. That was it.'

'We're in this apartment on condition that we fix it up,' Shoshona says. 'We've no idea how, and no materials.'

'I like the idea of being pure,' says Tasha. 'There's faithful here, and other faithfuls opposite, and some without, but they have patrons and a flag. The faithful know we're not. Not to anything. Maybe they don't care. We are not pure, our presence is an insult, we're part of what they suffer, and we're an obstacle if things go well.'

'They can't go well. You don't know anyone it's ever gone well for,' Shoshona says. 'Those people who might do well – we're invisible to them. Two more castaways – who needs us?'

'The wind blew us here, not me,' says Tasha. 'We're two black balls, big as bird-shot, specks of snot up a big dirty nose. We'll be picked or snorted. We shan't be blown away – we'll starve by our own efforts.'

'We can't live out of rubbish-bins,' Shoshona says. 'The competition has the edge on us.'

'We can't go North or South or East,' says Tasha. 'It must be the sea again.'

'It's too bad,' Shoshona says. 'There's everything here – all faiths, most countries, no faiths, a country close to unviable ... and yet, the table's set, and there's no food, no money to buy it, nothing even for the tips....'

'Must we end like this?' asks Tasha. 'The city flattened, no cash, no work, and all divided by our superstitions?'

'It started so,' Shoshona says. 'The Tower of Babylon. Sabotage or subsidence, or hand of God.... It keeps on ending just like that....'

There's people coming in to shore in little boats. The boats are left untended on the sand, and when it's dark, Tasha and Shoshona – they think, how easy to embark, explore some more.

*

'The big guys,' Chico says. 'Want dominion in the universe. Deliveries at your door – if you have one. Otherwise – your acid lake will do. They're stupid. I'm a deep thinker. I don't waste cash on rocketting and falling back to earth. The message of Icarus – the final splash that people took for some big fish ... they were not wrong. The fish was Icarus, landed, frozen, filleted....

'Queen Victoria had vast lands gifted to her ... she never left her bed; no ant-proof boxes, no cleft sticks. I doubt she even coloured in her atlas. Like drunken Alexander, it was enough to have the Kops and Drifts named after her, her kids; rolled out like hot *panini*, parented by who knows who – the ghillies, retainers of all stripes and tartans....

'No, Olbek: we must choose a different way to appropriate the stars. By no means going there, planting a flag that lasts a tick, frizzling the flag and pole and boy-scout holding it....'

We laugh. 'No,' he goes on. 'They burnt my house. I thought to educate the world, sent teachers, missionaries everywhere – a waste! I shan't concede another fire. Forget the space – emptiness, expanding, infinite, does not attract investment. We can devise....' He ponders. 'Viridium, palladium. Suppose I take an option on everything there is, was, and shall be in the universe. What could that cost?'

'Would there be a use?' I ask, forever provident.

'Everything is put there for a purpose and a use,' says Chico. 'All the holy books agree.... They're ours, belong to humans, as a gift. Don't need a thank you – just get stuck in.' He takes out his nose-ring. Brass, it seems. 'If those minerals made better nose-rings, that didn't green your nose.... We could monitor supplies.... There's former agents on the loose, or lam – we could engage....'

'No, no,' I shout, 'Those loons, the CIA and FSB – they sell you countries and you have to pay for wars eternal to get hold of them.... This is the big time, Chico – act cautiously....'

I'm kidding, naturally – but he says. 'These universal contracts ... any shyster lawyer can draw you one. If there's dispute, your rivals will pay you cash to drop your claim.'

I think this over. 'Nose-rings don't interest,' I say. 'Maybe my option could be for all the monkeys and the parrots in the universe. If they're found, we'd hop from star to star – platform to platform, that is; each little world we can explore – and they'd be mine! Like all the Indians and Africans were hers, the Queen's.... Every monkey, every parrot, on every star.... Of course, they'd be left where they were, you couldn't put them up.... But if you needed one or two.... Minerals can't speak, Chico, but I would generate affect....'

We laugh, embrace each other – Chico says. 'Yes, it seems a joke, a nonsense.... But it's absolutely so. No rocket, no lifetime journeys – just attorneys. A morning, a signature, a loan, and we are set for life, and even after.... You could add tigers and pumas too....'

I'm giddy with delight – 'And mermaids!' I say. 'Not to mention fabulous beasts – the senmurgh, super-bird.... I could corner every one....'

'Of course, of course you could,' says Chico, hugging me, kissing the crown of my head.

*

My lawyer seals my document. 'Pay as you leave,' he says. 'And mind the stairs – there's no light on the bend. I hope you're sure your counsellor, your friend, has not led you by the nose....'

'Time will tell,' I say. 'It rarely does, but in this case – we have a pact with time and space, and judgment is ensured. As my friend says, and every holy book confirms. Judgment is certain, final, and is good – over the whole universe....'

'You know,' says Chico, as we celebrate and josh each other, whacking about us with our parchment attestations.... 'Queen Victoria, who owned a good part of the world, and almost all its people – she was less than one metre tall! A timid sort, she'd sneak for refuge underneath the kilts of ghillies and meal-dealers – and yet, and yet! What a tycoon *avant la lettre*! A trader, enslaver and buyer of the world – those penny blacks, a bundle, with the discount – yours at three hundred to the pound ... sterling.'

'Here, there's the rule of law,' says Olbek, 'So, our contracts are secure.'

*

Euphoria! Even without the frogs.

*

Shoshona sees all round – as they seek a fruitful landing place – the war of civilisations. No one puts money on the Greeks, though they invented dinner parties and the conversations no one afterwards remembers, unless there's been an argument, a fight. The Syrians – no match for the Serbian and Croatian militias they meet with – they are exquisite people, talented, refined. The Afghans are more resilient.... A new, post-scientific renaissance seems in wait; the midwife – not force, but restraint....

'Maybe we should go to Rome, Tasha,' Shoshona says. 'Though I know you think the buildings are too tall, and dark inside....'

'Look, Shoshona,' Tasha says. 'My legs are black.' And so they are.

'I hadn't noticed, Tasha,' says Shoshona, 'Are you sure?'

It's serious, the boat is tiny, so's the diet. So many potential causes – even destiny. To cut them off, the legs ... there is no knife, and even then.... It's tricky. There's wire. You wrap it round, tighten with a stick – the sea is full of those.... To seal the stumps with tar – is genius. There's tar too, on the sea. It doesn't work. Tasha is terrified, as she bleeds out. If only Olbek were here, instead of laughing with Chico about his universal properties.... He has experience in saving me, she thinks.... Shoshona believes in ghosts, as well as rights. When Tasha's gone, her ghost remains. a 'Tasha'. Shoshona talks to it, as if it were alive.

Shoshona's never been to Rome, never been rooked in Italy, so has no doubts. 'We'll call in there....'

She's internationally wise – an expert.

For sure, even if Turks and Iranians go West, the Syrians have the strongest chance of making a distinctive civilisation – though they've no cash, and technology is not their thing.... They're not in Syria, of course, like Greeks were not in Greece, Romans not in Rome....

*

'Ghosts don't have rights,' Shoshona says. She doesn't know; she thinks. Rights are invisible, a consequence. They must exist somewhere, if you believe equality is thinkable. Are ghosts equal? Tasha's just fine, as she is, without a touch of theory, which has gone by, passé. And, fortunately, everybody knows the little country where they were, although it holds all faiths, all nationalities, in person or as proxies – it has no secrets. Everybody knows it's broke, unviable. No mystery, no threat, and no defence.

'If we had turned up north,' she thinks, 'And gone to Russia, or Ukraine – any secrets that we learned would cost us dear. Who knows if they can torture ghosts? – for sure, they can imprison them. A touch of Russia, red or black, you never scrub it off.'

'If we had landed on those shores,' she says to Tasha, 'Coming off a little boat, they'd think us frogmen – or frogladies. And when we left, we'd be suspects for certain, all over everywhere, for evermore. The prey of everyone....'

And she laughs, and Tasha too. If Olbek had been there, he'd have joined in – such irony! He and Chico – not spies, not commandos, not yet at least – but frogmen to the core!

'Tasha,' Shoshona says. 'We're clean. We have no secrets yet, no plan. But, if we go upriver, into the Vatican – we'll find there's secrets everywhere, and plots, even if there is no plan.'

*

The problem is – they won't let Shoshona in. Tasha, yes. Rome's full of ghosts. Shoshona'll have to pay, and maybe even do a service to the bad guys, carry a package in, or something like....

'Forgive me,' Tasha says. 'If I tell you, Shoshona, you have a vulgar side. You like the risk of feeling you matter somewhat. It isn't so. The game between countries, secrets, intelligence – it has no worth. It's only about victims, lots of them. An opening, knocking the little whites and blacks – the pieces, off the board, off the table. Have done with it! All those ghosts, living and dead, where we've been – and still you're not an expert. If you don't respect me, I'll have to let you go. You've only me.'

*

Solange is a phenomenologist. 'Rights,' she says. 'Are metaphysical. If they are anything, they're politics.'

She talks about the life-world and its structuring, the social creation of reality, and Valentin is silenced by her rush of commonsense, sophisticated and, given the settlement and its foundations, quite out of place.

'You guys should build a boat,' Solange says. 'And then we'd all move on.'

Valentin's humiliated, but he wants to leave as much as she.... He even joins the movement Nooshi runs, that 'In us all, there is some Nooshi.'

Solange is full of enterprise. There is a boat, a boatman, but he'll only take one passenger, and that one must be dead, or catatonic.

*

She lures the boatman off his craft – maybe she flashes him. Maybe it's the gift of wine. Not resinated.

She and Nooshi jump into his dugout while he is up the slope, and pissed. Phenomenology has proved its worth.

'"Natural ingenuousness" – that is their fault,' she says. 'The guys here didn't accept that past is past, it's so for science, and philosophy. The solution is the human one – eliminate the boatman, learn to navigate yourself, trust to geometry and Galileo; don't put to sea when waves are high.'

'I'm lucky to have you, Solange,' Nooshi says. 'I'd still be stuck where I was before, and before that too.'

'Yes, Nooshi,' Solange says. 'You're an Everywoman, Everyman as well.'

*

'Maybe,' Shoshona thinks, 'I should drop off poor Tasha's ghost, back in the settlement. That was the alternative world, a place inspiring us to start again. It was a punishment, an education, that there was no other path.

'Now, Tasha's done. Only a resurrection can put her upright once again.... She could rest here, in indeterminacy. In her depth, for certain. Where I have been – there wasn't much philosophy, and travelling the world, I see it isn't anywhere unless you bring it with you....'

Solange and Nooshi meet Shoshona pulling into shore, with Tasha's ghost on board.

'Ahoy!' they shout, all of them, in chorus. There is no plan, there's nothing more that they can say. There's a dilemma. If they travel off together – the canoe holds two, the dinghy – probably can't take three, plus a slim ghost. It's a conundrum. 'If I leave Tasha,' Shoshona thinks, 'And don't let Valentin on board.... We'll sink.'

All in the same boat? Perhaps. Impossible. 'If I squeeze Tasha in and drop off Valentin somewhere ... there's Chico too....'

'It's like the puzzle of the ferry, the sheep, the fox, the onion – and the ferryman. How did he acquire his mission? And the incompatibles? How does he bring them safe across...? That is another unverifiable tale....'

'Keep Valentin away,' Shoshona says. 'If only we had Chico here – a titanium boat ... if only he had access to the metal, we could all travel to infinity....'

And so they could.

'Carry poor Tasha up the slope,' Solange says. 'Don't linger, Shoshona – you know, once you take the other path, wherever and whatever it may be, you can't get off. Don't do an "in memoriam" for the dear ghost, it won't be heard,' and she shoos Shoshona to the bank.

Shoshona hesitates, and as she lifts poor Tasha's ghost above her head to keep her from the waves – quick as a mamba, Solange strikes – hustles Nooshi off the dugout, into the empty dinghy, and off they roar!

'See, Nooshi,' Solange says. 'That's how the puzzle's solved.'

'And the boatman?' Nooshi asks.

'Well said,' Solange says. 'The boatman retrieves his canoe. Thanks to me – I reconcile both property and justice. Those too might seem incompatible – but every sailor knows, you must tie twenty knots or else your boat comes undone ... and you must learn to untie each one. My head is full of string, Nooshi – string theories, the almost-latest in the physics field. I tie and untie, and the boatman does his job when there's cadavers or arrivals. The firmest knot I can't undo, is what binds him to his miserable task....'

'Oh Solange,' says Nooshi, much distressed. 'You're not to blame – for anything.'

It's a good basis, that, for intimacy.

*

'People who have no wish to learn,' Solange says, on full throttle, baiting some hooks and dangling them for fish – 'always look for lessons life will impart. Is it a scandal, Nooshi, that one can last quite well for ninety years never having read a book, had a belief or lost one, taken a side? ... woken in the dark, an unknown head beside yours on a bed...?

'Life goes around. Shoshona is lucky – once more, back where she wanted to escape. The settlement! Always a settlement, everywhere – getting out and sneaking in.... Next time, she'll do it properly. We don't all have the chance....'

'Indeed we don't,' says Nooshi. 'Though I feel fortunate. I've never repeated an experience.'

'Perhaps you forgot,' says Solange, scattering a school of dolphins with her prow.

*

'It's time,' says Solange, 'The wretched of the earth should have their day. We'll see Chico, recovered from his wretchedness – he's an entrepreneur. I can help him with his cause: he'll help with mine. I need my independence – yours as well, of course, dear Nooshi ... to write, to speak, to earn, to farm, to walk, to listen to the birds.... Time, Nooshi, that's what I need....'

'Is it time, Solange?' asks Nooshi. 'Old people should accomplish so much more, they've had the time....'

'More than what?' Solange asks, sharply. 'We all want settling, assurance, for the rest of our lives. It's from lack of a resource that people don't do what they might. You need a person who can subsidise the talented. The money....'

'Is it to spend?' asks Nooshi. 'They say it's not. It's power, but do you use money to buy power, or is that what money is?'

'It's more complex,' Solange says. 'But yes, of course.'

'If old people are more accomplished,' Nooshi says. 'It's better to be very old. You've had more time, and now it's done. You can evaluate anything you've been.'

'When you're young, you have more time, but it's not there, and so – there's nothing to be done.... Potential has no price, no value....' says Solange.

'There's something there that I don't grasp,' Nooshi says.

'You don't need to, Nooshi dear,' Solange says. 'It's me that tries to get the funds.'

'Chico has much bigger thoughts, it seems to me,' says Nooshi. 'Than hiring help. Then there is Tasha. How to explain to Olbek, her pallor, ghostliness, not being anywhere at all, but in the settlement again.... Shoshona too. It's quite a tragic story that, for him. How they ended up back there, when he had taken risks to save them both. And – the settlement. What squalor. What an opportunity is squandered there...!'

'It needs some pub, is all,' Solange says.

'Unless there's secrets,' Nooshi says. 'Publicise them, it all falls down....'

'Leave it to me, my dear,' Solange says, ramming the dinghy's bow to where she espies Chico and Olbek lounging on the shore.

*

'Shoshona and Tasha – had a bad trip,' Solange says. 'They sought refuge, a solace – back, over there....' She points.

'I'm not part of that,' I say. 'I'm very close to Tasha, but she's no feelings, or else too many – so many, she can't express....'

‘Does that matter?’ Nooshi asks. ‘When musicians do publicity, they talk of emotions because people who don’t know think there’s music and there is emotion, separate. Musicians don’t think of warmth and passion when they play – anxiety or euphoria perhaps, but all emotion’s already in the music. It’s like that with Tasha – you should recognise, Olbek, there’s just one package, all inside....’

‘Well, too late for all that now,’ says Solange, urging everything along. ‘The settlement’s not for Olbek. It promises simplicity, but it’s all tied up in ancient thinking, greedy personalities, misbelievers in what they do....’

‘It’s not belief,’ says Chico, ‘It’s understanding. Much more serious.’

‘Ah yes,’ says Solange. ‘Very true. You see life to the bottom of the mug....’

‘The dregs?’ he asks, and laughs. ‘My life was finished. All I have is what came after. The full account, the bill, the autopsy.’

‘We’re agreed,’ I say. ‘We shan’t go back to the settlement. It’s antiquity, and everybody there is a cadaver, waiting for the boat. And what is new – their trip, the city that exploded.... Wow! That’s something new – the bombers will get through! – and no one heard them for the noise....’

‘Nooshi and I,’ Solange breaks in, ‘We’ll go where you suggest ... but we’re at a climacteric in our life. There’s the foundation to be laid – we look for rock, the sand is fine against the earthquakes, but you need granite beneath you – so’s you can build and build again....’

‘I see you’re architecture buffs,’ says Chico. ‘Which pleases you the most – the build or the destroy? The point you make, the criticism? – or the mess the builders interpret from your plans?’

'You sound like you're an expert, lying there with almost nothing on and much surplus stuff to hide,' says Solange, needled.

'I lived in long houses,' Chico said, 'until there were no people left. Then I would have sought out architects, but I had ideas instead....'

'But you guys doss down in these beach shacks for tourists – if ever tourists came again, this place would be demolished....' Solange says.

I feel Chico needs some help. 'Chico is right,' I say. 'Ideas are good – trouble comes with the beliefs....'

'This isn't where I want to go,' Solange says to Nooshi.

'How do you two get on?' Nooshi asks, pushing me and Chico away from Solange. 'You're critical, dissatisfied. Creative. What have you got from yourselves, each other – apart from Chico's fortune, naturally....'

'Oh,' says Chico, laughing, 'We don't have cash. We have options. Everyone has options, but mostly they can't take them up. When can you cash them in? Not many do, not many can. you'd say they were the putrefying ones.... The body lives on, the will has disappeared – laid low by friendly fire. They didn't ask, they fell in the forest, the poison made them streaked and tawny, they stank for a while, were eaten clean, and polished – their documents went back in the pile.

'The hunter who kills an animal must first accept his own death. Accept, and undergo, submit. It's an exchange, death is. One dies, another, to all intents identical, springs up. Everyone is doubled. Hunter and prey, victim and victim.

'There's ghosts – the ghosts don't die, you made the pact, you're not a ghost, Solange. And if you seem to die ... you are a hunter and a peccary. You will be gone – completely, not an odour left, no memory. People you've not looked into – they become the ghosts.... You have an open mind about them, they're uncertainties. To you, not to themselves, of course.

You're not like that, Solange. You're a green leaf turning brown....'

'No,' says Nooshi, 'I'm not there, not with you, Chico. You've gone beyond me.'

'Solange will protect,' says Chico. 'Not like Olbek. Not like me. Solange feels guilty, I don't know why. Perhaps she loves hereself so much she can't forgive her infidelities. She's much attached to Nooshi. It's fatal. Olbek and me – we're clean, no guilt, so no compassion.'

'I'm here!' Solange shouts. 'It's just that you can't tell, no one can tell from looking at each other – I might have walked on Mars ... been left for dead and buried in a pit, in all my clothes, and other people in all theirs, we wore all we had when we were driven from our homes, but didn't think to take a pot or pan.... I pretended, crawled out, dead.... I wore a *tailleur,* sat in a limousine, parleyed for an hour a week to bring food to you starving doomed indigents and indigenes, and when it didn't work I didn't cry, not once....

'I know, Chico, how to make you big – bigger than Babar the elephant, more footsore than if you wore red shoes, more wretched than the match-girl, more gullible than Riding Hood, more cunning than the forty-first thief.... I'm gross and greedy, but – I am a genius. Without me, Chico, you're a wormy side of beef....'

'I know, Solange,' says Chico, embracing her, running his small hands over her large breasts, 'You have the job! There is no job.'

We stand frozen, like kids in a game.

'Don't try to change things, Solange,' Chico says. 'They'll change by themselves.'

'What will you do, Chico, if they don't rocket the miners up, and your options lapse?' asks Nooshi.

'Oh well,' says Chico, 'I've had bad deals throughout my life. I guess I'll have to go back – do good. Campaign.'

*

'These dinners,' Shoshona thinks. 'They are a game the Master always wins. Suppose we have a challenge, with a prize. The prize is easy – me and Tasha take a cruise. The game – it should be complicated – some Greek tags, perhaps – structures that you must solidify – after a while, they melt. I'd call it "Ruins", but that implies a negative. To me, making a good ruin is a sign it's time for something new. Nothing takes the place of anything – in the long term, everything winds down. It's physics. The deserts expand, the rivers dry. We eat the locusts, the bees die.

'Or else it rains incessantly – we all build arks. The world is sea, we float and eat the fish....

'So – to keep us happy and amused – we must concoct the games....'

'In your plans, Shoshona, there's always a desperation, at the end,' Tasha's ghost suggests.

'It's true, Tasha,' Shoshona says. 'If escape again, not having destinations – it could all end like you, caught on the beach, and Olbek not culturally trained to rescue weaker people....'

'If you have to appear weak to have your life saved,' Tasha says. 'It's better not.'

'You say that, Tasha, because your legs went bad while I was steering, looking the stars – compensating for the roundness of the earth, the linearity of life and legs,' Shoshona says, much irritated.

*

'If you want new games,' says Valentin, 'Don't base them on the structures of your brain. No chess or *Go* – the one whose brain is better wired will win, and once you know how yours was fixed, there is no fun, no skill. It's like a pianist, playing Alkan or Nancarrow – all lies in your ganglia. Listening – the music's trite. I can write a piece for panpipes Tasha couldn't play, however wonderful her brain – but hearing it, it's nothing much....'

'No,' says Shoshona, 'I want to exclude dexterity. I want memories only I can have ... interpretations of a history hidden in a grave-pit....'

'Oh, lighten up, my love,' says Tasha's ghost, quite jovially. 'Philosophy's a game when people steer themselves, are steered, to a predestined destination. A form of words, presented as a form of mind. A trick, that is. It's like Monopoly, except when money is involved, it's obvious who's lost, they're broke. But in the world, winning in the money game – what does it mean? More than you need? Taking from those who need it more? More than you can spend? Having no one to leave your stash to when you die – or going demented, needing someone you don't know to spend it all for you?'

'It will involve making a story whose conclusion lets me out,' Shoshona says. 'A story that resolves itself – only by letting me depart; a boat, my dear, seaworthy, a compass, a radio for Berber songs ... no complicated switchery I can't manipulate.'

'Yes,' says Valentin. 'That might be yours, a story that does everything you think is good for you. It would sell no copies – you'd possess the only one, though written brilliantly.... But if it is a game, you can't decide the winner from before the start. I might require a tale that takes account of beauty, truth and justice....'

'Oh Valentin,' Shoshona laughs. 'That's for Olympians! All I want is getting out of this discursive place, when everything concludes and nothing starts....'

'It's ridiculous,' says Valentin. 'It reminds me of 'they talk about their lives – to have lived is not enough for them.' Must we hear about the Camaro your father bought for you, as a reward, or compensation for what he did to you?'

'Not a Camaro,' says Shoshona – 'I don't drive, and the roads are rackety. Don't take the highway, it doesn't lead anywhere – just to political cash.'

'There's money in games, and gaming,' Valentin says. 'The book always wins – but it doesn't mean the individual never does. Why don't you ask why the boatman doesn't let you take the canoe, Shoshona, drop off Tasha's ghost, bring the canoe back, and have the boatman take you where you want – far from Tasha's ghost if you prefer.... So, the incompatibles are ferried out, the puzzle's solved.'

'It's difficult,' Shoshona says. 'That story's difficult. It's not up to the boatman. He believes. He believes his mission is divine, and ordered from Above. You can't get him to change who and when he takes away.... One at a time, and in his care – it is canonical. You see, it isn't trivial at all – not like truth and beauty, those slip down like oysters, snails ... or justice, if you wear a wig and gown – and have a prison handy. His belief is set in tales. It's concrete. No puzzle, no solution.'

'You can't do stories,' Valentin says, amused, frustrated. 'You're too literal.'

'Stories don't do anything, we've just seen,' says Tasha's ghost. 'Look at Chekhov. Escapes impossible. And the Revolution – was that a story? The boat – it wasn't the Potemkin, it was the Twelve Apostles, dredged up. Not the deceiver-prince – the story's the deceit. Stories illuminate when they deceive, they're traps for rats – the rats are smart, the traps trap cats!

'Horses are more fun.

'There's many more people arriving here – all moderns, but mostly they don't believe in anything. Not in the new, not in transcending it, nor ignoring it. I could be wrong. I know – modernity's not about the new, it's about accepting what is present, and understanding the slime-pit it's just come from.

'Perhaps they believe in everything. Everyone is modern anyway, you suffer it, or laugh.

'The beach is full of boats abandoned, scuttled ... you could fix one up, but wherever you go, you'll be a modern. There's nothing left, you can't be disillusioned, you had none, no illusions. But – there was maybe one. Velocity. You could have driven that Camaro anywhere, on the desert – mind the candlesticks – you could rumble on for ever....'

'For you and Shoshona, stories are no use,' says Valentin, 'They only grow upwards, like magic beans. Horses, you can ride on the flat, or over jumps – and they can get you out of here, the back way. And yet – listen, Tasha's ghost – when you were caught, imprisoned by the tide – if you'd climbed up, up the cliff, you could have avoided drowning, avoided Olbek, avoided being weak. There's always an escape, if you think hard. The beach – a strand, between the solid and the fluid – an area of uncertainty, of contradiction – sand for cement, sand for castles. Where once we lazed and bronzed – now it's our Maginot where we await defeat, recession. Sea-rise. Our limit, our retreat. And yet – look up! Those cliffs are rugged, full of handholds ... like Shoshona's dad,' and he giggles.

'I didn't think of it,' says Tasha's ghost. 'In the long run, it would have made no difference. Not to me.'

'That's the lesson, then,' says Valentin. 'I've dealt with destiny and games. You can't get out, Shoshona, unless the boatman is convinced he must take you, and then you'd have to leave poor Tasha's ghost behind, so in the end ... you're stuck. The boatman takes you only when you're dead.'

'It means a horse,' says Tasha's ghost.

'This place,' Shoshona tells Tasha's ghost, 'Is squalid. All the time that you could want – but the food! I have to scrabble to get by – no cash, no nothing.... No respect, no future. Perhaps – this is the future?'

'Well,' says Tasha's ghost, 'I don't cost you anything, Shoshona.'

*

The beach huts – you can say they're safe. No stairs to fall down, the roofs light, replaceable. They'd fly away, not fall on you. But – something is lacking. You only face one way – into the waves, the instability, the repetition. There's never a 'what next?' – you know.

'We design our lives,' Olbek says. 'It takes our concentration. However hard you try, the unexpected ... not what you hope for, the unforeseen that brings you unexpected pleasure.... Often the planned life is hard – avoiding the routines, you miss out on security and cash: you're vulnerable.

'Other people – must be left to make their own design. Don't interfere, and anyway, aside from being an unwanted meddler, other people have such big demands on cash and time.... If they can't run their existences – maybe flooded, in a camp, or starving – we suffer.' And Olbek looks round the little group for some agreement, some dissent, an understanding.

'Waiting for the good times,' Chico says, reluctantly, 'Gets on my nerves.'

'Oh, I know exactly what I want,' Solange says. 'And exactly how it will not happen. I plan for the second best – and even that will take some luck.'

*

Ah, the Settlement. You want to leave, but there you are – all places are much like the Settlement – a movie set; one day Zagreb, the next Zagorsk. Really, you want to leave yourself and grow. You can't. Shoshona's finding this....

'A horse!' Shoshona shouts. 'My virtue and my heritage – for a horse!'

'Hush!' says Valentin. 'We only take promises that are notarised. But – once Oskar had a horse – in case he wanted to escape. A quarter horse – we put the four of them together – off a quadriga, ran like a wave.... But it grew fat. He fed it snails – justice and equity – it put on weight, we housed it in a shack....'

And there it is. A cart horse.

'No saddle,' says Shoshona. 'I'll grasp its mane.'

'Oh, it's not a goer,' Oskar says, joining them, preparing that the horse, at last, will meet its destiny ... a race, a sacrifice, was it to Apollo? Neptune? Or to the sacred rose? 'We have no cart. No metalled road. Besides, we moderns wouldn't cut down trees to make the cart, and as for leather reins.... To be free, a community that self-regulates, we must await the boatman. When our choices have been made, he'll bear us all away ... no fuss, no fee. The obols are on the collectivity....'

'It is with these,' says Valentin, holding a bunch of – red nails? Horns from satanic fauns? 'We'll make him trot. Hot chilli peppers. You stuff them in the horse exactly where you wouldn't want them for yourself.... Just let him see them, hold them out – they're better than a coca snort – he'll remember Attic winds, the sea, the sea! And off!'

With one bound, the horse indeed – is off. Shoshona holds the mane, and Tasha's ghost clings to the tail.

Feed a graminivore with gramineae. If you feed a horse with snails – the dialectics of nature spots the contradiction – and the horse will speed.

Up the slope into the trees, and then there's scrub, at last a rackety road – past the abandoned Roxy, past the shuttered betting shop, electronics boarded up, the mango stall quite fruitless....

'Civilisation!' Shoshona shouts, 'It can't be far ... hold tight, Tasha, my dear, salvation awaits, and time to reflect on all the risks I took for you....'

But Tasha's ghost has lost its hold, has tumbled off. She's somewhere in the scrub ... or in the trees ... or maybe rolled back down the slope, into the settlement, where dinner is about to start ... the snails, like salt and pepper pots slowly circumambulate, justice and freedom leave their trail, and Shoshona rushes on, she cannot slow or steer; the horse – driven by his alarm, the snails long gone, the chilli – firing him up, perhaps a wonder diet, unexpectedly a find.... His technique? An antique stretching out, the gallop elongated....

Then, on and on, along the rackety road, the sandy track, over the brackish runlet....

There in the distance, she sees the shine of Chico's nose-ring ... then Olbek, Solange, Nooshi too.

'It's formulaic, but it works,' Shoshona thinks. 'Alas, poor Tasha's ghost, gone to find another path, another life – but all the rest! We've aged, accomplished nothing, but we're vigourous and sharp. We run, escape, the road is circular – and here we were, and here we are. Now, the climax, the adventure with us five ... canonic number ... with a ghost, we were three pairs ... now, we're a winning hand at five card stud….'

And she drops, invisible and immortal, off the horse.

*

'What shall we do with him?' Nooshi asks, patting the horse. He steams. 'Maybe – race him. He could enjoy that, now, he might even win.'

'Can we trust each other?' Chico asks. 'To do the best by him. The oats? The gold cup? The curry combing, and the colic scares? There's division ... that's the hardest operation in arithmetic. It's easier to let him run, just loose him, freedom ... all that stuff....'

'We've given up our merely big ambitions, hoping that only leaves the biggest one,' says Olbek. 'We've been trapped, lost our inheritance, or found we weren't entitled. Our hunger, though, to leave a trace, is ever with us. But – still, we're vulnerable. Most people still have to face the disasters we moderns write about, hoping for us, they're past ... but it doesn't mean the trials are finished for us, indeed.... Remember Adam, in the creation myth – a wife, a garden, with a gardener. A pensioner's delight. Who'd have thought it was a fantasy, a nursery tale. Behold! the naked spouse, the snake – a sex toy probably... maybe what they did was wrong, though there are hints.... Misogyny, of course. The gardener turns out to be a Pasdaran, a fink – and orders "out you go, my friend, my first clay puppet toy, into the desert, your stupid bride to chide you, a crushing sense of guilt, no woodcraft or survival skills, no nothing". The gardener, the trickster, sloping off to hide....'

'The fantasies. The talking beasts, princesses – crones in drag – you think it is reality. It *is*, together with the taradiddles, the magic cakes and powders you consume.

'They never stop,' says Solange. 'It's like Mah Jong, you have to build a wall, and when it gets knocked down, you advance, consolidate. You must remember, that it never finishes. Unless you set an arbitrary end, it goes on and on. You don't know if, when you're long dead, something will be different. There's no discovery you make that changes rules – you weren't there when they were made, and if you had been ... it'd have been Olbek to the rescue once again – your unasked, unplanned, human nature makes you hop, prostrate yourself. We're yea-sayers. Into the trap you leap, no second thoughts. You take the consequences on the chin, don't question how the real is fabulous, is metaphor. 'Successful guys make sausages – and losers compose symphonies.' Nature, instinct. They're the default. Not thought, not reasoning.

'Like the horse's fear, instinct sometimes helps you fly....'

'Flee,' says Olbek. 'But we'll have learned, I'm sure. Not from what we were taught, but from the kicking we got in the playground after class.'

'Hey!' says Shoshona. 'It's *my* horse. He need not have galloped – that was his gift, no one was after us. He wanted to have a game with me, that's all.

'All the challenges you see ahead – we'll meet them, one by one, each one of us alone. Trust me – everything that's lost won't disappear. it ends up with the dealer. That's what you play for. There's no mystery.'

'You convince me, Shoshona,' Chico says. 'But I don't understand it, not a bit. It seemed we play to win, be rich, yet you say the cash goes to the dealer....'

'That's the rule,' Shoshona says. 'We don't know ourselves, trust anybody but the dealer – no time, no interest. We blunder on – that's the best way. We don't know each other, except, perhaps, for Nooshi.... She sees everyone for clear, and in return they ignore her. We're too concerned with our own strategies, the fortunes, reputations, even the philanthropy we plan.'

'We could get to know each other better,' I say. 'And everything else too. You can spend a life poking at a germ, or putting a harness on a slice of space.... See where it moves, what boils in it, makes crusts.... Chico, if we all stroke....'

I don't say 'frogs', I'm prudent. 'Shut up, Olbek,' Chico says. 'Go on that tack, I'll kill you.'

'Ooh drugs!' says Nooshi, clasping her hands and making them a mystic knot. 'I don't do drugs, but if you're all are....'

'You see?' Chicho whispers, hissing like a scorpion. 'Keep your fucking mouth barricaded. We may want to know the others, they may be our lost loves – but knowing isn't sharing. Nooshi's false naive, Solange collects jobs, can't do them, gets given titles, honours, to get rid of her. The queen of surfaces, universally known as knowing nothing, a boombox without content. Shoshona – her name, her parents – looks like she has structures. Something to look for. Something to make you envy. But names are all she has. She's the spoonful of tar in her empty barrel – she's slick! See how she amputated poor Tasha...! Pintos, Mustangs – she doesn't ride them, they're the motors people buy for her ... a trader in replicas of what she hasn't been.... A bottle of brown stuff, perfume, makes you remember ... all the roses of Bulgaria.'

'If it's so,' I ask, 'How can we work with them?'

'I'm warning you, Olbek,' Chico says. 'That's all. The more you know, the less you'll want of them. Keep your distance, be alert. They're all warriors, they each want to end alive and on the winning side.'

'I'm not a warrior, Chico,' I say.

'Then, they'll be finding out about you. You don't need to do anything. Be you,' he says. 'The frogs – they're you and me. We aren't about fashion, or what's happening; the great screw of the moment. If you need a telling metaphor – think "Tasha's legs". They ended it for her. If you want to know what people want and cannot have – ask an American. Allegiances – for the next while, ours will be with each other.'

'What you are loyal to – it isn't allies,' I say. 'Your allies are recorded, and you pay for them. The rest is ephemeral, loyalties.'

'I said allegiances,' Chico says. 'It's stronger; while one lasts, you have to pledge.'

'The spirit of the times,' I say. 'We should tune into that.'

'It can't be us,' says Chico. 'This place is devastated, anarchoid. It isn't anywhere, it's somewhere quite distinct, but it is nondescript. It isn't what you want. Here, if you protest, they don't take your liberty, they take your livelihood. You aren't locked up, not like over there,' and he gestures broadly, 'you are locked in.

'No one trusts anyone, what you do outside yourself has no significance, we've come from everywhere, there's nowhere left to go. Be content. Our little band can find a grove, collect some ospreys, different kinds of vodka – then, pass on. What's done ... we always try undoing it. Obsession ... to excavate, restore, return.'

'Return means going back to where we know it's hopeless, and it means coming back here,' I say. 'Chico, my soul is dark, real dark. I'd do dark things. The speed, the odds. I've done them.... Still, we have our options....'

'Absolutely. Yes.' Chico says.

*

'How will a change of hegemony affect?' I ask Chico. 'Those people we have now – they have the power, knowledge, even the cash, to make anything at all happen to you, even nothing.'

'It will come,' says Chico, 'It won't save anything I'd have wanted to remain. What's gone, went long ago. Can we remain outside, can we do a deal, pretend we don't know what's hegemony, and how we need it, to serve us better. Will it feed us, talk more honestly? Will the "us" be different?'

'The projects will be different. No options – but ours were fantasy,' I say. 'Lots of fantasies will turn out to be fantasies.'

'We'll remember my lost home, and you'll remember Tasha, lost in the scrub,' Chico says. 'This place will be built over, the settlement closed – unproductive, an illusion that anyone at all makes history all the time, is equal and powerful too....'

'I shan't miss what goes,' I say. 'Not at all. Though I may resent what comes. Can we still duck out, Chico? Will the sun set today and give us some hope for a tomorrow's sunrise? We didn't get what we wanted, lots didn't, but we were lucky, they didn't see us sneak away, and live on little....'

'We live on Solange now,' says Chico. 'She backs creatives – like us. We're all supposed to be creative, or at least appreciate and buy.... Solange doesn't listen to what Nooshi says about us. She's accumulated some resources, and she doesn't discriminate – she likes a turn of ankle and of phrase.'

'Shoshona might cling on,' I say. 'She needs continuity, needs a platform to situate herself, her causes. You lost your story long ago, Chico, so being a hegemon was your sole prospect.... Vanity, my dear, just vanity.'

'What we have to do, we must do quickly,' he says. 'We may have no chance in future. It won't be better, you can bet. Try to be on the winning side. We must decide what it's to be for us, and do it quick – no brakes, no safety straps.'

'There are comrades,' I say. 'We don't have any. You lose anyway, now or after. Your friends go down with you....'

'Whatever I do,' he says. 'I do to win. That's discipline.'

'The promise of capitalism,' I say. 'If anyone had noticed promises while the whole world was transformed – was to bring riches. Instead, it brought the rich. And hierarchy, disorder, and the rest. Shall we have communism? Know what it is, what it is not? Will it be order, hierarchy, repression – and communists?

'America? – it was a tossed salad – slaves and fugitives and millionaires. China now – it always was the centre of the world....'

'We must prepare to watch in safety – the birth throes, they call it. We've no swift horse running in this race,' says Chico.

'You could say we're ideal for the new, having lost our prospects in the old.'

'The big war, the drastic famine, necessary labour – it's not easy for us to plan,' I say. 'We tiptoe round holes in the road, subsidences, disasters long announced. There's world's end to consider too.'

'There's been Vietnam, Beirut, Somalia,' Chico says. 'Syria – just a start....' He counts off on his fingers, desists. 'We know how things can go. Tasha's been lost – that was an accident that followed accident.

'I won't continue – it's best for us to stand aside. Big wheels revolve, the change will come, whether we press for it or not, when we are long long dead.... What will be the theme? Thoughts of autocrats and books unquestionable? You could do a jig to it, Olbek, for sure....'

'You're not a nullity,' I say. 'You're in transition, but you're on a side ... you add your weight....'

'I did, I did,' he says. 'I played my part. And so, Olbek, did you – confused and ineffective though you are, and who knows what you did or thought you did.... At least there was your Tasha, saved from the wave ... and wandering now, quite lost. Both of you – undecided. "Ask us later".'

*

'Still watching it spin round, you two?' Solange asks. 'You need to get the world beneath your feet, be part of it, the giddy movement....' She laughs, but not with us. 'I have the project in my mind,' she says.

'Wait!' Chico says. 'Remember – we do not love, we have no secret place to come from, no garden, no family. We have emotions, but no cat, no dog, no favourite book or cliché, we dodged our army, faked what we could....'

'Oh come,' says Solange. 'Olbek and Tasha? – a love worth three operas. Epics all round! There was the universal garden in the Settlement – that everybody ran from. You are not victims, you empathise with those, but do all you can not to be victimised....

'It isn't easy to see what history me and you four can make ... and not forgetting Tasha's ghost....'

'It doesn't matter,' I say. 'So long as you have a way to set things right.'

'Yes, that I have,' she says.

'Forgive me, Solange,' Chico says. 'But you sound stupid.'

'It doesn't matter if she sets things right,' I say.

'What's the answer?' Chico asks. 'It's easy to give an answer if there's no question. What form does your answer take, Solange? Lectures, a book, a movement? Something you read on telephones? To set it right, all of it...?'

'Yes,' says Nooshi, 'It's telephones.'

'We'll think about it,' Chico says, and whispers to me, 'It's more publicity. Let's take Shoshona, head off on our own, we three....'

'When the rain stops....' I say. It doesn't stop. The Settlement slides down to the water, through the mangrove, under ... the great slither, shacks and snails. No one dies, so no one calls the boatman. He's useless. He can die, and no one knows.

It's gone, all the people too; the rules – and soon you forget the names, the project.... What was it? Symposia? To work out principles, the purpose, like the book of dodgy dialogues had said – though it was out of date, a piece of bourgeois real-estate, real as only it is real – fragments of one many possible worlds, a bull-filled field of utopian experimentation. All washed away, that class of dullards and geniuses bussed off. Try again. Or not. It's old hat.

The rains, the droughts – the waters with no fish, the waters full of those big flowering medusas, the multicoloured babies diving in, retrieving nickels – each with a doctorate lying unused in its envelope....

'The snails have multiplied,' says Chico, 'It's called a bloom. We'll forget their names, the people, what they were for, why they couldn't be ferried off.... Maybe the village was for rehab? Maybe a sponsored project, shrimp farm, intensive manioc, a penal settlement, soldiers on the lam – resisting, dodging drafts ... living well, living worse, just living. Working. Tourists and refugees – they don't, they can't work. work is like Carthage – to be utterly destroyed. Look where it's got us! Each of us a bit of everything.

'All slid, ended in the water.'

'While we wait until the rain stops, gives way to its opposite, the natural dialectic – let's try interpretation. Hermeneutics. Not something the Settlement was keen on,' I say. 'Rain makes things grow and is the death of us. You could say our pounding heart, the pressure, the inner heat – they should be signs of vigour. But they aren't, they're signs of the end. Us and the rain. The flood that doesn't stop this time. No outrunning it, no swift steeds, racers, dolphins, pigeons, acquaintances of humankind – no winning way. Rain or sun. unruly growth at first, irrelevant and hedonistic, evil knowing what is good for it.... Is there a meaning underneath the meaning, the significance...?'

'No,' says Chico. 'I get the point. Talking is about continuing. If the rain continues, we can't go on talking. Shoshona's mustang is a car – they come in boxes, kits. She could buy one, and we three could bounce off in it – it helped to make the rain. There is a special dance for it, not to be abused ... out in the desert you don't need rain anyway, it would melt your grave-mound, the *kurgan*. We know *what*'s coming, Olbek, it's the *when*. You can't interpret that.

Philosophy is the menu of the life you will not have – science tells you why you won't, can't. That's it. Solange is right – the message is 'we're in the same sinking boat, let's sing a rousing song together, the words are the same in every language.''

'It doesn't matter, Chico,' I say. 'Languages are all the same, but the soldiers don't come to speak in tongues. It's all the rest, what they're carrying – not words.'

'Oh, there's no soldiers, Olbek,' Chico says. 'The trucks can't get through the floods. Now, the couscous will be ruined with the wet.'

*

'The Mustang came,' Shoshona says. 'In its loose-box – I bolted it together. It has enduring faults – a light back end – that's how Tasha got flung off. And narrow factory tyres – no grip! I'll see to that, although I'm not Comanche. Maybe you two are.... Your conversation is traditional, you're patients, terminal, you won't be fit to fight. Whatever's new you won't be on its side.'

'Let's escape Solange,' says Chico. 'The hectoring! Too bad we can't take Nooshi, she knows all about interpreting. She's the wall creating different rooms.'

'I usually go on trips with brainy guys,' Shoshona says. 'We play Wordcraft, there's Zelenka on the stereo, and we are three in bed: the last's the weakest part. But you two guys fall down in everything.'

'Of course,' says Chico, 'We've all had that life of yours – it won't repeat.'

'We can go anywhere,' Shoshona says. 'This motor's wood-burning. Not the trees where Tasha is – that's a sacred grove. Pellets – like the owls make.'

Far behind, there's Nooshi, waving frantically. 'We won't go back,' Shoshona says. 'She's a mouthpiece for Solange, and Solange says only what millions will understand ... there's no point is listening, and going back means listening. We've heard everything said since we were born, that's the technology, what education gives you – the standard. repetition. That's why Olbek couldn't teach anybody anything – they'd heard it before and so had he. There's no communication. That's the flaw – communication means a passage of something different: a passage of the same, which is all we have, is raindrops on a window-pane.'

*

'You don't have a map, Shoshona, that's an atlas,' Chico says.

'Well,' she says. 'You know all the countries, Chico. A road's a road. I'm interested in percentages, not places. How much of the world we've searched.'

'Searched for what?' I ask, knowing it's a silly question.

'For what we haven't found,' Chico jumps in, and we three laugh. 'Wait!' he says. 'We've run out of trees ... the horse needs filling....' There's a mescal pump – we fill him up. have a glass ourselves. It's too hot for the frogs,' he says. 'They've shrivelled – maybe gone extinct....'

He shows us a tobacco tin, three or four 'T' shapes, like dessicated mushrooms, mescalin – orange and green and red. Four dried-up paws for roots.

'Slow, quick, stop,' says Chico, touching each in turn. 'They give you peace. It's too early for any of them now. When we reach the end – one each....'

'You guys,' Shoshona says, waggling the wheel to make the car skip high. 'You relish the past and your absent places in it. You're conservatives, living in the mud; the has-been soil. Yet you talk of socialism, living in the future – and how hard it is both ways, conservative and socialist, to live in nowhere. And yet you'd hate to be thought liberals – living as you will, free to make catastrophes and then be caged when everything falls down ... but doing what you want, celebrating your tiny wills, and fuck everybody else.... And yet there's no experiment. It's just "do as you want" and hope you'll be done to you as you wish. That's you two, for sure, your likeness, and your plan. And yet you know you will be caught, you'll overdo it, so will all the rest.... It's a way of escaping guilt, for taking the money if you can. Lots and lots, if you're not restrained. But why? Mostly you want trivial things, but if someone has ambitions, excess, or folly – it's the end! Those are genocidal messiahs! They sink the boat with greed and corpses!

'Conservatives and socialists are ready with their sabres and their chains, but they have reasons, pretexts, justifications. you are nihilists, full of hope, and expectations of ... nothing. The end. Let someone else have a go....'

'Where does the atlas say we'll find a haven?' Chico asks.

'You've had your rants,' Shoshona says. 'It's my turn now.'

There'll be some landscape soon. Here, there's stands of tall yellowed grass, a rutted road.

*

'Chico – they took everything you had,' Shoshona says. 'You have been colonised. They gave you lessons – sacrifice, a bloody cross, and writing down your protestations in a language not your own.

'Olbek – won't work. Your forebears were those who worked, slaved, and formed a class. Then – not they, but you, gave up. Preferred a humble hedonism and uncertainty; rhetoric to power. The general strike, taking over ... where did that go? You tricked yourselves. You didn't persevere, you went and fought in someone else's wars.

'And now – these quibbles over Tasha, and her ghost that's gone – where? Into the sacred grove, the big expanse, a plain all taboo now ... a soggy desert.

'I shan't be tricked! Not like you! I have a name, no place, no cause, no duties – nothing. I must search for everything, my past that there is not, a future I'll make by and for myself....'

*

Shoshona speeds up, the Mustang bucks and skitters – on, on, we go, a ride to the abyss ... at least, surely, there'll be a gas station, a woodpile....

'The sea, the sea,' she shouts – 'I had adventures for nothing, nothing at all, that you'd have paid to watch. What do you think I do in life – titillate old rich men, steal their money?'

'No, Shoshona,' Chico says. 'You have class. So do we – we'd not mix with that other sort. You and I carry totems and graveyards. We buckle under their weight.'

'You're wrong,' she says. 'No weight. I'm not that person, you invented her, and she was bored with you. I'm with Olbek, weightless. I have no depth, no substance – that's the best, people worship people just like me, they quote from them, shout at them, "*kekekekex*", I am everything they hope for.... And what is more – I crossed the sea, saved Tasha, cut her legs off – she was my sacrifice, and it made me an immortal!'

She spins the wheel, but the car can't rise out of the ruts.... 'Let's stop when we see a shack with food,' says Olbek. 'The horse is tired, and I am hungry.'

The signs says 'Cocoanuts'. There's a brown pan with hot brown oil.

'Those are crickets,' says the lady. 'We're sober,' says Shoshona. 'Put vodka in the glasses, and hang crickets – locusts – round the edge, like question-marks.'

'No,' the lady says. 'There's no questions, the road is long, longer than you've imagined, so they're commas.'

We get back on the Mustang. 'We forgot to feed you,' says Shoshona to the horse, 'We were so thirsty – and a wee bit apprehensive – those guys, insatiable as locusts, putting an edge on their machetes....'

'They might have cut our legs off,' I say, to lighten up.

'There's no need,' Shoshona says. 'It's automatic change, you don't need feet, the road's too long to walk along. Relax. You haven't learnt anything it's worth forgetting. And, we still have my project, remember.'

'If anyone can make the trip,' says Chico, sucking up to her – 'It's you, Shoshona. You and the horse are one.'

She presses on. 'That vodka and locust cocktail – doesn't fill you up,' she says. 'On to the next!'

'The project, Shoshona!' I insist.

'Discovery,' she says. 'It is what invention is. and invention is creation. So – we'll go see the mountains – the greatest creation of our humankind.... Over there,' she points, to shiny grey shapes – 'The Andes, the only chain created by a pressure, not a crash. They're shapely, not just bits of stone thrown up. The rest is disappointing – ahead, the Rockies, then over there....' and she lets go the wheel – 'Alps and Atlas – product of collisions. Maybe the Tien Shan is less a scene of violence, but the Himalayas – pink with the refuse of our climbers – what disasters they have seen.... All ends just in a pile of pointy rocks. Over in the sea,' and she gestures – 'Knobs of stone, like dinos' backbones, islands half submerged and then – Pacific! Sunken craters, steaming like pustules in a soupy sea....'

'And that is all?' asks Chico. 'That's the world – imploded, ridged and sterile.... That's the project, that's our world? See it, appropriate it....'

'Those are the best parts,' says Shoshona. 'I haven't taken you to see the *kurgans*, the mounds of clay where we once lived like termites ... busy and motivated....'

'All this is ours?' I ask, knowing that it is. 'There's rivers and deserts to come. 'The beetle bar – we're known already, we could return, fill up there.... It's legendary, all you need to see the scene is horse and rider....'

'Of course, people have been thoughtless and messy,' Shoshona says. 'But in the early cities, we could keep things clean....'

'Wait!' says Chico. 'We don't need another nature tale, about what's left when we are gone.... Our profligacy and trend to self-annihilation has undone us all. There's a more enticing theme. This began with saving lives – a life. Tasha's ... her reasons for so wishing it; and Olbek's doubts.'

'Oh, everything's about everything, or almost so,' Shoshona says, kicking at the Mustang's tyres. 'Where there's no one, you can bet they've met an end you wouldn't want yourself.'

*

'There's not much room for three,' says Chico.

'Leave your inner selves on the back seat,' Shoshona says. 'What's left can sleep beneath this tree – the pods up there, they don't look ripe, they shouldn't fall on you by night....'

'I don't think they are pods,' I say. 'Pod-shaped – but it is fur. Bats or foxes, I suspect....'

'Here's a tip,' Chico says. 'If you can't sleep, devise a game where all the cards are five of clubs – or sometimes they're called flowers. There's no significance, no symbolism. It calms the spirit, a casual suit....'

We both think of Mount Fuji, not part of a chain, but a spirit, floating above itself. No natural significance at all.

Shoshona sleeps behind the wheel – and in the morning she, with the horse, are gone.

'She means us to look for her – to show we appreciate,' I say. 'Besides – the pods were busy all the night – snacking, flying and chatting, happiness unrestrained, but chirruping....'

'Don't be too sure,' says Chico. 'I'd sooner let her go, taking our inner selves as a memento. Shoshona tends to the side of Thanatos. Seated in the symposium, not eating, and at the end she calls the chef – next time will she bestow a taller pie-crust hat, or will his head be served, a pomegranate in his mouth and myrtles or whortleberries for his eyes...?'

'She's slick, for sure,' I say. 'It's true. She's well-read. If you must, take Ockam's razor literally, a snicker-snee "off goes her head"....'

We laugh. I have a small revelation. 'But – you know, in the end, Chico, we've nothing. I saved a life – the life went bleeding in the sea. What was it, is it, worth? A life saved, or lost, as they all are – what can the value be? The worth, the sense?

'And you, Chico, like me, we sleep beneath the stars – it's poetry. But we saw the world, Shoshona drove us over it ... yesterday, the mountains, tomorrow, possibly – the seas. Forget the deserts. It's all ours – but she owns it all. What for? She has your project, Chico – why? What will she do with it? Meanwhile – we have nothing. Only the poetry, if we care to write it down....'

'The poetry is everything, Olbek,' says Chico, looking disappointed, cheated. 'But, you'rc right – it's vapours from the oracle, her pot. A touch of skin, from frogs....'

We've nowhere to go. She doesn't come. We can't start walking – everywhere is far far off.

'We could eat dates and locusts, have food brought by storks,' Chico says. 'But there's no palms.

No anything. Nature says – 'everyone eats everyone'. That's what has happened here.'

'We could eat the pods,' I say. 'They eat all the time. But I don't fancy it – the wings are skin, the bodies meager, like crayfish, transparent.... And how'd we climb the tree?'

'She'll come back, if she can and if she wants,' says Chico. 'Money would be of no use to us. A telephone? Even without an answer ... it's an empty sound, but if you die, you leave a tune, so people know. No funny tricks – a requiem.'

We settle, grow carapaces, dry out, brittle and brown, our spit is thick and grey like mushroom soup – less nourishing. Chrysalides, cocoons – we are the creatures in their grave-clothes, not in the swaddling phase.

*

'It's quite ridiculous. I'd no idea, intention. What a stupidity,' Shoshona says. 'Just went for a trot.... And now, here's Chico – quite dead, passed from is to was – no river, no boatman, nothing to pay, no customs, and no passport. Free as the wind.'

'He knew so many songs and shuffles – he was a box of games,' I say. 'Just silence now; no summary, no doubt, no fear, no stoicism.'

'Oh, you're romantic, Olbek,' Shoshona says. 'Terror. That's death. Both come, together. If you're awake, you're terrified. There's nothing more terrifying than the fall ... eternal....'

I start to contradict. She shushes me. 'You don't know, Olbek, you've just read the stuff. I've seen it, I've been at the edge and going down. Terror. That is what one feels, and what you'll feel. It stays with you, the first and last sensation, emotion if you will – at birth, you cry and scream – time takes it out of you, and leaves you with its silence, silence for the first time ever.'

It's so. The pods stir on their branches, up there, there must be a breeze, they dream, re-fold their wings like turning a new page.

'What was he, Chico, like?' Shoshona asks, as if she'd never met him.

'Most people are buffoon or dictator, usually they're both,' I say. 'Then there's the happy nondescripts – he was striving to be one of those.'

He lies, a brown curled leaf. He was my friend – he could be all of what he saw his chances were. Nothing – just nothing. That's the achievement.

'It's up to us,' Shoshona says. 'To give a shape to what we've started being.'

'You weren't here,' I say. 'You could be being anything.'

*

I don't ask. Dumping the horse – for simplicity, or for profit? Because love ends?

She says. 'Horses run away. It isn't personal. They remember – it's false. They weren't happy in the wild. They're not happy now. That's why they run. You can't say "escape", because they'll be caught and it will be worse. No one holds them – on the contrary, we want them to race!'

'Chico had the same idea,' I say. 'He had a scheme – to restore something original. But original means something else – not as it was, but something as it's never been. He'd never been in the forcst, but he knew, he thought, what it could be like ... its fulfilment....'

'No one knows it, and living it, it's everyday,' says Shoshona, quite tart. 'The fulfilment is invented long long after. I know. I have this name. I don't have its past, or its present. I have to make up something else....'

'That's what Chico realised,' I say. 'He could have been a big cheese in that symbolic past, but in the symbolic present – he was nothing much.'

'Rather pathetic,' says Shoshona. 'You too, Olbek – your plan came from saving Tasha – but she didn't know danger or safety, so for her there could be no plan. You were blocked.... You're a nullity, a blank sheet – people trust you to write their memoirs on.'

'You're a modern, Shoshona,' I say. 'You know what you are. You anticipate the judgement – the rest of us must wait, a summary, a memoir, necrology, whatever measures what we were against what we hoped to be.'

'I don't see you as a hopeful type, Olbek,' Shoshona says. 'I studied; – *you* believe what comes. I make my biography – you don't know what your life has been. Someone will have to make a quilt, and it will have your parts in little squares, even your private parts. You won't recognise yourself, but you won't be here.'

'You want the story, Shoshona,' I say. 'You're determined. You could have put in at a hundred places with Tasha, but you had to bring her, a corpse, back to the settlement.'

'Oh, the Settlement,' she laughs. 'You make it sound like an experiment. Rehab, a comune. It was the best – supposed to be. Profound.... And those hundred ports we passed. Each of them – Odessa, Haifa, Limassol, Rhodes, Alexandria, Oran, Valencia – no, you make me laugh! Each slippery with blood, and I could go on and on reciting.... Marseille, Tripoli.... Not one place to land a suffering, confused, expiring person!'

'I know,' I say. 'The boatman told me, the Settlement is the place where everybody hopes to go to, to avoid death under the sun. But it didn't work out. It began as a *stanitsa*, ended as a halt. And don't tell me you're a humanitarian, Shoshona. You select humans, put them on a ladder – the ones at the top lean down and eat the bottom ones. You think having friends means having enemies, as many....'

'You're right, of course,' she says. 'I don't love everyone, and so – I have to judge. Solange gave that up – she wanted to send messages instead. From the start, I know I have my enemies. Finding friends – it's long, exhausting.'

'Chico?' I ask. 'He was my friend. What shall we do with him? I don't have enemies, everyone I know who is alive, eats well, is full....'

'If you've so little, Olbek,' Shoshona says. 'If you no longer have your enemies, you're thick with parasites. And Chico – he's not here. Do you have a tale he told, we'd carve it … somewhere?'

'No,' I say. 'He's this brown leaf. It might be customary, to have him resting here.... The pods – they'll clean him up....'

'He's dead,' Shoshona says. 'Not resting. Custom? You need a lot of people before there's custom. You need a tribe, a clan. He had you and me. We leave him – what more could he expect?'

'We could pretend,' I say. 'The forest. Like it was. I never saw it. Set it around him.'

She laughs. 'A forest? Like you have? We all have one – mine's full of enemies. Perhaps that's what they're for, forests,' and she laughs and laughs, it's irritating, and I nearly ask her – 'where's the horse? what did you do to him?' And don't! Don't ask her why she left us here to starve. Knowing why – it doesn't help at all.

'You think you know the value of a life?' she asks, 'Because you saved one. With me, you'll find out much much more....'

'A life is its context too,' I say. 'Tasha's like me. Possibly like you – no context.'

'You want happiness, Olbek, or its pursuit. Don't expect it's in my gift, or my desire,' she says.

'So,' I say. 'We evaluate the contexts. It may put us in some danger. Jail, perhaps.'

'We'll go where it all takes us,' says Shoshona, 'The waves – beat on the shore, but don't climb up the beach. Relax, my friend.'

*

'We've made ourselves experiments, Olbek,' Shoshona says. 'That's a great step. The living have no fixed point – the images change and depart incessantly, some as if by hallucination, mostly by the passage of the train, the post-chaise, the *tarantasse,* relays of ponies, trampling the landscape into its definitive state. For a long time, only the dead – excuse the reference! – had the fixity, the concentration, of a single frozen image ... "the vision the dead contemplate for ever...." But, of course – we don't know what that vision is!'

We look back at the stand of trees – the pods, swinging unconcerned, it seems ... the cadaver, my friend, my guide and inspiration – like a failed chrysalis.... No mystery, no mystery at all.

No horse, no car. 'We walk,' Shoshona says, determined. 'That's the modern way.'

Walk far enough, you come to water, and a boat – inevitable.

'We, humans, can be one,' she says. 'A single people, settled wherever is habitable upon the earth. For a year? Less? Much much more? It's irrelevant. All the choices have been smoothed away, we are under threat, but also liberated.... We are burnished, machined. We're mobile – each generation learns a different set of referents – the countries, occupations, locations ... they resemble one another, but tomorrow we may have to move, to run, pick up that bundle – *en marche* – find a new everything which we've already seen and known, coveted, despised and feared, tumble from riches into poverty and back again ... from lawful protest into terrorism, autonomy to autocracy, tolerance to bigotry – we're spies and spied, controllers and controlled....'

'I know all that, Shoshona. Maybe it will be like that, it isn't so today,' I say. 'Not everywhere. Not here. Not yet.'

'Exactly, Olbek. To make the species act as one, defend itself,' she says. '... the rhetoric is soft, but it's a war. Many! Most people are my enemies, although they tire the day with saying how we must co-exist and compromise. For sure – we're all complicit in all our friends and enemies do....'

'We've colonised the world,' I say. 'The animals toil and die on our enormous latifundia. Enslaved, consumed. It's complete, but not enough. There's more. The problem is – I'm already mostly what a citizen of this controlled, chaotic, anarchic and repressive world will be. If I accept – release myself, like a bubble in champagne – I am effaced. I have no affect, and no belief at all. No tenure, nothing permanent, nothing worthy of an argument. It isn't bad, or sad – it's nullity. The more I believe in stuff – the more unlikely, false, and ephemeral it becomes.'

'That's your problem, Olbek,' Shoshona says. 'I can't help you, you have to suffer what shows up, just like the rest of us.'

'I have this premonition,' I tell her as we stumble on, the rutted road, narrow and dry – 'That you have in mind to found another Settlement. This one – big as the world. Possibly – the world. No boatman, no Oskar, and certainly – no Valentin. A settlement can be small and crabbed, a throwback, a village deserted by its nomads – alive one day a year when we all come back to dance ... or huge, with palisades and marble floors....'

'Yes, yes,' she says. 'It would depend who wins the war – those who wanted liberty and found the yoke, those who submitted to the dynasties and ended up with privilege.... It all depends how you understand the contradiction, live in it....'

'This is how it may turn out,' I say. 'It's not how you started off.... You wanted, or accepted, standardisation ... the homogeneous person....'

'And its opposite,' she says. 'I didn't *want* it. Didn't want anything. I fought because it's right. It's here. I didn't make the consequence; the labyrinths.'

'I'm right, then?' I ask, 'A Settlement?'

'That's all there is,' she says. 'It's how we are. We live in them, and with our human flocks we trek from one to other. Almost identical....'

'Conviction is ridiculous. And – conviction's essential, without it there's no personality or character,' I say.

'Hurry, Olbek,' Shoshona says. 'It's getting dark. See – the rookeries are filling up,' and she points up to the black trees. 'They don't mind the rain – we need umbrella leaves....'

'The car, Shoshona,' I say. 'That you sold, or crashed. That was stolen, broke irreparably....'

'Something like that,' she says, pushing me beneath a spreading fern, taking off my clothes, settling my head on the folded parcel that they make.

And did she sing?

*

'Are those the birds that bring us food?' I ask. 'I'm starved!'

'No, those are the indifferent ones,' she says. 'Don't take it bad – it's not hostility. Besides, they are not edible.'

'I'm not your citizen, Shoshona,' I say. 'The money from the horse won't keep us both. I can be anything, but not yours.'

'Like doing what?' she asks, amused. 'Working with animals? Shooting poachers, smashing drag-nets? As they say, "the oyster is your world"?'

'I'm unused,' I say. 'Or rather, I'm shakeable. A kaleidoscope. Unflinching. A brave little soldier, like we have to be. No feeling good, and no retiring. Nothing "for life".'

'Exactly,' Shoshona says. 'You're good for anything. You don't know "good for what", and so no use for Solange, who'd give eternal peace.'

Shoshona means, when everyone counts for one, no more than one – I am the One. But that tells me nothing, of the value of a life. Each is the same as all the other ones – but....

'Here's a stall,' she says. 'A bowl of dall? Some wild *finocchio* seeds?'

'You could recruit, Shoshona, and forget me,' I say. 'There's the displaced, the flooded, the starved and roasted, under the yoke, the sword, the pestilence, all those women languishing beneath the wrath of God. Think of it, of them. Just for a start, plucked randomly, from a tall hat....'

*

'I know,' she says. 'More people want to leave from where they are than I could hold. It would be the world again, my settlement would be extreme success and failure – both at once. It won't be done. It's you, Olbek – I need you as my friend. Forget the rest – that's what a life is worth....'

It's not what I had thought. She goes on – 'Suppose we reach the water. There's a flat-bottomed boat; a pole. You'll have to be the motor. We could cut the pole in halves, share, but then they wouldn't reach the bottom. Nothing would go on, if we aren't friends. And think! How terrible – me, helpless in the boat, if we were enemies.'

'If there is food,' I say, 'I'll get you there.'

'I believe in you, Shoshona,' I say. 'In your extraordinary power. Ambition, and desire.'

'If you believe in the wretched of the earth,' she says. 'That's what there is, that's what it is about. My power ... it all depends. If you don't recognise the wretched, that they exist, then you're not with me, Olbek.'

'Remember Tasha. You save, hold, and then let go,' I say.

Was it like that, Tasha's abandonment? Doubt saves your life and ruins it.

I say – 'It's too much like Chico, and his plan to compensate for everything that has been and would be in the future....'

'I don't invent,' she says. 'If I did, it would be unlike anything you can imagine. Here's the boat and here's the pole – over there's the shore. It's easy, easier than using oars. Just don't fall in.'

If you fall in, release the pole.

*

'You must be the boatman,' says Tamara. She's new. She wears outgrown clothes.

'No, I have the boat, but not the mission,' I say.

'I'll say it different,' she says. 'You *must* be the boatman. Every gathering needs one – a conference, a hunting party, a pool, a party....'

'The hope,' I say. 'Flesh on flesh, and if not – the boatman.'

'You have the gift,' she says. 'Most people evade hard questions – they're unanswerable. Any answer is unsatisfactory. But you go head on, try, fail, go round again....'

'I've no finesse, I know,' I say. 'But like they say, all the facts belong to the problem, not to its solution. It's true, inescapable, and unsatisfactory.'

'Unresolvable,' she says. 'I don't want to see you, Olbek, with the boat, not for ages.'

'With Shoshona,' I say. 'I may need a larger boat. A timetable. Why are you here, Tamara? I've been here, or in somewhere like, long ago. So, what's new, Tamara?'

'Oh,' she says, lightly, 'I've been all over. Slept in tents – not as romantic as the tepees Shoshona didn't sleep in.'

'I wonder who starts all these settlements,' I say. 'Once, it was pirates, brigands, missionaries. Lawyers. Guys drawing straight lines on a map. Then the little wayward ones, the communes, moderns, post-moderns, antis ... goats and chickens were the crucial elements.... Then there's Shoshona, the self-displaced; aliens, looking for a continuity. Now this. She'll start another settlement – just watch. And you?'

'Something different, and when it turns out to be the same, they give you back the passport. You look for a hospital to fix you up,' she says.

'I didn't want anything that wasn't already in my head,' I say. 'Though I usually don't tell. I saved a life – by chance. It wandered on.... What am I owed? Nothing? Am I in credit – abstractedly, of course. An apology? What's that worth – for a bundle, dead souls, tied and weighed like dried tobacco leaves...'

'Abstractly,' she says. 'You're asking what is any life worth, but you mean – what is yours worth...?'

'It's the same,' I say. 'That's what I think.'

*

'Well,' she says. 'If it matters to you, it must matter. I get by without a thought of it. Of course, there's circumstances ... those are concrete, you are abstract. You'll be misunderstood. You want a price, a weight, on lives – you think in forests, but – forests are made of trees.'

‘It’s not just you and me, I say. ‘It’s how to organise these settlements. All settlements are there to pose a question, a problem, and a method – most disappear. But that’s the point – where do you settle? The first step always is deciding why you’re there – who started off as brigand, pirate, lawyer....’

‘Here, it’s being done in style,’ she says. ‘Spaces for eating; for belief and disbelief, separatism and hugger-muggering.’

‘It’s in Shoshona’s blood,’ I say. ‘She’s not Comanche, but they came long long ago from China, I’m convinced....’

‘Mongolia,’ Tamara says. ‘Almost everybody came from there.’

‘Wherever she came from, Shoshona’s tireless,’ I say. ‘Unflinching. A weak spot is music – she doesn’t know where it’s all leading. And of course – we all get bored here. Does that mean we’re worth less? On the beach, in an emergency, you can’t tell who’s bored or just improvident. Are the bored ones worth less here? In general? Do we need think, and hope to know?’

‘I’ve a right to get bored,’ she says, laughing. ‘And to anything else.’

‘I share Shoshona’s vision, share it completely,’ I say. ‘But with Shoshona, you won’t just get bored, you’ll protest. I believe in visions while they last – a few minutes. Shoshona’s has no term, it doesn’t fade, it sharpens.’

‘After the protest, we shall need a bigger boat,’ Tamara says.

*

We’re fortunate to have the boat, I think. Saving lives – they say it’s been discussed, decided there’s no answer definitive. So – each life is worthy, worth something, but we see them washed away all over, driven to the edge.... Ought we intervene, in all and every case, like I did with Tasha – or leave it to impulse, wringing of hands – like I might have done with Tasha? They all say 'intervene', and no one does....

Life's not the start and finish – it's the in-between. Take the rich peasants and the bednyaks – some of each appearing worthy, others less ... but surely you can't ask, evaluate, discriminate....

Here, I'm sure, they know all this, have lectures on it while the people doze.... Tamara is right – being the boatman's a necessary, a worthy, trade. Involving no judgements. None at all.

*

'All want to be in a settlement that suits,' Shoshona says, addressing a big crowd, intimate as if there was just one individual, or two. 'You're lucky. This is it. You're precious to me, every one of you. The tide comes in two times a day, you must avoid encirclement; that comes by chance; the boat is moored not far away, it's flat-bottomed, so it only moves when there's no swell. It's not a life-boat,' and she laughs, 'It is quite the opposite.'

Tamara. She could be my new country, the good one, where we all speak to one another, and we scrutinise Shoshona ... maybe she's too unconcerned and autocratic, and there's slides of mud, opinions too – they end up in the rubbish heaps that rise and rise to overshade the grimy buildings....

How I love Tasha, now she's dead.

Tamara is annoyed, disturbed, but absolutely normal, laughs and smiles, and sometimes hugs....

'Shoshona doesn't explicate,' I tell Tamara, as we sit entwined, sat high on the harbour wall, watching the flat grey sea. 'But anyway, I love you coming here to pass the time with me.'

She takes my hand, grips it in both of hers. ‘I can’t always be here,’ she says. ‘I’ve business with the counsellors. It’s only flirt with them, like me with you....’

‘Shoshona doesn’t need those counsellors,’ I say. ‘She knows exactly what she wants. I guess people like to think there’s different points of view, discussion, detail. All that....’

Folly. A parliament of nightingales?

Besides, we must persist, the settlement needs reproduction if the land’s to prosper now.

‘Well, Olbek,’ she asks, ‘The value of a life? What’s your conclusion? Suppose I ask Shoshona, what then? Who’s the judge?’

‘With the boat, there’s only load to watch,’ I say. ‘Each life is a different weight – so, that’s not a stable measure. I’m with you, but you can’t determine what my life is worth. Only I can, and even so, what does it signify?’

‘This time,’ Tamara says, kissing my cheek, ‘I’m sure it will be good.’

MEMOIRS, MEMORIALS

'You were a spy? Almost everybody was those days,' they ask.

'I spied,' I say. 'With my little eyes. But for myself, my satisfaction.'

I fell in love with Russians, with Russian women, Soviet women. It cost me my career, my livelihood – and of course they never really knew, about my love. It's always unrequited, because it's imagination, the best of what humanity can manage. They told me they were manufacturing the future, and I was complicit, pretended it was so. It was their work. Everything was work for them.... That future ended when socialism finished. But I worked on. There's always something else, there's always pieces left to piece together.

Foreigners? Tricky. Some are diamonds, mostly glass. I was curious to know – everything. That's what true spying means.

Spying isn't ideological, everybody steals and lies and cheats. It's like the army. Espionage is curiosity. Peeking in your host's closet – it means you both have a touch of class – he to have a closet, you to be invited. Spying on the poor, it makes no sense. You need a roomful of mysteries, hinting at heights unseen, a ceiling in penumbra; a fresco? 'the judgement of mankind'.

I took Nina round the Uffizi – I love kitsch. There's all our present century in those old crusts, the Venus au gratin, *a Primavera not found in Italy, but in a supermarket; the*

Caravaggios – scary movies, clunky production values worked to death. The great masters – they'd exhausted our entertainment, its shapes and colours, long ago; knew our weakness, all of it and only that – the flesh, the vice, the shadows, horrors – then, for Italy, their inspiration, half a millennium of decline, of repetition, a bastard 'Italy' born a cripple, deaf, blind and twisted.

Prince, courtier – crime and vice. Then, deflating versions of the mafia boss and counsellor, forever imitations, taradiddles....

The apotheosis was the mountebank, the Leader; seller of shirts, pincher of bums, a maniac killing blacks – the gas, the bomb, gun, rope – as if he'd invented all of them!

Italy should have ended there, in the abyss, Abyssinia. Tumbled in, regiments of lead soldiers into the crucible....

'That's what "post" means,' Nina said. 'Imperialism, communism, democracy – all post. Bodies all over. They make our crops grow. Don't expatiate. Adventures always come, unstoppable. Do not encourage anything. Head down. Don't break the seals fixed to the past. It seeps out anyway. Don't ask me. Nothing. Don't ask.'

*

That's all he left – my inspiration, guide. Lover of the enemy – not my enemy – mine live next door. He left the faith he thought everyone should have. Illusions. More than enough of them. Malcolm! And for foreign travel – Albert? Albertine. Two cold fish named after him ... names to pass under.

Chasing his butterflies. Died netted, fluttering on his further shore. Loneliness; any woman, just anyone would do.

The future didn't come, no one expects it now. And did they then?

If you go to school, they'd like you to believe, be credulous. but really, there's no future, just growing old. No one trusts in the present, though you have to work in it for ever so you can eat. The past.... It's not inviting. So that leaves sport. No education needed. It makes narcissists – and if you don't likc your body, it's better to forget all that – the bullies and the boredom, find what pleases you, by yourself. Only – I don't run fast, not fast enough.

Tell me one thing I'd know if I had stayed at school, and now don't know.... I do know many things about my world, its roundness, collisions, its jagged corners I'd not have known.... The land crabs crawling to the edge, the fighting bulls crated up, the war – dust to dust, the blocks of desolation – termite hills sucked empty, spurts of air, of foam, my comrades who I'd never see, indifferent to me and all the busy people here making the cash that ended up in blasts and flames.... A different world, not teachable, but mine, inside me, a body slender that's taken refuge deep in me, that pushes up against my heart and lungs, making a space for his beat, his breath, weighing me down ... no gun now, seems he is on pills, a radio – once it gave orders, now it's tunes.... Small; my passenger, burning out, wax draining off, light dwindling. He was the one brought up to believe in the future.

It's no one my old mentor, Malcolm, would recognise. That seductive devil – with his party, partying, betraying – a traitor to art history. He, she, Albert-Albertine – my growth within, twisting like a root. A growth on my past, my future, the foetal stripling deep in me.

Malcolm. Find something worthy you might betray – then refuse. Be loyal.

My world – I live in it, own nothing of it, don't speak its languages, wear its clothes, see its water-courses, don't bring goats down to drink, nothing ... the foetus that I bear can die or wither, I can do nothing, maybe grieve, but it's also a relief not to bear it – I speak my own language, in the street and on the manif there's many dialects, we grasp a phrase or two, there's not many of us, few of us believe – we haven't studied what you need to know to believe in what's unknown here, other suns and other planets, other cities. Causes change continually, but there's always a right side for you. You can live on very little, though it's not good for you. It will kill you.

Your world stays with you, like a crab's shell, as you traipse round looking for a bigger one. A smaller one.

Being a militant for people – soon, getting away from everybody seems the best. Best for them.

There's always new people, sharper, laughing more, contemptuous and tough. They run over you – pigs do that, ants, horses too. New causes; the old cause changing shape, sloughing many skins.

I thought Malcolm knew all sides, had the foresight ... to do everything, enjoy, and yet to have the life, the power – to show a way.

*

'You like beautiful things?' he, Mirko, asks. It sounds like a come-on, in a way....

'No,' I say. 'I don't buy. I despise collectors. Buying stuff for you would mean fakes, cops and stupid prices. I won't do it, and I know – it all falls on my head.'

'No,' says the guy. 'Not things. People. Beautiful poor people.'

He's evidently rich, or acting it – vicuna accessories.

'You'd go into the wretched places, scout around. Find me lovely people – even families ... who're desperate and clueless. People with stories, or that you can hang your stories on. Write them, film them. Pay them and sell them. Bring them here, or if they're stuck, paint them where they are – add goats and camels, a trade, a document.'

'The market's full,' I say. 'That kind of person springs up everywhere – just need a camera, and there they are, unasked, unaware – just poor and stuck in where they are.'

'If you're wondering,' he says. 'It's easy to cheat me of my cash, but you still have to bring results.'

'I remember you,' I say. 'Mirko? When I was a bird of augury, hopping from counter to bar and tiny table, you were around. Your court, your sycophants – your courtiers, wanting approval, place, a jewel, a word on a barmat.... You were the judge, a pawky judge, withholding judgment but giving little sentences.'

'Judges don't judge,' he says. 'They apply criteria. The stallholder doesn't adjudicate a kilogram, he weighs out a kilo of courgettes.'

'Your plan....' I say –

'Is unconfessable,' he says. 'It's like the races. Everyone is trained, deserves; only one wins – horse, dog, motorbike. The rule's the same for anything that competes – and everyone you'll meet competes, even if they've lost their hope. For you, nothing that differentiates is fair. It's true, and it's not relevant.'

'I don't do business, Mirko,' I say. 'Bringing people here – they're not a spokesman, an example – they are performers.'

He doesn't react. 'I recognise your genius, Uwe,' he says. 'You've not done anything, but you're unique – skipping an education, you've saved years, the field is far behind, at book and test. You're running free, free as a fighting beast.'

'Before we go on,' I say. 'I stumble at "beautiful". I tend to modernism. Sceptical, I ask, 'Why is there beauty?' There must be an answer, and I know it will not please. Especially if it's magic, metaphysical, or made for your convenience. Relative? Or customary. To beguile us all, give taste – a common feeling for the species.... *How* is there beauty? That's easy, but manifold. Start from our love of symmetry, its usefulness – two matching eyes, a nose that lets you see in stereo and kiss untrammelled ... two of many things inside – each has a spare, or an auxiliary. Then there's the festas – man and woman on the throne, big god and little god, lots of angels – encircling, stamping, or round the throne. Sex and desire – have them coincide for once. Relax, transform – "look at the sunset", time for bed. Is "beauty" there already, or must we find, create, it? Nudity – embroidered frocks....'

'Yes, yes,' he says. 'I think you understand both language and our common sense. You have in mind appealing people, conveying their emotions, not their hopelessness. People who have faces able to pass customs – arousing pity, sympathy ... honest and open, but not too stupid. Ambitious and harmless. People who won't be deported – anyway, not at once.'

'It's disgusting,' I say. 'Trash colonialism. Like the Kanaks, on exhibition – show what they were not, peaceful and resigned.'

'Well,' he says. 'You're right, of course. But it's your chance to be a judge. Do something big and generous, not costing you. You'd be an agent, but – the casting director no one recognises, who determines a success. Me – the philanthropist. The subjects – your choice – their choice. Tell their story, then back they go. Stay, and be militants or do whatever; be Harkis, take the chance. Not everyone can read the history, the stages of development, false ceilings, disappearing floors.... You'd be a little dirty and a little clean – a new experience, unobserved by all but you.'

'No, forget it, Mirko,' I say.

'You don't negotiate,' he says. 'That's very good. Suppose – put another way – you do what I say and have it turn out in your way. Your witnesses, Uwe. Have them say what suits....'

'I'm not sure,' I say. 'I'm not sure that works.'

'Oh, Uwe,' Mirko says, and laughs. 'Self-knowledge! It's the death, the death of everyone. Don't waste your time on it. Other people will tell you all you want to know about yourself, and much much more.... People are people, if they don't say what they feel aloud, they'll tell you what you want, and think whatever at all they want inside!'

*

I take my stand, my principle. No slaving, no publicity.

'You eat all wrong, Uwe,' Mirko says. 'Without passion, eat as if tomorrow cooked food could come again. If there is time, don't finish off your glass. Let it sit, and warm. That way, ice melts.'

'That's it,' I ask, 'The secret of social class?'

'That's it,' he says. 'It shows you've credit, calm. Voltaire told me – have burrows all around, well stocked, and you won't need to run. Just let go. Drop down, like in a stage trap....'

'Forest and jungle, Mirko,' I say. 'Suppose I'm in those parts – how would I choose my people, and their tale?' I ask. 'Their dislike and hatred forms around the landscape, their eyes....'

'Everyone loves somewhere,' Mirko says. 'That they've lost, or hope it may exist some day.... Show what may be unattainable, but not what's gone distant or that looms too near....'

'You're a romantic, Mirko,' I tell him. 'Working hard – means you're in the struggling class. Most people fail, how much it hurts depends on where you are, and who will help.... If I bring families....'

'You're right,' he says. 'Families aren't cute. Too much decay, bad lines on face and hands.... The kids – most fail, that's true of everywhere. We don't want ones that's tried at school. The clever ones won't need to strive. And if their family can't thrust them up – they're anyway where they should be, among the ordinaries, the also-rans, the simple soldiers, the good, the honest ... disappointments to themselves, and me. What we want....'

'Is the exception, Mirko,' I say. 'The person destined to repeat a life of flop and flail – instead, a revelation! They see the picture whole, become original – they fly! Their plumage glistens, in their claws – they hold the crown, the grail, the platinum credit card....'

'Exactly so,' he says. 'Although....'

'Yes, I know,' I say. 'They are insufferable, cultured vulgarians, much richer than we'll ever be, worldly wise, god-fearing too.... Do we want to mix with those, and speed them on?'

He is downcast. 'Athletes? Footballers? Freaks who have a body that does one thing well? How dull!'

'You want a star, waiting to be born, you'll bring it forth, give it number and name. It warms whatever surrounds it. maybe there is nothing, a channel no one watches.... Or splendour! *Lux!* A human lantern, phosphorous....' I say.

'You didn't know, Uwe, your life would be just this,' says Mirko, patting my shoulder. 'Did you think you'd be a warrior? Poet? Something more, or in between? No, you're a talent scout. That's what self-education and the street prepared you for.'

He laughs. Is that a tear?

'Mostly, we exploit,' he says, consoling. 'It's how we got to where we are.'

*

A ... mythical ruler was said to have owned twenty sheep. Each day he ate nineteen of them, but the next day there were twenty again.

D. Simov

No one knows where I came from. Most people start that way ... peoples ... often the founder is precocious – walks and rules from birth. It may be that I'm not the seeker of the person who gives interviews, has the moving story – but am that person. I'd be recognised, not need to spin, ingratiate. There's no difference, if you're the first, self-educate – you might be mythic, a simple soul, or be grounding something new, its shape becoming clear long after ... all the brave people, all their horned animals ... if you are or were the first, you could have been anything at all. A figment or a bully. A river, a rock, a carpet. A bird.

That's what Mirko wanted, though he is ignorant, self-centred, had no idea what he hoped to see.

The new sensibility needs a fresh population – they all start with one – or at the most, with two.

*

'You wanted to found a new people, Mirko,' I say, I ask.

'A sensibility,' he says. 'No more. Not a nation, a nationality, not a world – a soul. As if you're Malcolm-Albert, being dealt women like a hand at gin. I seek a soul, a *dusha.* All those Russian women to love, to love him. I'd include Russian men, but – that's tough, that's very tough. There's some beautiful, of course, but time! Ah, time! Those calloused hands, the chin-brush ... the booze, those sausages....

'A soul, a sensibility – not the body, those come willy-nilly. A way of seeing, of internalising....'

'Malcolm lodged,' I say. 'He was a layabout, an end-of-roader, picked up stories that he passed off as his own ... or got from books. The cameos came from bars and brothels. A torch-singer with flaming hair, guys with real Pattanas, those blades go up, twisting behind your ribs – or admirals who lost their fleets.... Origins – those he knew about, and destinies, especially his own. When he'd pissed off people here, Malcolm went elsewhere as 'Albert', like the Belgian king, or like it is in Proust.

'Another genius – good riddance, that's the epitaph. He lodged where I did – the greatest person I shall know.'

Mirko's enterprise – the adolescent dream, find people who will like you, not those milling round who don't notice who you are, and if they do, don't care.

'Some ideas, Mirko,' I start off, 'That seem quite innocent, straightforward, you agree with them, you follow principles if there are some. And you encounter great hostility. People with nothing die fighting communism – an economic system which proposes the impossible – give power to people who have nothing. Or have least. And from the start – there is the Party. I'd go into that, to make a simple system work, I say. We'd both be in, Mirko, that's for sure.

'But, as you know, my friend – philosophy may die, but philosophers do not. Philosophers, I mean, who understand the world, and want to change it all! They see how simple ideas, even with a flaw or set of flaws, can spark, enflame emotions. Philosophers, like you and me – we have the strongest emotions of them all, even if what we believe is unbelievable, what we want's an illusion from the start. We're passionate, Mirko – like my dearest friend, Malcolm or whatever else he said he was – not that he had ideas you could write down, or put on walls or posters – he lived, tried to live, exactly what it was he wanted....

‘Is your idea like that, I wonder. Simple and leaky, attractive but flaccid ... and yet it would create a tempest. Discriminatory, elitist, populist, and visionary.... Without a mechanism of measurement or realisation, vague, vapid.... Onc world – a species change....’

‘Some animals form gangs, some flocks. Some have harems, some nurseries. Some give their similars a helping paw. We have societies,’ says Mirko. ‘We think they’re hives or termite hills. It isn’t so. We don’t have divisions of simplicity – drones and queens, that stuff. We discriminate at sight – colour, age and sex ... and then the classification starts. the basic categories multiply. Shade, years borne well or not, sex plotted on continua of all techniques and preference ... language, its use, intelligence and training.... In the end, no one sees a human as a species equal. Let’s say – a cat to cats is “cat”. No man is woman to all men, or woman man to woman....’

‘It’s a great start,’ I say. ‘That is your nub. It’s exactly what I said – people will form fours and fives to contest what you say, deny equality. Equal treatment is a patronage, or deference.... They’ll hate you, Mirko, persecute you, dance on your early grave.’

‘Help me, Uwe,’ Mirko says. ‘Help me work it out, start to find our followers.’

‘It isn’t so, that man’s a wolf to man,’ I say. ‘Wolves don’t eat men – besides, wolves have a sense of humour, and of play. Food is their gripe. Do we forgive them for their passion for a hierarchy? And in return be grateful for their music, their songs – huge concert halls, the mountains, rivers filled with relays, choirs in accord, a sonorous telegraph....’

‘Passion, Uwe,’ Mirko says. ‘Stick to that. Lose the rest – it’s dross. Tailings.’

*

We set out, seeking the sources of our admiration for Malcolm-Albert. 'Vice, crime, love – all together,' Mirko says. 'We shall go horse-riding,' and he winks. It was Malcolm's word for sex, unadorned but indeterminate; extended, he'd explain when he returned from weekends in some capital – Budapest, for choice, and sometimes Warsaw. All together, the sex, the louche life, victimless unpunished crimes – he described the hotel-brothel, where everybody had to sing to get a room, a bill, and every Sunday there was Verdi's Requiem, that monster cabin-trunk of costumes, patchouli and corroded dented bombardons – left and right-handed for the ambidextrous soloists ... with thin liver-coloured lips attached.... Spasms, flailing like the German woman Lola in the film – an emblem for the wars, the frantic peace ... and song! Beat out those rhythms!

'Suppose we love the same person?' Mirko asks.

'Not to would be odd,' I say. 'Don't ask, don't tell. That is the rule.'

Mirko is five years older than me, but what five years! The long years. Before he talks, and walks, controls his sphincter – the forest fires begin, the cold war melts. We learn to applaud rhythmically, there is that plot to sink Cuba in the seaweed ocean.... Mirko wears the maturity of those years worn and swirled as if it is his dressing-gown.

'Why is the soul sad?' they may ask, 'Because there's nothing left but reason' – that's the reply.

We make progress with the origins. In the train, Mirko reads from his favourite book, how 'remnants were noted as slaves being sold in market where the "light colour" of their skin (described as *namry*, although the word might also be translated to mean "bright" or "intelligent") was commented upon.'

'Exactly so,' says Mirko. 'That is what we're up against. Those people disappear from the record too. That's what it says.'

Our weekend in Marseille, following the example of Albert-Albertine, lamenting the pawky imaginary of a century ago – there's every shade here, of intelligence and brightness – horse-riding nomads, like Mirko and me – we make a stir! All trades here date back before Assyrian kings! No one is surprised that we're such dandies, but we don't fit – two curious drifters on a strict timetable, making a confederation? Looking for travellers, busting up the clans? Starting an empire that rests on grass? Buying some.... Toiling slightly pissed up steep stairs in collapsing houses, maybe there is something here of Malcolm's spirit – when we find there's not, we go scuttering laughing down the stairs....

'There's everything of everyone here,' Mirko says. 'It could start in this city, whores and chancers, a confederation of all the shades and shadows, something huge, really big, unknown but enormous, probably for centuries, then gone, disappeared for ever, and starting up, quite unconnected, somewhere else we shouldn't want to go.... No sentiment about the businesses, the sex, the pills, dark slabs of hash for cash.... We are not hypocrites and dreamers, Uwe – what you do you do to live.... Except, they all speak the same language here, and we don't understand a word. Indo-European? Maybe not. We're not experts – we don't know.'

'It's always like this, Mirko,' I say. 'You mustn't admit to it.'

'Sex,' Mirko muses. 'Language, even if it's incomprehensible, you understand it, why it's used. But sex – what's it for? If I felt like it – what then? Babies left all over? Houses, families, granny demented on the stoup, feeding the chickens handfuls of dry pebbles now and then....'

'Mirko,' I say. 'It's wonderful being with you, your money, and there's wretched people we fools make fools of, and so long as you can pay ... it's good. Life is life, unwinding, leading the dance. The cops are here to give us protection, if we talk good and don't stagger, take pills, all that.... But you, personally, are quite a bore. Malcom wasn't, because he found the person he was talking to was usually a drag, and he walked off. You don't.

'People here are camorristi, they use the law for their own ends. We can't expect the cops to give us protection because we're customers in things that can't be sold and trades that aren't for things at all.'

'You're self-educated, Uwe,' Mirko says. 'That must be the first step. It always has been. Anyone who founds a state.... It's an obligatory passage....'

The *putes* in streets that otherwise would seem abandoned look twelve years old, their pimps a little less. One of the pimps, one with golden hair, is reading La Rochefoucauld – 'Required pimp reading,' Mirko says. '"If you think you love your mistress for her love of you, you're quite mistaken."'

'The *putes* are self-educated too, Mirko,' I say. 'We could take one home with us – they will take cash....'

'Oh, cash is all I take with me on these expeditions, Uwe,' Mirko says. 'Cash is best down here. The problem is, the cops need to be paid if we remove a *pute*. We don't want anyone to think we're hostaging or stealing goods.... Anyway, to pursue your point – Uwe, it's not about age, but about experience. The Romantics should have taught you this. Of course, you were not there in class. These *putes* know what a good time is, love too – but they won't give it you.'

'Where does that leave us, then, Mirko?' I ask.

'The forest people.' Mirko says. 'These city kids are wild – they're cubs, the grown ones are the prototypes, they have no choice but to resemble them. We need to find the adults credulous, ingenuous, lost. at sea, or on the run....

'The early horse – in the Americas was "hunted to extinction in that world zone by about 10,000 years ago" ... and when it was reintroduced, Comanche and Apache took to it – but in the forest ... the horse is useless. All our history, Uwe, over here, starts with horse-riding, and even better for the trade, the two-hump camels – they, their businesses, are us. Let's begin elsewhere, without the horse....'

'Perhaps it's so, Mirko,' I say. 'Forest people don't do much. They're smart. They hide.'

'I want to see the manatees, the dolphins; see wise people, just for once,' he says.

'We'll go see the Mundukuru, see where the civilisations began,' I say. 'Except – we can't call on them. We're failing! They were our source. We can't go back and start again, or take their genius to replace ours – especially when we've taken cover from them ... their trees, Mirko.... We might confirm a past, give them a medal for their persistence ... but it's all gone, we can't make a future out of it. It's us – we are their future. Leave them to struggle on....'

'I'm sure Malcolm was there,' says Mirko dreaming – those first nights in Manaus....

'Maybe he speculated? Bought dodgy land with dodgy credit – the papers pledged against some further dodgy deals,' I say. 'Those days – they bought and sold quite indiscriminate ... people and things. He was a human, after all.'

'Yes,' Mirko says. 'All too human, that's for sure. I've checked the price of land – Parà is largely taken, and there's the law, if you're unlucky or a timid sort....'

'You're losing vision, Mirko,' I tell him, quite apalled. 'The weekend in Marseille has changed you, changed you utterly....'

'Oh no!' he says. 'But you must build with what you have, with what there is. With clay, and cowrie shells for eyes, a straw will prick out nostrils, an axe will cut a mouth – a sharp knife gives you language.... Sight. How does that come – if indeed it must. Appetite comes with the mouth. The craw – it is survival. For the eyes ... alas, there is no hope. They give no life, they make no change – they're slaves unto what's pre-constituted: reality. Reactionary, suffering, in blue or brown. They're passive, rheumy – they decay. Tears, Uwe, that's what eyes express. Someone, something, has figured out the real. The real coheres, it's colours, sounds – they are consistent, sometimes they attract. If they don't – too bad! It's all that you can see! The real persists – if you are blind, it doesn't change a thing. You don't need eyes, or vision – it's all there, preconstituted – deny it, contest the existence of the real – and they shut you up, or chain you to the door.'

*

'No doubt, Malcolm was the precursor, the messenger,' I say. 'He saw how life could be quite different – a fluid and fantastic cast on everything: new people, pliable and lovable. But – some things about him sound quite louche. There used to be a character – stage-door johnnies they were called – dressed in splendid togs, gone shiny, but real class,' I say. 'They disappeared decades ago. They hung around, after the play, the musical, review – for leading ladies, or just leads, then when those left, the chorus too. Offered a drink, and hoped for sex, and longed for love....'

'I laugh,' says Mirko. 'That isn't him at all. He was a visionary, not a hanger-on, an importuner. Mountains climbed, insurrections inflamed, yaks herded, deserts irrigated – don't you recall, all those adventures as he retailed to you,

Uwe, and re-confirmed across the world?... A stupa in Mongolia, memorial plaque in Bogotà....'

'Yes, yes,' I say. 'His spirit, presence – it's all documented, moulded into clay and terra cotta....'

'You miss the point, Uwe,' Mirko says, squinting at me. 'These categories – you can use them in a pejorative sense, of course. What Malcolm did was show a way; constructed nothing, changed no one but himself.

'The drama, spectacle ... he wanted a testimony of what remained: after the play, the opera – what had changed, what was there left, what sign, what contour.... In the public – not a trace. But the performers? What transformed in them, going on stage, singing, dancing – year after year. The legs grow heavier, high kicks, high jinks – grow leaden, the voice, grows pebbly. The song issues from the lips as if it struggles over a bed of marbles, rises from a pot of brawn.... Emotion conjured from the box of tricks – over and over ... to what end? With what plan, and what conviction?

'Creation, Uwe. Inspiration? Forget the mystery of where it comes from – a tiny mystery, since it seems universal, we all have gnawed a slice of muse, emergency ration, the lyre, the mask – part of the uniform we're issued with, like straps to blanco, boots to bull.... The ageing diva, those venerable Toscas, thrown down from the Tarpeian rock a hundred times.... Is it all puffery? The maestro, whipping on musicians like spavined nags, heaving on a fairy coach that's fashioned out of wind ... is it all flimflam, a slick accord between him and the audience – greatness, transcendence, exhilaration? Or a fraud – a transitory self-abuse that leaves us as we were, we are?

'That is the point, my friend. There's the question, posed and tested – not resolved, of course. But that is why his fever, drive, impress us. His stickiness, obsessiveness. The unanswered question, he'd have called it....'

'Something of the messiah, do you think?' I ask.

'Be very careful,' Mirko says. 'Messiahs bring nothing tangible, and the consequences are terrible, much worse than you can imagine, and the spark-plug's gone long long before. Let's call him – a visionary. And I know – those bring trouble too. We would have more peaceful lives as millionaires....'

'Let's stick to what we have begun,' I say. 'At least until we need more cash.'

'We mustn't sacrifice ourselves,' he says. 'He didn't miss a trick himself – shovelling guano, mining scraps of gold – he'd seen it all, and didn't recommend them, not hard work, nor poverty.... Driving a truck on a dusty shelf, over the ravine – you need a flask of raki, or poor eyes....'

'Now,' I say. 'Don't confuse me. We're about a new sensibility – not love or tolerance or empathy. Those have been tried, and now – enough! Awareness....'

'No!' he shouts. 'Cretin! Humans have been aware since the savannah days! It's a change to our nature, idiot!

'I have a potato field, left in the peaks near Machu Picchu. Let's dig the tubers up and make a fortune.... Potatoes ... an easy food, found easily. Let's start from that abundance ... Malcolm bought the patch, you have the paper here....'

It is the document – written with points on leather, or just on skin.

'We could sell the skin, and save ourselves the trip,' I say.

'No, no,' says Mirko. 'Thoroughness. That is the commandment. Digging: that's how people can grasp the past.'

*

It's very high up. The soil is fibrous, dark, like grandfather's tobacco in his jar. The potatoes are not in file, but brood where they were tossed, lay, and sprang, not at all like dragons' teeth. More like dragons' *crottes.*

'Remind me what this does for us,' I ask Mirko. 'The digging and the altitude, the sickness....'

'It shows the document was original, legal....' he says. 'Unless someone says it's not.'

'We could be harvesting for someone else?' I ask. 'The cops could come....'

'Some say that's what life's for,' he says. 'Plant for yourself, have somebody much younger dig and make the soup. A pity I am not your father. Can't be helped.'

We're short of breath. Our legs won't straighten out. Many of the vegetables have rotted, there's empty skins, like Danish pastries – 'Found in a bog,' says Mirko, and we laugh, and lie exhausted.

'Put them in these sacks,' says Mirko, 'Some women porters can be found. They need the cash, we need the relax. Hard work – it's best farmed out. Women included in the workforce – it's an international goal....'

The porters want more cash –

'Alas,' Mirko says to them, 'We don't know the going rate so we can't over-pay. If you prefer, we'll put these tubers back – they'll sprout, we'll come another year, and so and so. Another, and another year, more potatoes every time, all reinvested till there's a potato capital ... that we could make a currency, more sought after than gold and silver, and you, my friends, with your experience of carrying sacks of them, would all be millionaires ... enough you pocket some.... Here in the mountains, you won't need to mine. Just scratch the soil and lift....'

'If you've cash to last the week,' I say. 'What's left can go to french fries. Crisps. That's what Malcolm wanted – a new way of living, seeing things.... Just think – a currency you can pan-fry, deep-fry, roast or bubble, mash, even use as darning tool, or mushroom, to mend your socks....

'Marx, or perhaps Engels, said you peasants were like potatoes in a sack. So, there you are! Malcolm, our inspiration, had a touch of Irish in him, the national emblem.... A human currency – a person's individual and economic worth – potatoes! Forget the cowrie shells, Yap's stone discs – carry a sack of spuds when you go to buy your Maserati, the dealers will go wild...!'

'Hush, Uwe,' Mirko days. 'You confuse the deal. It's carrying dead weight down this mountain path.'

'It's true,' I say. 'Machu Picchu possibly collapsed after a crisis in the currency. Maybe the year's crop failed – you can strike up gold from worn-out solidi, or bullion – potatoes, though, may not renew....'

'Leave it, Uwe,' Mirko shouts. 'Dollars are good for all of us, Malcolm too. The city, Machu Picchu, was probably deserted at some visionary's call. "I have a vision" – if we stay – disaster! Follow me, down from the heights, into the trees....' and never hear of them again. We must be very very careful, Uwe. Malcolm lacked – above all – charm. Charisma. If he diddled you, there was no lightness – straight fraud. Honesty is monochrome, and never coveted.'

'The grey huddled city, where we can hardly breathe,' I say. 'You may be right, Mirko – the people left from accidie, from fear ... a pestilence of mind, a completeness without end, without a goal, a purpose....'

'Potato futures? Did Malcolm bet on those?' Mirko speculates.

'There's fortunes made of crisps,' I say. 'Malcolm always turned desires into paper. He invented his own time, own times. When we get down to where the air is thick and sticks inside our honeycombs, we breathe like bright young animals with songs and dances to waste ... young hares, you and I,

Mirko. Of course – we made no contact, have no contacts – but we learned.'

*

Our appointment is in Braşov. Malcolm-Albert was here when there were forests, castles, darkness.

Mirko says, 'There'd have been limousines. People wore gloves for everything. And hats. The cars were made of iron, and cracked from stem to stern. The bourgeoisie wore beige, the peasants – white, trilbies dark with sweat.'

'Ah, the smells, Mirko,' I say. 'The farmyard, before chemicals. All in heaps – the grain, the hay, the dung, the cockerels and the chickens, the labourers, the owners, the cow matriarch, the bull, the bully. The blue eyes, the women. and the shifty men.'

'No,' Mirko says. 'You've placed him wrong. He was post-war. In uniform, perhaps, handing over influence to people no one trusted. A commission – looking for facts: unavailing. How those battledresses chafed! Officers had silk shirts.... We could find a farmhouse, look like investors, use a spyglass. Have fun not being us....'

'I'd like that,' I say, uncertainly. 'My friend – he was small, low-built – a greco-roman wrestler. Like Astaire said, the secret is not leaving the ground, but being very fast and clear. That's how you wrestle, and do the other things – be a soldier, a DJ. And then – you enjoy the trees, and if they've gone, enjoy where they once were. The most beautiful land....'

'OK,' says Mirko, 'Your friend will find the farmhouse – deserted, whitewashed, a frieze of painted celandines....'

It's not at all like that.

'Listen to the people,' Mirko says. 'How they shout! They don't want this tawdry stuff, the other countries it comes from, the gas stations and the commerce. It's like the book says, they want to circle round and stamp.'

'I'm not sure you've grasped everything, Mirko,' I say. 'There's Oedipus. They're sure it happened here. You should read Jocasta's tale – it puts a different sheen on things. These were Greeks, then French, and they have this difficult Latin to master, partially is how they do it, and you've not started – and it's time to leave already....'

'That's the way with countries,' he says. 'I've often said they should be abolished, and let's appreciate the space.'

*

We walk along the road – asphalted, it's smooth as someone's back. I think, we must get involved with different people, eccentric, poor – just....

'Please help me,' says Mirko, in a small voice, 'I'm falling down.'

'Try not to make a fuss,' I say. 'I was just thinking.... It's the height, or age. You need a rest from digging....'

'No,' he says. 'It's all those and worse. It feels like I'm going into history, but not knowing whose....'

'Be sure,' I say. 'It's all yours, personal.' He can't answer. It's the last thing he wants, even if he could reason.

That's it. The end, of Mirko, and the things we've done together – the whole interpretative slant, narration, point of view. 'Come on old horse,' I say, pulling him on to the sidewalk, 'Pasture!' He's already there.

I remember him saying 'Walls have ears, but potatoes have eyes.'

I laugh. Maybe he too laughs.

More will come to me in time, I expect. Does Malcolm disappear with Mirko too? It's a temptation.

'Just leave me here,' says Mirko's corpse. 'I'm not much use to anyone. It's harder to move me if I'm stiff....'

'I'd like to, Mirko, but....' I say. 'If I run, the pistols of suspicion threaten me.'

'See if the cops take credit cards,' Mirko's corpse says, chuckling. 'I'm an unknown soldier, on an unknown side, struck down by unknown force. If you must, honour me on wood, not stone – and not with a cross. I suggest a pineal eye – Blake's God.... Let them ponder what I signified!'

'Don't laugh, Mirko,' I say. 'It sounds like a death rattling. And Blake employed dividers for his senile geometer....'

'Oh, I'm sure there was a third eye somewhere. Dividers – that is genius Everything and everyone – divided! Genius, though one would expect no less!' And Mirko's corpse and I enjoy a hearty laugh. It's a mistake. Death has no sense of humour.

The cops interrogate in squads. Each knows a different law, and each knows a different phrase that sounds like maybe in my tongue. '"*Gutta cavat lapidem*",' I say. 'You wear me down, until I am no more.'

It's unavailing. No one knows what has happening – except that Latin has evolved into Romanian. It's of no help, no help at all.

They close me in, for the night. 'Mirko!' I say. He's next door – there's no radiator, so I can't tap out in Morse, that language everyone forgot. 'I can't do all this alone, what shall I do?'

'You ask me, Uwe,' he replies, 'As if death is a state for pondering in, maturing judgements. No – you rot, you stink, you're undefended and infested. They cut you up, laugh at your penis and your gut, and spill your brains upon the floor. Companionship, my friend? Trust to luck, not to yourself, and keep your money in your shoe.'

From the slab comes advice more sound and sonorous than ever I received from life.

'Are you cold, Mirko?' I call out.

'Yes, it's good. When they finish with you, they'll warm me up....' he says. 'That won't be good.'

It's the last time that we speak.

*

Dying. It's a great test, losing everything, reality, yourself, the spinning of the universe, all movement – of the sun, of blood. I wonder if I'll manage it. I'm not good at challenges. Malcolm has preceded me – maybe on the walls, his scratches.

A guy wakes me, though I'm not asleep. His uniform says 'trusty'. A prisoner? A cop? Both of these?

'Are you afraid?' he asks. 'You know what the police do. For themselves, or as accomplices. They have those leaded sticks, they have the law, you common types have given all your powers to parties, to dictators, to people you don't know, who don't know you. Are you afraid?'

'Yes,' I say. 'I'm terrified. And what are you?'

'If I were you,' he says. 'I'd not be confident that I will tell the truth. Or know it, or am bothered. Bothered about anything that has a label like you like to put, as protection, like a hex sign on your head.... "Protect me from the passing day ... protect me from order on its march." Today it's facho, tomorrow liberal, next day some guy says he's socialist, but not like what you thought you were; you should comply with all of these....'

'Yes, yes,' I say. 'I know all that. Order rules. If it doesn't, our neighbour will skin my cat and then skin me, and so ... you will skin me, then my cat ... order wins, it is the banker, the house, the dealer – gives out the genes and lineage....'

The guy laughs. 'You're paranoid,' he says. 'That's good, that's very good. Too bad for you – you killed your friend. He was your lover, didn't love; your boss, your underling, your competitor, your friend, your enemy. You took the easy route, the hardest choice – and killed him. Maybe not. Not all things interconnect. We have you now. We always have. Peru? China and Paris, all in a day – la Cina è vicina, *after all. Where next? We'll see you come and go, evade your tax, sell your drugs, swap your party card for candy-floss, flush your allegiance, philosophy, your principles; leave explosives in the gents, kidnap and throttle, rape and traffic, give refuge, love and be generous, forge your documents, love what you must not, hate and revenge, engage in* faide, *hate blacks, hate whites, love everyone, stab catholics, dissolve your nephew in the acid bath, cut off that soldier's legs, commit suicide in the meat grinder ... let me hang you from an oak, a baobab, and take your food, your animals, your children, country, your dignity, your sperm....*

'And what will you do about all that?'

'I know, I know,' I say. 'I told you. I know all that. I'm terrified of you and me, of my resentment, of justice, of my sad existence, my rebellion and my conformity....'

'You're on the path to innocence, my friend,' he says. 'A full confession does the trick. Accept the punishment, be a man, be a woman, be what you want, accept anything you get, it's for your good and bad, but don't complain. It irritates....'

*

A group, a country, ready beside me – for the message not to be ignored, but to inspire? All the rest – the war, the fire, the famine and the pestilence, have come and wait. They roam and rage as if they're lions in a cage. Our whitecoats have diminished threats in different immaterial ways – treaties and treatises, warnings and movies.... In jail, we're all a hero, freedom fighters, persecuted ... you grow to fit the part.

I can't do everything myself – I need at least a mate, a lover or a pet – a horse, perhaps, a camel, or a yak....

They're satisfied with Mirko's death. Two culprits are too hard for explanation – so they let me go. Mircea takes me to his home – I'm useful ... a crook with contacts and a passport. He dazes me – all the kids and cousins he hasn't – might have – had. I glaze over, as he climbs the family tree and gibbers, shakes the branches.... Down they drop, his antecedents....

There's a run, a spate, of kids – small white boys, like those white sprats in French River, Canada – you could walk across on them, dry-shod, at the right time, if you weighed about four grams – but impressive! – all white and male.... All white and poor. Must be a backward part of Europe. Then, of course, I think – Mirko!

I ask the guy who follows – chases? – them. 'Around me, is there a reek of death?'

'There's one such around us all,' he says. 'But universal stench – it's impolite to single out one guy when it's on us from our birth.

'One of those spratlings might be mine. With procreation, evolution is reversed – it's one step forward, two steps back. An infinite regression, each child needs teaching everything, they are you right back at the beginning, they die, and by the end, they know much less than us....'

In the cell, there must always be a confidant – not wholly trusted, but essential. Then inseparable, loved. Mine is Mircea. More courageous than me, living more of my life than maybe I shall have.

'See!' he says. 'Those kids are a flock, like one in panic, but this is fun, or hunger, penury.... I ought to recognise one or more wee sprat that's mine, but they're so similar.... That's good, but, it seems, not very good.'

'I understand,' I say, forgetting Mirko's cadaver for the while, and where they store it, the temperature, like it was the globe ... human activity determining not life, but how quick will be the deliquescence....

I say, 'You're looking for the link – the special bond that should exist between you, the child, and its destiny, which is to break free, eventually, bearing no scars, no traumas, and no quirks ... yours, but unidentifiable as such. Credit for the good bits, denial of the bad....'

'Free will,' he says. 'But money and influence on my side. Perpetual need on his....'

'This is banal, Mircea,' I tell him. 'We had a similar problem in Peru. Potatoes. When do you harvest them, their price and value – their being yours,' I say, 'And loved as such, the connection broken in the sack and on the market stall ... the chipper and the fryer, the gouging, consumption....'

He laughs. 'And can you recognise which ones are yours?'

'Not when they're scrubbed or peeled,' I say, joining his merriment, 'But clad in the black fibrous soil, the blackness, clinging, penetrating, the smell of dank and latency.... And after all ... who else's?'

'Yes,' he says. 'Tubers. That you don't remember planting.'

'Each potato,' I say, suddenly serious, 'Sees back to its creation....'

'God gave them eyes for that,' Mircea says.

'Each child,' I say, pressing ahead, 'Is old as its species, and with all flaws that will bring it to its end – the shaky genes, short life, poor comprehension, suicidal, homicidal, tendencies.... You are that child, Mircea. You can't escape, your son will not improve yourself, your vision, your shaping hand – turned to yourself, as it might be – is ineffectual on you, on him. We see, even – yes, we see ourselves. Like all the rest – what we see is outside, it cannot be a part of us, we cannot introduce the object in the subject. The subject – us –

transforms, it cooks! the object as it is internalised. Unrecognisable! The goose that's cooked can't honk, lay eggs or strut. It's a poor reduced thing. Landscape seen – cannot be part of us. The child – cannot re-enter. Yet, like the landscape, it is created by the flux – old as the hills, primordial as the mushroom....'

'All this is true, or could be so,' he says. 'Remember – your friend is dead. Do what we all do with dead friends. Practise the ritual. The cops suspect there's been some dirty deal. That leaves emotions in them you will never feel. Perhaps you'll wonder – "Did your feelings for your friend – attraction, repulsion, irritation, distance – contribute to his end?" Certainly they made his life less happy, less serene. So what? you say.'

'Your child's a thief,' I say. 'You punished him – held him to the fire, chained him, beat him. You live in a broken hut, you raped his mother, did some time for that or something similar – he stole to eat, he ate to steal, he beat his granny, but with her dementia, it didn't leave a mark. Is it guilt or fear you feel, Mircea? He's big now, hates you, everyone – he'll take your eye out with his genuine Pattana blade ... you told him to be good, but basted him with bad....'

'We parents,' Mircea says. 'We try. We get the blame. It's solace, even if the rest is true.'

*

'Sheep's head soup,' says Petru, Mircea's brother. We three are the only ones in the house. Round the table. 'Mircea is a black sheep, and this,' and Petru holds the white sheep skull high, 'Is a white sheep. They each once had a realm. Where did they go?'

'They bunked with everybody else. They went nowhere, they're all here, all us, cousins, but not kissing ones,' says Mircea.

'Take me West,' says Petru. 'Get me away from Mircea and his awful family,' and we all laugh.

'There's always pardon,' Mircea says. 'Even the law, especially religion: they give it you, it doesn't hurt, or cost.

'I'll be clean, Uwe, then I'll come with you. Yes; sensibility. We're reduced quite bad – so, let's be sensitive to everyone, surroundings. be less destructive, greedy – all that. Let's be what the TV tells us. Maybe the snow will come.'

'Oh,' I say. 'I forgive you, though the details are obscure. I too must flee suspicion, find a place where I can forget my friend, as if he's never been.... You can't be guilty of what you don't remember....'

'Don't bet on that. Pascal says, 'bet on yes and no'. You may forgive Mircea for what you don't know he did,' says Petru. 'But you won't travel with him. Maybe you will with me.... That's how it goes....'

And so it does.

Petru can travel where he likes. 'You can get in,' Petru says. 'It's getting out, if they don't want you, that's the prob. Besides – you are a crank, Uwe. This sensibility...!'

'You're wrong, Petru,' I say. 'With Mirko we discovered work and wealth, how these don't function where we were. My problem is publicity. A crock of poison, that! Spread it around....'

'And kill the grass,' says Petru. 'The birds and bees as well. Then it's your turn....'

'No, no,' I say. 'The substance kills, not telling tales about it.'

I can go West. I want to go East – it's more adventurous. 'No,' Petru says. 'Hardship has eaten what you want to see.'

‘What have you done, Petru,’ I ask. ‘A gang? Contraband? What mask would you wear in theatre, in Noh?’

‘Oh, an old woman with a face of oak,’ he says. ‘An earthworm.’

‘A demon or a snake,’ I say. ‘Maybe Mircea was a better bet.’

I miss Mirko.

People are logs in backwaters. You push them, and they wallow, the water stinks, the bark peels off, and underneath there is more bark. We sleep rough, and Petru rumbles all night, a cat. He wakes happy. He wants nothing, will take everything that comes or goes.

‘My trade,’ he says, ‘is trade. I switch, transform, transmogrify – you see, Uwe, trade is exchange of unlike for unlike that reaches out to make unlike like like. Remember – ‘how to make a ton of steel into a ton of grain’ – trade does it all the time. Unlikenesses become equivalents – you don’t need passages through currency.... Of course, when you begin – with pearls for oil, denim for opium – all that, and futures, telegraphs, *things* move around. But you can also swap in ways that nothing moves, and no one moves them.’

‘I know all that,’ I say. ‘Images come in. Especially images of people, ideas, continents. You can collect them, stick them in albums, or on your bedroom wall. And then there’s politics – what kind of merchandise is that, its price, its weight, heft.... And prisoners. I’m sensitive to them....’

‘Yes, Uwe,’ Petru says. ‘The fear. You’re right to have it, lucky to have so much it’s with you all the night, your sweat of terror. How I envy your stock of fear, your knowing what can happen, where, and how, to be exchanged and ransomed, how transformation in one place hits everyone as if a dodgem on the track became gigantic, maybe instead – it withers – and all the rest ... react, follow, shudder with the cold; tremble ... when it’s torrid.’

'Those pinball ramps,' I say. 'When millions are racked up, and stacked, but you are always number four in history, there is no number one to meet or joust, it's printed on before you play ... a giant, quite hypothetical, in the programme, and who never TILTs.'

'Well,' Petru says. 'That's quite another thing. What's profit, what is loss. You're paranoid, Uwe, that's good and right, so you win all the time, it takes your health, your life – it shows you're on the ball, and smart, upgraded, a red-hot pepper in the soup....'

'I believe in winning, Petru,' I say. 'What an improved sensibility, though, could see as profit – I'm not sure. No, not so. I'm sure – that I don't know. We all must change how we perceive and sense. A guy walks down the street, a hand falls off. You don't just carry on, and say – "I'm prudent. For myself, I have a spare." At least, you oughtn't to....'

We laugh. 'It's so,' says Petru. 'You might even say, "How fortunate – I'm a tough guy, it's good it should be happening to me, and I can guess who made it drop off that other guy".... Gets angry, "Revenge!" but takes it philosophically. And maybe the bastard'll make a leg fall off some guy you haven't met, don't want to either....'

'Well, Petru, that deals with wars and trade, and what we all might eat, all that,' I say. 'You understand me perfectly – if we don't want that crap – of stoicism, of history, vendetta, feeling smart while coughing blood – we need a different panoply, reactions better targeted ... but....'

'But – what am I contributing?' he asks. 'That is your question. I see the need for it. If we're to avoid extinction – we must solve the questions that you raise.'

'What does "taking things philosophically" signify?' I ask. 'That sounds like Mircea's faith in pardon....'

'I've suffered terribly from Mircea,' he says. 'It leaves me open to blackmail. To show he's bad and I'm good, I have to do all kinds of dirty work.'

What that is, he doesn't say; and if I'm part of it. That night, as he is purring on, I filch his documents. 'Security' it says: as his profession. Qualification – 'sneak'.

When he wakes, he says. 'Don't heat up, Uwe. Security is precious, we all seek it – and when you talk of sensibility, there can be no prejudice: not against anyone. You can't object to me. Or anybody.'

Suppose he's right. We're all alike, like grains, or filings. And yet – how can I seek inspiration with a cop, possibly one that's being turned, possibly been set to watch me – to watch all of us. What is his brief, and who sends these guys?...

We do, of course.

There's lots of Kazaks on a course to drive big trucks. I swarm aboard one, piracy in my head.

'I love your country....' I begin. The camels there, at least.

'I'm here because it can't love me,' the guy starts off – and then, oh no! – there's Petru, in the cab with us.

'Don't patronise,' he says. 'And don't ingratiate. I'm here protecting you ... from me, my lookalikes – you're never free. Not that we're free ourselves – we cops, we are the tools ... the artisans are you! You use us.... Or – you're the materials, the objects – doesn't matter, not a bit, which way you look at it.!'

We ponder this. It's not true. It's true, of course – everything is true, except we're not the ones to judge. We don't have reason on our side – just hearsay and some shards of our experience, worked into our favour, naturally ... true reason could be just approximate as well. Inhuman – metaphysical. We are not worthy of the truth, nor know it when it smacks our face. You need to call philosophers in to counsel you, and to find they can't.

'Look at that skein of priests,' Petru says. 'Allsorts. All super-sexed – they start off so, then laden with the fantasy and guilt – they sublimate. The spiritual – the cloud. They can't, of course, control themselves. A swap of devils! Sex or the supernatural! They try to shut sex in the goaty stall – get it behind them, if you will ... straight, gay, or tutti frutti, they dodge it all until – oh no! There's all those choirboys, servers, groups of delight, the young, the gullible, the lollypops, the sherbert, liquorice.... Life is a confectioner's, the jars are full of aphrodisiacs – pray, invoke, it all peps up the moment when....'

'You were a seminarist,' I say. 'Like Baffone. The personality shaped in theology and frigid beds – it bursts out everywhere – moustaches, urges of all kinds, the massacres, anathemas ... they sprout. The best thing is....'

'Yes,' he says. 'Of course. The singing. Though Baffone – Stalin – I never heard him sing.'

We leave it there. The truck has crossed a frontier, maybe four or five. Petru jumps down.

He doesn't disappear. He stares. The truck is stopped. Bekzat, the driver says – 'You cop guys will have me drive to Venus! You'll never find what you can't recognise.'

'There's nothing lost.' I say. 'There's nowhere it might be....'

'The cops find anything, they say, even if it wasn't lost,' says Bezkat, and he laughs.

'What it is,' I say, thinking of Malcolm and his busy wanderings – 'is looking for the way of finding things. Something is lost, or somewhere else. It's what you know is missing, so what counts – is finding ways of finding what you know's not there.'

'Kazakhstan,' Bezkat says, 'can seem quite flat. Mostly – that's what it is. And yet, you're right – flatness is not what Kazakhstan *is*. "Flat"'s not its quiddity. The camels....'

'Yes,' I say. 'When you see a camel on the steppe – the flatness disappears. You observe quite something else.'

*

Petru shouts up – 'I'm off to pick plums. Watch this guy, Bezkat – as close as you can.'

He dwindles in the rear mirrors.... 'I'll watch you, Uwe,' Bezkat says. 'So close, you'll lose your distance from me. You could be Petru now. Maybe – you are.'

He's lifted Petru's documents. 'You are my security, Petru,' he tells me. 'A cop in the cab – is worth a basketful of plums.'

'Either of us, Bezkat,' I say. 'Could be the cop Petru.'

'Indeed,' says Bezkat, and I think of Malcolm – very sure of who he was but flexible with names.

Of course – I followed in Malcom's wake. I've become Petru. Perhaps for ages – I've been Malcolm too.

'If the plum-picker was Petru, and not his brother – his likeness,' Bezkat says. 'We could be him as well. Anyway – I drive, you sit and be Petru, and the other guy picks plums and gets insulted. Apples are best, though plums are good to eat. Apples – they reveal what's evil if you eat them. It's as good a way as any to have you pick a side.'

'Best not pick anything yourself....' I say. 'Let's get intimate, Bezkat – avoiding anything physical. I once loved a woman – ah! how it stung! She wore black, and lived on the same street – a tree name, I remember. Pine? Or Ash? And was it wealth, or family that meant we couldn't socialise – until one day she said, 'Uwe, let's make love. We can't be friends, so let's bed down....'

'"Reflect!" I said. "It's maybe not a good idea...."

'"It's not an idea," she said. "Not an idea at all."

'It ended there. We separated – and ever since, distinguishing ideas from all the rest has been my weakest point,' I say.

'That's quite pathetic,' Bezkat says.

'Yes,' I say. 'She closed the door, I never saw her, never more....'

We're stopped. Control of documents, and I jump down. The cab door closes – the truck departs. I never see Bezkat again. 'never more'. It seems that for emergencies, I'm Petru now.

*

Yet – I think of Malcolm; and I see Mirko's cadaver – as it's set up in a lecture room, ready for a thousand cuts. The choicest bits are destined for the eager students – vying for a liver, kidney or a head, like cats outside the butcher's window....

This interchangeability, though, of names, of persons, trades and prejudice ... in a way, a distant way, it heralds the new sensibility. A trace, at least. We can – we must – become not Doktor Caligari, but each other. A trick, a tribute, a new avenue, an alleyway....

They used to say, 'you can do anything' – and it was a lie. But if you can be anyone? Resemble any standard person on a document? Be the Other, your *semblable.*

Everyone, of course, is different, has something special to be remembered by – Malcolm, those paper shirt-fronts, gone out of style long since. Mirko, salt sprats with vodka, Petru, stuffed cabbage rolls, and Mircea – *castraveţi* – gherkins. Defining, humanising.

The officer – how apt he's 'customs' – shouts at me, as I stand thoughtful: 'dirty gypsy Romanian! go back home, home to your sty!'

'I'm a colleague, colleague,' I say, show my Petru photo, and he backs off.

*

Hey colleague.... It comes from many sides. 'Live, let live. Don't let them change you! Don't eat and drink official stuff, it changes you, you become another. Don't sign up. Your blood – it's zombie blood. Don't accept the poverty, the rules ... the lies. Live as we always have, be a man, a woman.'

I don't understand. 'Hey, colleague,' I shout back. 'I'm not Shia, though I respect.... I'm not religious, not at all, but I respect, and I believe ... I want to be a millionaire, just like you, I want to strut the stage, kick high and higher, just like you, and show my face, put money where my mouth is, swallow my oysters live, pluck my turkey when it's time, my spider-monkeys when it's not – I want to see their slender arms stick out the curry sauce, their shaven faces just like mine, like the primal, the prime minister. like my woman and my man.

'Then run!' he says, my colleague, my brother, lookalike. 'Run with us, and make things like they were, should be, will be. The simple life, tattooed like cannibals, bright as suns – and take the airport and the station, the roads that lead out and in....'

'Is that gunfire, colleague?' I shout out. 'I'm not a communist, but I thought – is there emergency or not?' 'No, no,' I hear. 'The emergency is them! The whitecoats and the sheep. It's an invention – theirs!'

'I've only this,' I say,' my service pistol, no bullets, and it's rusty too.'

'That's the best kind,' the shout comes back – 'They'll run away, they have no stomach! They are sports, the monsters, liars and corrupt. They sold out to the Chinese, the Chinese law!'

'Oh yes,' I say. 'We're all corrupt. We were, we strayed. You, me, and everyone. We all flock where the money is.... But ... if I join you, and we take everything, and eat and drink, have sex in the park, and skin a deer and barbecue – we'll have the money, everything, the power, the current, futures, all the bonds and titles – we'll all be in delicious bondage, sex, we'll all be lords and ladies, live as the great Creator wanted us....'

'Join!' I hear. 'Your roots! you know them, hobbling you, they're creamy white, you're not....'

'I'm not so sure,' I say, although it seems they're running fast, there's victory in their breath, shooting in the air and crucifying as they go – there's little aeroplanes that's flying off, there isn't answering fire, but much confusion, crowds lining up, flags with writing on, and bands begin to play Jelly Rolls, shops close and open like fans on midsummer's day, or fans with arms in synchrony, enthusiasm a sweaty poppet, russet hair – the oaks are on fire, the flames....

'This, this,' – is how we're meant to be.

'I may look as if I'm Shia, but it's an illusion, guys,' I say. 'I over-egg, enthuse.... I understand you, you are like I was in school, things must go on just as they've been for centuries, invent and grow – that's what we had to do ... guddle the catfish and the alligators, save your sister's honour, cut the usurpers balls off, have him bleed out on the palace lawn....'

*

'Everything's been trashed,' I say.

'Not here,' a woman says. 'It's over there. Nothing will happen here.'

She's right. I never went to school. I don't know how to become bigger, stronger than I am. There's no one running, and I don't have a gun, no choice, no passion. Take what comes – there's nothing else, for no one, everyone's the same, or maybe some want fast and some want slow, and so ... it stalls.

'You were ranting,' says the woman, 'It's quite worrying, because I don't know how to help you, you are one of them, a cop, and should be used to people passionate and running. I could have you chained and sectioned. No one will look for you – the ward's locked for a thousand years. Anyway, it's much too late. You're what you're born, Yazidi, Shia or Ismaili, and besides, the fighting isn't here, it's manifs here, and over there it's guns and not about the being what you are, or wanting to be rich or poor or clean or pissed, spaced out, or up your rope.... The same, if you're Tadjik or Hazara. Or from the South. I thought you needed help, but obviously you don't.'

Malcolm, I think, was always being helped by unknown people, lifted out from where he fell, his sensibility uncompromised.... He had the recipe, and I....

'No,' I say. 'I'm just the same as you. I remember those wet summers, the wasps drowned in jars of beer, the hollyhocks, the boabab trees, the camels and red squirrels, croquet and christenings, and flagellation, pink ice-cream. It's not religion, colour, sex, anything like that. It's forward with it all, hot and poor and difficult; we're peasants with our savings in the seed bank ... or back, disaster and enjoying it ... we're peasants with the holy book tattooed on our prick.'

She stares at me. I couldn't formulate it well, there's no one running here, the buses and the planes – yes, they run, there's pink ice-cream, there's no dispute ... we all believe in dialogue, we never speak....

'It's not for real,' I say. 'It's just an exercise, to test your readiness for what may come.'

'I'm just the same as you,' she says. 'I'm not from here. Except – I'm not a cop, I don't have qualifications, not like you.'

'My card, my photo,' I say. 'I'm not sure they count.... If I'm on the wrong side, what does it mean – the cops are after us?'

'It's always a possibility,' she says, looking awkward and shuffling away. 'It's something you must always bear in mind. You wouldn't know, of course, being one. You've taken sides.'

'We must....' I start.

'Then run!' she says. 'Run fast with them, run or you won't catch anything.'

'That's obvious,' I say, not moving, 'I want to catch a slice of civilisation. Haven't eaten since Braşov. I need to know what I'm fighting for. against.'

'Just to be safe,' she says. 'I'll hand you in.'

'What for?' I ask. 'Opinions? I'm unlettered. But everyone's unschooled in future things. Everyone is communist now – a plan, new laws and prohibitions, people shifted here and there – all for a hope! The future – may we have one! All participating, everyone to take the blame ... and sometimes praise....'

'Yes, yes,' she says. 'It's the way you put it, Petru – being a renegade.... You've not done anything, but you've asked for reckoning....'

'It's true,' I say, trying to defend myself – 'There's maybe no new sensibility. Not possible, not relevant, no way of facing the unknown ... it's always been unknown, the what's to come, but now, it seems.... Alas, poor Malcolm showed the way, and stumbled, fell, and yes – the day-to-day quite often made him deviate.'

I see some cops – I drop Petru's documents down a drain. It's better not to have an identity – even a false one – that's too respectable.

'I need someone,' I tell Petrunya, the woman's neighbour who's been listening to everything.... 'To treat me as newborn, to tell me what I have to do when the future comes. I know there have been interviews, big numbers. Sacrifice and virtuous life – but me! What do I do? No one has told me, and I've turned away when someone tried....'

'You need a lover,' says Petrunya, 'to take your mind off, on to his or hers. Not me! I know too much about you, and besides – I don't love, it's a labyrinth, a disappointment, a plum that won't mature ... you have to eat it unripe, serpent-green – and when it matures, it drops off – squash! – on to the ground. Inedible, expired.'

'I know,' I say. 'It's what we all must face, none more often than dear Malcolm. the morning after, how to face the day and take the condemnation for what you did the night before....'

'I have the one for you,' Petrunya says. 'Babigul. And she has lovely twins. But first – the cops. They'll check you out.'

'Wait,' I say. 'I can't take on anyone. It's not the twins, I have no prejudice. I'll tell her, thank you, if you think it's right.'

'Oh,' says Petrunya, 'There's a husband too. The question is – she doesn't speak your language. She started a Romanian, but then they left. Like you. So – no use.'

'I know what I want to do,' I say. 'I've made a few shots, not got far. But – this would be a deviation, unmotivated.'

'People need people,' says Petrunya. 'You must be strong, to have so little and keep going. You come on like a lion, then you worry, and it all falls down. You, me, most everyone.

'Babigul would understand.'

'I'm sure,' I say. 'But she's been spoken for.'

'Oh,' says Petrunya, 'He's never there. He's into dirty tricks – currency, people. It does well but won't end good. She's yawing like a sea-boat. Seeking a shelter, but the rudder's lost. You're not a port, my dear – maybe you're a buoy.'

We laugh.

'There's no war here,' she says. 'There's casualties and walking wounded. People chased and fleeing, making their Parthian shots. If there was war, you and you other boys would all be equal, eat the same crap food, die the same crap deaths, inflict the same crap rapes and wounds and fear and jubilation ... if the machines can win for you.

'Intelligence – that's what you give up when you put on the grey and green, and get the bonnet with the cock-a-hoop tied on.'

'You have to be prepared for that,' I say. 'I am. Everyone that's born should be. The fear, the feeling good – those reveal the secrets of what's going on, but – it's fairyland. The secrets last while the parade goes on – then you're back to guys who climb up ropes, jump through fire, and ladies who pack bombs.'

We laugh some more. Petrunya's a good sort, and I could fancy her, we're both sat here until a squad of cops might invent some law, maybe beat up on me, maybe on her for treachery.

'I'm supposed to know about police work,' I say. 'If they hurt you bad, they have to keep you in until you look normal enough to leave, if you're alive.

'It's strange. They like to pass their time with crooks and crocks.... They enjoy making monsters, keeping them for company.'

'Go with nature,' says Petrunya. 'Nature is trees who feel and talk, then there's our nature – we humans, we aspire, contest. Walk with our legs. Don't force the boundaries, my dear!'

'Don't be afraid, cop,' says Babigul. 'You are the bait. Petrunya wants to kill them all, the cops. She hands guys in, to get an insight, to wheedle, gain confidence. It was too much, you being Petru, like you're the first part of her, her name. It all fits.... You're almost her, and yet you're not at all; nor are you you. And not Zamfir, her man. Shopping you, my dear, is handing herself in and cleansing all responsibility. Yet if you're not you, you're not anyone at all....'

'But I've done nothing wrong,' I say. 'Even much that's good. Or – I've done lots that's wrong, but don't deserve a punishment. Everybody's bad. What do you expect, and how'll you change it?'

'You're my type,' says Babigul, 'A vagabond. Unconnected; come from somewhere, going nowhere. They'll likely beat up on you. Your politics – they're odd, undefined. You're angry?'

'Yes,' I say. 'The laws, the gyring round, the arrogant guys in lace-up boots and Glocks – if she wants help shooting, count me in.... Her mission must be to kill them all....'

'You're unreliable,' says Babigul, 'I'm used to that. Petrunya too; – she and I, it's best when we are bunkies. But there's guys like you that fall off trucks, that have to be accommodated.... See, when she hands you in, it means a lot to you, and next to nix to her.'

Now, that is true. That's what the movies say. That is the truth that's evident and people sail around it as if it was a buoy. Keep it in view, don't hit it, or you'll sink. Homicide or suicide – those are the destinations on the ticket God gave us when we went through the garden gate.... Your spirit, destiny, and luck. we all have these, they guarantee no hour of life....

'Malcolm was always being handed in, or handed on. Albert or Albertine – when you're in Calais, you can be anyone at all. He was one of those old guys with hang-ropes round their necks.... Covered in birdshit, long gone green with being in the rain.

'If you want a new order,' says Babigul, ladling out some gzougou, 'You must be rid of the old. Everyone. I can say that, my dear, and be heard but get away with it. You can't,' she says, twisting my ear. 'You're loose. Like a tile blown off the roof and flipflapping all the way down into the road. The arcana in your memory! A student of holy books; sent down for fondling on the tram.... A suspect....'

'Be rid of them all?' I ask. 'The enforcers. Bullets or barbed wire?

'We're not alone,' Petrunya says. 'Us two. We'll call on anyone who wants a cleaning, *chistka*, purging of the bullies, the armed people who face us down, at times they billy us, at other times – they bully us. Enough.'

'I hadn't thought,' I say. 'My fault! I should have realised the liberation, creation of new sensibilities – requires this cleansing. I'd closed my eyes to details – re-education, patriotic labour, all the necessary stuff. I'm not a part of that, let's hope it's over quick and largely invisible.'

'Don't worry, dear,' says Babigul. 'We're sensible already. We know exactly what to do.'

'I love gzougou,' I say. 'You're not converted, Babigul – usually there's a time you eat it, not every meal....'

'Oh Uwe!' Petrunya laughs. 'The new sensibility doesn't use a calendar. The counting off of days – like irksome tasks, the cadencing of joy and sorrow, a day for this, for that!

'*We*'d celebrate each spin of earth. We eat your food and sing your songs, and fuck you! if you think we do it wrong! There's new criteria for everything, new interdictions, new permissions. Each day is precious, unlabelled, untimed – a day to make and save the future.... What more could you want?'

One of the twins, Radu – a vulgar, philistine type, says. 'Ma has a deputy,' and winks.

Certainly, a politician comes to call, stays, and there's a rumpling sound, and Babigul laughs and smoothes herself when he has gone. He's a support. With money.

Radu says. 'We have to kill and kill, until there's nothing left, and we are top. That is our way.'

‘If there was the Securitate still,’ Petrunya says, and laughs. ‘I’d feed you to them as a snack, Radu.’

‘His brother, his sister,’ I say. ‘Perhaps she or he is not so smart....’

‘Radu?’ asks Babigul. ‘They’re all as bad as one another. Radu should see the world....’

‘Alas,’ I say, appalled, ‘I don’t bring the world with me. Someone – a guide – will come along.... take the Radus....’

We all laugh. ‘Radus are twinned through radiation, that’s what it means,’ Petrunya says.

It’s clear, Radu is toxic, but I’ll load him on my back if necessary, to get away. Here there’s a smell of Malcolm in his poorer days, when resentment and desire for massacres predominate.

‘I’m useful to you,’ says Radu. ‘I’m young – that scares people, scares them off. I’m a source of energy – that helps you, since you’re struggling with your age already. I’m toxic, like all the energy we have invented – I give cancers. That sorts people out, without discriminating.’

‘I grant you, Radu,’ I say. ‘You’re the power I need. But what use am I to you? I don’t know what or how you know. I’m sure you don’t want to see the old buildings made into heritage, larded and farded, ticketed and tocketed with know-all guides and all restored ... you can’t go back and live in those times, you don’t know how to fence, or kill a pig.’

‘Babigul knows all about killing pigs,’ Radu says. ‘Best not get close when she and Petrunya start cutting with their sabres....’

And we laugh. It’ll be a good adventure – like Malcolm’s, ending before dawn.

‘I’m the future, concentrated,’ Radu says. ‘Like all futures, I started with a bang and end with cancers.’

‘What I need,’ I say. ‘Is being able to get out of countries. Especially where there’s been a revolution. I’m sure with a mother like Babigul, you're a revolutionary. So am I. It's when they start to lose the drift, and sink to earth....'

'Leave me in Slovakia,' Radu says. That I shall do.

'A village,' he says. 'With Romans – Romany. What are they, Uwe? Roman colonists coming from the East, where Rome was the indivisible city, magic, floating – Byzantines visiting, giving the name, Fromo Kesaro, Caesar of Rome, to the chief.... Or Afghans. those Ghaznavid armies, defeated by the Mongols, fleeing to the West – the Wessies, always those beaten elsewhere, looking for a patch of land, then finding boats and going further on, Westward Ho! Until they fell off the world....'

'I'll help you, Radu, but you've gone far beyond me, what I know,' I say. 'I'm still in disappointment – Petrunya and Babigul – they were on my side, seeking new sensibility, earning little from their present state ... and yet....'

'Too human.' Radu says. 'Too like everyone and unlike you. Unlike me. You can't take consequences, Uwe. You missed many many days at school ... and all the details passed you by. Your vision – as you approach the revelation, brighter and brighter it will grow, and you'll stumble, fall on the grass.... Your genius will weigh heavy on you. Malcolm the messiah of evolutionary adaptation – it's brilliant, and you'll promote it although it turns out different from what you'll want....'

'Your life among the Romans, Radu,' I say, unwilling to engage in criticism – 'Those Slovak villages.... Not easy. Capricious, even....'

'Without going to the moon,' he says. 'It's the nearest thing to not being here, or where I was.

'You're outside, looking in, and no one cares, no one hopes that you will change, be someone else, or be like them.'

'Keep your secrets, Radu,' I say. 'Some things you can't answer, so you mustn't fudge. Sex, ethnicity....'

'No,' he says. 'They won't pin me down. If it limits me, what I can get, where I can go – it didn't bother Romans, so it ought not bother me. Romany, Romanians – busted empires, everywhere is full of them.'

'It didn't bother Malcolm,' I tell him. '"Where the bee sucks", he said. 'And, "My language marks my species, like the mynah birds' arpeggios marks theirs – if you don't grasp my words, I've gestures...." You're right to criticise me and Malcolm, Radu, I'm convinced. The faults are there, you can do better.... But no one ever does. If they did, everything would improve, always, until ... but it does not. Now – they'll ask you – what you believe in.'

He's looking up the ridges of the baby mountains. There's some low constructions, people, all very young, in clothes too big for them, too small.

Radu has followed fashions, not all consistent – his hair cut one way, the tattoos going from bravado demons to equations, parrots, and blue flowers.

'Listen!' I say, and grasp his thin arm – 'Be very prudent, if they catch you and put you in the files – their questions and your answers make you a personage, a character in theatre, a doppelganger, your shadow – even if you're in a ballet – be aware! Those questions – they cut slices from your soul. As for religion – the unknown and unknowable are always pretext for a war.... Be an animist, like me, it's free and silent....'

But he's already slipped away and gone ... up the muddy hill.

*

'... finding their place in the world....'

Finding the centre, for Malcolm, like the Hopi, like the first Americans – plotting the year, the day, by the sun, the solstices – it was all they thought about. Each day for them, for him –

dawn and dusk the centre. It absorbed them, the approach, the search.... The task of the day, for moderns – it is work. Malcolm didn't do much work, nothing regular or clockbound. There was the fight to wake, hot bright streets to plod along – and then the dark. The passages, the caves, the voices of the moribund, roaring in the pubs, the louche ladies in the clubs, the music, like you hear in conches blown, or in a flower's bell.

I'd ask him, if he were here alive – though I might find a way to ask him dead, unquiet, ever quick to tell a tale, exchange, conceal – the secrets of the dead, how they live with what they know.... I'd ask him. 'The cities you frequent, the mountains, the red birds, the forests ... where are they? Are they full of....'

'Of Indians?' he'd laugh. 'Indians you find in India, you funny boy! Finding the centre, my place in the world. That's my occupation, and it should be yours. What else matters? The cycle of the sun, the years, life, death – the six directions – you should try them all.... Get them in balance....

'The conch is a portal....'

I doubt that he sounded one – but the potlatch ... those, he believed in, every passage, every celebration and ceremony ... hierarchies, new chiefs, the smoke, the drink – at dawn legless, like the quetzlcoatl....

It's a dead end. Useless to seek a parallel. The sun is everyone's. The voracious consumer, the jaguar – is no one's. The jaguar – or something similar – consumed Malcolm. Eaten by nothing – you're dead, but still alive – it's mathematics.

Evolution is a force, like dialectics. Everyone is part of it, subject to it – nature, culture. Those cycles – sun, moon, years, days – those reveal nothing. Those are the flies around the light. How does the light work? No deal. Nothing. It's no help. It does nothing, it's always been there, a word, waiting for itself. The force, that's what you need to know about, that's what drives you, changes your shape – from dapper and sleek to bent and foul.... Evolutionary adaptation – that takes the force – you can't imagine it, or reproduce it, colouring your hair, making your wrinkles, coking your organs, inflating your children, making them fertile, sprinkling inkblots on your brain, making you snarl and weep.

The force kills you – at the start, it makes you. ready to be lit, warmed up – a blob of wax, a cotton wick to burn right through. It kills you, out you flicker, an erratic flame – it kills you, kills everyone, never missed one in millennia, wherever they were hid, however strong, inventive ... and not just you, but every jaguar and every scarab, each yellow rope of milli-legs, each veined orange eye – every specimen of everything, it kills. It is the only device that always works, needs no maintenance, and kills you as you fly high over Jerusalem, or swim in the dark beneath the ice, hide your thin, fragile legs under a rock from midday sun, or in your warm bed as you dream of sex and cosseting.

*

'Kostadin – Guide' it says, there's nothing much to see, still less that needs a guiding.

'He'll be back,' says Kostadin. 'You seek love, I'm sure. He too. Two seekers – surely they will find each other.'

'Oh no,' I say, grasping the theme. 'He could have been my son, my brother. Neighbour, even. Radu – the runaway, who's found his niche. And love? Is that what you can seek and find? Or only seek?'

'Aha!' says Kostadin. 'Philosophy! Now, that's another thing to seek. What you find – is yours alone. Another might say it's just a pebble or – a sunbeam.'

'My inspiration,' I say, off guard, 'Malcolm – you'd think him probably a wastrel, spiv, spy, man about town, a hanger-on, a broken dandy. He speaks to us, he even shows a way ... resilience, acceptance, striving ... I think what Malcolm sought was never love, but – beauty. That's easy to find because it always changes shape. So – losing it is easier than losing love. It doesn't need a brain, a guide, a mug-shot – that's why people pay for beauty much more than they would pay for love.'

'For sure, your boy appreciates your passions and your doubts ... you are his beacon, the angel with feathers reaching to the ground. His ground....' says Kostadin.

'No,' I say. 'He's nobody's. I was convenient, I ferried him from alien shore to where he'd be a curiosity. He likes that. It's him.'

'At all events, you need a guide,' says Kostadin. 'Name me as yours. I'll be what your messiah never was – spiritual and secular both. The world is full of one or other. Your chief, Malcolm, was a secular incarnation – prime quality. I'm what you want – you'll never find a better one. I'm not immortal – just more immortal than you are....

'Just sign here, "I delegate myself...."'

To humour him, I sign. He stamps my signature, and pulls out waxing paraphernalia – drops a red hotspot on my name. There's lots of people round. 'His soul!' I hear. 'His soul, his soul – he delegates himself to Kostadin,' they whisper.

'What does that mean?' I ask.

'Nothing,' says Kostadin. 'It's just an old law. Ridiculous. It says you're mine – body and what's left, if there is any more.... If you want, we'll get you out of what you've signed. It takes a little while – maybe we made an error – the sealing, our mixing blood, you being adopted as my son, though I'm your heir....'

'At least that's right,' I say. 'If I die first, I leave you – everybody – nothing at all....'

'Oh,' says Kostadin, 'It isn't that – it's you working for me all the time before you croak. Ridiculous – but there it is. the law. Your choice.'

'So,' I say. 'I can go off, ignore it all? Value Malcolm? Or despise him, like I sometimes do, more and more....'

'Malcolm's nobody. There's no religious clause,' says Kostadin. 'Believe whatever trickles in. The relationship is legal, it's continental, guaranteed, it follows you wherever – but it's symbolic. You earn cash – I take it, give it almost all back to you.'

'That sounds like wages – but I'm not working for you....' I say.

'Well, in a way you are,' he says. 'We all work for everyone – in a way. Don't stress yourself, don't trouble. Don't be a silly guy who says you make your rules, there's no society, you decide what you do and who you work for. Of course it's so, and not so, if you contradict and don't reason through. You're free to come and go. No one impedes you. But you signed, and I protect you, I look after you. I may suggest some things for you to do, and see you do them properly. It's not a mafia – it's all signed and sealed.'

'Yes,' I say. 'I did it. Now, I'd rather not have. I don't know you....'

'Well,' says Kostadin, 'Now's your chance! You can know me now. I'm not a state, a cop or boss. I'm someone who you trust, is all. Think of me as you would a friend, except it's better. Signed and sealed.'

'To get out of this,' I ask, 'What will you have me do?'

'Oh,' he says. 'From time to time. The thing you mustn't do is follow kooks who talk of freedom and repression, when by talking so, they show – it isn't so! Anything you do is bound by law, accepted by you, printed in this document....'

I start to feel terrified.

'If you don't know what you're looking for,' he goes on, 'Any way of looking for it must be as good as any other. This Malcolm – what would the meaning he may have sought look like if he found onc? What if thc meaning is dour and dire – unattainable by all except the witty Wittgensteins, the parfit Parfitts...? Or the Few? By lot?'

And he laughs – alone. He goes on –

'Imagine, Uwe, that for the progressive world, after enforcing fevered work – the model turns to promoting passivity, to idleness, to holidays and staying cool? You'd stand out – you don't seek work, and yet you're active to a fault. You're not the one to follow a messiah, still less to be one. You're flawed. Anomalous from the start.'

'Yes,' I say. 'You're right. The hunt's the thing. The feast is dull, a gorge on death. The hare ... his stringy thighs remind you of the springy sex you missed out on, the turkey's drooping breast recalls a love eternal forfeited....

'Yes, to eat the wild stuff you have duped and snared – that is the great macabre! The lives of others, sauced with your losses, your faux pas – all served with farce and sage....

'"Eat, you fool! The game! You've lost, eat, puke – the game has the last grave laugh...."'

*

I climb the hill. Radu is there – 'What can Kostadin require of me, Radu?' I ask.

'Anything,' says Radu. 'Anybody can. Can ask any thing at any time.'

'Can I refuse?' I ask.

'Any time. Anybody can,' he says.

'And can he do anything to me?' I ask.

'Anything. At any time,' he says. 'We all can.'

We pause. Then he says. 'Why did you sign? It makes no difference, that's old stuff – but you are bound to him.'

'You're bound to your friends here,' I say.

'I'm happy,' Radu says. 'We have nothing, we're the wretched of the earth. This is the place where I am happy.'

'I'm bound,' I say. 'I am not happy.'

'I know what makes everybody happy,' says Radu. 'We watch the movie in the open. Every two weeks, brought in a van. "Kurenai no buta" – "Red Pig".'

'What's it about?' I ask. 'I'd heard of it, but....'

'Friendship, aeroplanes and anti-fascism,' says Radu. 'It's just the best movie ever. And islands.'

'In any case,' I say. 'Kostadin. Whatever he asks, if I do it or refuse – I have a premonition. I won't make it through the winter, through to next year. So, it matters less and less. Maybe this premonition is all I've caught from Malcolm. But he had a good time with it.... His dream of plenty, going on for ever – socialism, the USSR! The best he could imagine – not only for himself, but all those women too. Skipping communism's difficult bits ... on to being a critical critic, man about town. Evenings with opinions and a glass. Bodies – human bodies, any age or shape – he loved them.

'Most things don't work, don't be discouraged. Who remembers it anyway, dead, all dead, losers all? Don't bet on yourself – it's a rule! Win some? People don't remember those. It all seems eccentric: random.'

'Oh no,' says Radu. 'The Malcolms come through, through everything. Dragons' false teeth, perhaps, sown in a pretty pot.

'Those old guys who fought and croaked and drank and screwed – they played it well. They lost, but kept their honour.... Like in the movie, there's even at the end a glimpse of the Red Pig. It goes on and on. Better and better – just older and older, but a movie doesn't need show that.'

'You're no help to me, Radu,' I say.

'See what Kostadin wants, do it, and you're out,' says Radu, scuttling back up the scarp. To the village on the hill.

'You never thought I was a help,' he says. 'I've a woman now – Iris. I tell her about the project, and Petrunya, Babigul. She thinks they're splendid. Real pioneers. Like the chained women on the railings. On the griddle. And another thing – you know I'm twins – well, here, we're all twins. Twinned. We belong with the indigenes, the Xokleng, in Brazil.'

'I know all about them,' I say. 'They have a marvellous colour sense.'

'We have no goal,' he says. 'No meaning to impose. All our disputes are about trivialities, and we expect no help, no sympathy from anyone. It is ideal. True, it's muddy. But that's nature's way....'

*

'You're in the second rank,' says Kostadin to me. 'You know what you are for?'

'When the first rankers drop, we step forward, take their place,' I say.

'No,' he says. 'When guys in the first files turn to run, you're there to shoot them. That's your job, and why I put the best guys in the front.'

'That way,' I say. 'We lose in quick-quick time.'

'Not me,' he says. 'I am the general. If we lose, I'll be a general, you'll be dead. Moreover, I get to tell the history.'

'I've heard that, Kostadin,' I say. 'Next to yours, though, mine's the best job. The second class. us, the Chekists. Punishers, survivors.'

'It's just examples, Uwe,' says Kostadin. 'Go along with what you signed, you've nothing better, and it's interesting.... Paid as well.'

'You will bury me, Kostadin,' I say. 'I feel your fingers round my heart.'

'Then what you were, are, is not worth anything. That's the lesson. A falling leaf. I can make a big fire with leaves like you,' he says.

*

Modern adventures – about money and territory, and people dropping dead. The deaths are not significant, or interesting, they happen all the time. Ventures. There's no confessions, no true ones. Truth costs money....

*

'It's no more than a favour, then you're on your own. Free,' says Kostadin. 'I owe this odious guy some cash – you take it to him, then you're done.'

'Torn up?' I ask. 'The document? It'll be tough – it's on donkey skin, you still see the tail and hear the bray.'

'Oh yes,' he says. 'Cancel the words – you're free.'

Mister K, the nondescript, the only person in the Balkans who will wear a suit.

I take the bag. 'Is it all good?' I ask, 'No slush?'

'Haha, says Kostadin. 'I haven't heard that word since I was starting out.'

*

The guy who takes the bag, he'll be denounced and taken in. Then *his* guys will take it out on me.

I take the bag, and hand it to a guy – the guy's guy. I'm innocent. I'm wise, though.

*

'This document,' the cop says. 'Your identity. It isn't good.'

'False?' I ask. 'It's surely not.'

'"Not good" doesn't mean it's false. People may be "not good" – it doesn't mean they're fakes,' the cop says. 'Usually, quite the contrary.'

'What do I do?' I ask. 'I belong here. If not here – just say! I'll go there....'

'Go back, that's all,' he says.

'I have no "back",' I say. 'Even my credo's wavering. My hand, my cards – they have no back. They're visible to everyone....'

'Belief in that old roué, Malcolm, is no excuse for anything,' he says. 'Not even stupidity. Back! Go back and start again.'

'Like in a board game, officer?' I ask.

'Yes – but it's you that shakes, and not the dice,' he says. 'Do it at once, or get banged up.'

*

I'm wrong. Everything I do is perverse. No religion and no ideologies, I thought – instead, I'd be inspired by Malcolm, the hedonist. 'Wrong' – I say to poor Mirko's spectral cadaver – 'I've been wrong, misguided, every way. Wrong – not unlucky, like you are. Wrong.'

Now – what is right? When you know what's wrong, what's right should be what's left, self-evident. I cannot work it out. I've done what Kostadin requested – I'm free of him, and being hunted down because of him.

My identity document – my identity – is under threat, so even the last hope, the law, is useless now. Or rather – it is after me.

After the Romanians, beautiful but flighty – should I try Radu's Romans, the village where no one is qualified to do anything at all, there being nothing to do that requires a qualification – and yet they live and sing and squabble, watch Red Pig...?

Renege? I could put Malcolm on a pyre and burn him – he wouldn't feel a thing, he's dead and if he's crucified, he'd just hang there, like they do, smile, look sweet, ask for a drink – and off I'd go, refreshed in the spirit – but of course, best not annoy the Romans....

Whichever way you twist – history will get you ... like going to Afghanistan, and Alexander's soldiers lie in wait, red hair, blue eyes, swallowed another sacred book you didn't write and don't believe....

The philosopher said, 'human life, lived intensely, and to the full, must always be unhappy. Other people make it so, and if you're on your own – it's you who makes unhappiness. It always ends with arms outstretched and empty – wanting the something more, the key. Useless. Besides, your pack is full of keys, they weigh you down. Something more? Inscrutable as birdsong.'

*

They come for me, three of them – vendetta. I was the artifice that brought down their boss. They're right to want vengeance. Do they have orders, will I ever see them ... make my case? I'm very frightened. Maybe they want to catch me, keep me alive. Or worse.

Radu's village is no more in sight – another country I can't enter. I'm not from here, the cops speak to me here in langauges they learn from tapes or discs – there's lots of grammar they don't know. They know some Choctaw, they've seen a pciture of Cahokia, city magnificent under grass –

maybe they'll go there on a holiday. A break from genocide? A few words in Q'eswacha, if I hear it right – there's Incas run the gas station, I run past, my legs wobbling, they wear those pointed woollen hats, they stare as I run by, into the field of maize. The maize – goes on and on, unchanging, intricate.

The avengers don't come in, don't chase after me. Perhaps they have a drone, looking down on me. Perhaps they're all around, more squads rushed in – surround the maize, the wonderful gift. We exchanged it for our catch – an emaciated falcon. It carries her, the goddess who brought the maize – way up, up into the blue, the mathematics ... the maize here seeming just a patch, not a field. On on it goes.

Like me – they weren't from here.

Of course – the first Americans, those Incas – with their human sacrifices ... some gourmet cannibalism, perhaps? They seem so distant. We've stopped the human sacrifices? It doesn't seem so. I might be one. No longer sacrificed to the sky, establishing my place upon the earth – but for reasons quite obscure, banal, or none. Usually ... none.

The cop said I'd prove my innocence if I would spy for them.

'I don't know how or what,' I said.

It's all knowledge, all intelligence, I guess. All good useful stuff. Not suspect, not harmful to anyone, not in the longest run. Everything you know that's valuable is buried with you every minute, eats you like quicklime. Get it out, cough it up....

Malcolm, the dirty devil – he might have thought he brought two worlds together, two cymbals – with a clash that rocked the planet. Or it was for cash? – playing off two corruptions?

On and on I run, the maize is thick, resistant. Above me – are those drones? Bees? – no, bees don't live here now ... those flapping wings.... Not the falcon ferrying the goddess; but mechanical.... How the emperors loved the clockwork toys, the flailing birds, the crawling scorpions ... the emperor Zhongzhong, at playtime....

I hear my enemies – fainter and fainter – the maize is endless – until it's not! I burst out, and – there's the old gas station, but it's not. No Incas, here, they're Malians, Dogons ... a sign says *ESSENCE*. Essence is what I need! I've found the country where....

'My friends,' I gasp, 'Give me an insight! What is the essence – does it lie within? Without? Do we seek it, maybe we are pregnant with it...? Is it us? Or you?'

'Oh,' they say, laughing, 'For the moment, the essence is with us!'

*

Spying. You are the arbiter and protagonist. Spy like Malcolm, scrupulously, for all sides.

Contact the cops. Forget enjoyment, peace to everyone and everything – and spy. If you should overstep – someone will save you, exchange you for someone else, give you more faces, documents, identities....

*

'I've seen this continent,' I tell the Malians, the essentialists. 'It's the best at reason and objectives – biggest massacres, wars of religion and extermination. But I've yet to find the place, the purpose....'

'You're wrong, Uwe,' says Mamadou, pumping gas. 'Places aren't *for* anything, you just live in them, until you must move on. Lives are the same: they're not *for* anything. You live in them until you die.'

'Yes,' I say. 'I thought I'd get philosophy from that. *Carpe diem*, for sure, and see how far you rock the boat before it sinks.... I thought the bit extra might be my discovery....'

'No,' says the lady, Oumou. 'The bit extra is my melon pie.'

It's very good. Original.

'All the people you have met, been defrauded by, or you stole parts of them, and envied them, and knew you couldn't follow where they found a niche,' says Mamadou, 'You're stuck with you yourself, and they've forgotten you....'

'Yes,' I say. 'And some are dead – Mirko, my friend. Some were fritillaries – wavering and frail – Mircea and Petru, almost they weren't anywhere and melted into one another....'

'Into you, I'll bet,' says Mamadou.

'And Radu, who is young and wise,' I say. 'And soon gets to be old and bitter, trapped, resentful and discriminated....'

'Try not to think too much,' says Oumou, giving me more pie. 'If we thought of where we are and where we were, and what's been lost ... what then?'

'No,' I say. 'If this is happiness for some, unhappiness for all the rest – it isn't worth the struggle. I'll pick up the fallen, carry those that lose their legs, their papers or their faith. But nothing more.'

'We'd take you on to help us pump *l'essence*,' says Mamadou. 'But, really – we don't want to. You're trouble. Lazy, too.'

'I'm versatile,' I say. 'I'm at the beginning.'

'And so you'll always be,' says Mamadou. 'We all are, everyone you've met – cunning, intelligent, riding reality, saddled and bridled – all at the beginning and will always be.'

'My friend Radu, went to live with Indians,' I say. 'They had the empire first, now – they are back, at the beginning. He knew....'

'That there's no such thing as melon pie,' Oumou says. 'But mine are excellent. Intelligence can get you far, but only – so and so.... The start, Uwe. We're all stuck there. Pumping the *essence*, seeing them drive away – and then they're back again. Empty. Fillup and empty – off they go and back they come. Everbody knows what *essence* is, and how it's infinite. Maybe it isn't good for you. Who knows – they're always emptied out, and back they come for more.... Don't think it's sad. You can't allow yourself to be depressed. After all – depression isn't cause, nor a solution. It's a hole you must avoid – it's plain enough....'

'I'm fine, Oumou,' I say. 'It's just – your knowing all this – how we never move, back to the start.... Experience told me this – and yet I didn't see....

'Doing a deal with the police; intelligence – maybe it's not so smart. It's a set-up, it can't ever work out right, you're not independent, you betray, and everybody knows. Their troubles are all down to you, making things hard for everyone, whatever side.... Whatever identity, it's never so significant – so long as you are insignificant! Who cares? Who bothers who or what you are?'

'Imagine, Uwe,' Oumou says. 'That you can't move around, can't travel, drift, meet us and all the rest. You can't switch imagination off – it all goes on, whatever and whoever rules.... Will you adjust? Survive? Speak?'

'I'll stay the same,' I say. 'Others won't know if I've changed. Do they know now?'

*

I imagine the re-educator. 'Don't you send me to a camp?' I ask.

'Patience,' he says.

Maybe it is 'she' – they stand behind a screen, so you can't tell, can't get revenge. They wear gender-neutral shoes in case you try to guess....

He or she goes on. 'You are a special case. You don't recognise the power, the healing, soothing force of regular, clock-timed work. But, you are familiar with our founding texts – superficial, distorted, naturally, but at least, you've dipped a toe in them.... You slack – but potentially – your head's a loose cannonball....'

'Oh, Schopenhauer?' I ask.

The pessimists – the realists – go down with everyone. It's those who thought there'd be a future infinite, to be invented by the best – those are the simpletons and traitors when it comes to real experiments.

'Work is obedience, recognition of responsibility and the needs of all the rest,' he says. Or she, or – it's irrelevant ... language congeals reality....

'Yes, that's three quite different things,' I say. 'I think in some way I'd go along with each of them – translated, naturally, into what I might have thought. Or – hadn't thought at all – I'm quite naive and unprepared....'

'We haven't time for that,' the re-educator says.

'And yet you should,' I say. 'For after all, that is your work.' My thrust – it doesn't score a point.

'I feel,' I say. 'You, not I, are here to make a case, and that it's me that takes the consequences.'

'I promise you,' he, or she, the re-educator says. 'It's better thus than in the camp.'

'There, you can learn a skill,' I say.

'It's not set up for that,' says the re-educator. 'And you are simple, Uwe. Bound to your stereotypes, picked up on unmade roads. Try something complicated – try Daghestan. Even Yemen. Things hang together in many different ways – it's not just you, falling off your branch, amnesiac.'

'Maybe it's work,' I say. 'Work to be able to enjoy. Malcolm went straight to enjoyment – but it still took hard work. Work to be a good citizen – is quite another goal.'

'Yes,' the re-educator says. 'There's a difference. Hedonism or rectitude. You'd maybe choose rectitude, if you had to – but you don't know how hard conformity can be.... Sacrifice, analysis, distinguishing. Malcolm didn't do that, and he didn't care for differences. States were states, politics meant power he didn't want, didn't have and never would. He couldn't expound and teach. Nor can you. Here, no one listens. Anywhere – any opinion that's deemed valid – must be enforced....'

'What?' I ask, alarmed. 'When can I leave?'

'You don't know it, but you don't want to leave. If you stay you may understand; if you leave, well....' he says, or she, whoever.

'I won't understand,' I finish for the re-educator. 'I'll only see a difference between two similar things, two systems that will kill us all to reach a similar conclusion.... West and East....'

'If you were American or Han, you'd grasp the outlines,' says the re-educator. 'But you put a stretch between your poor grasp, and the comprehensible. Vagabonds – that's your thing. Waifs and strays of vanished polities....'

'It could be Sufism,' I say. 'A caravan, hidden in dust.'

'Half hidden,' says the re-educator. 'We don't approach it. It's not minority – it's boiling. Red-hot. A challenge. Multiform, arcane, convincing. It's where the conflict is – best you talk of dust. Whether a continent is fixed on rectitude or holidays abroad – the marquee that we call "Sufism" – that's the war-tent. There are the generals, there's the map.'

'Oh,' I say. 'I never went to school. I don't know anything I didn't pick up in the street. Complexity seems just conjuring tricks.'

'That's why it's a waste to send you to a camp,' he or she says. 'Besides, they don't exist.'

'I fear no one,' I say. 'It's all a matter of being settled in – what you can tolerate in order to survive.'

'That too,' the re-educator says. 'You're for ever one of us, or one of them – inside the circle anyway, a mere trouble-maker, a sport, a black swan. You never see the other side....'

'Maybe I don't want to go there,' I tell him. 'Maybe I want no part of it, I don't believe or even flirt....'

'That's it,' says the re-educator, 'Exactly. We have a talk. You are convinced. That's it.'

*

That's it for him. Confession time for me? Unforced....

Mirko – can you talk frank and free to a cadaver? There was his woman – she wanted to run through the world. She the athlete – the cinders, asphalt, are the world, the track. Unless you fall, any surface is the same, if you are quick enough. Even grass, the flesh. Fall on that – it's a delight!

Run, run, a scissors: cutting a figure, cutting a rug, cutting and running.... Run so fast you're out of sight, sight unseen, all over in a Jack Flash.

Mirko – wanted to swallow it, the world. Have it for himself, inside. She? ... His woman? For her, being was a pleasure, gift, a nullity that makes a complement, makes up a compliment ... a shadow vertical, in a universe of nullity, non-sentient – space, with its grim contents, lava and acid, dark for a million years.... 'Want sex? – come, it'll be over in a twink, leaves no trace, does you no good, no bad. Get over it.'

For me, it was a simple betrayal. I could have lived my life with her – as traitor. Doubling the enjoyment, they say – secrecy, as Malcolm knew, is blank, unless it's shared and paid and whispered out.

She'd not be there, not be anywhere to leave an imprint.

*

Malcolm was voted in. War-maker, war-leader and -winner. Knew the ropes, slipped out of them. A great man, politico, a Prince – of lightness, knave of tarts. Man of the people, statesman, inspiration – pub-brawler, intellectual, lush. Our boss.

*

Can I confess? There's nothing to confess, and he, Mirko, can't be here. Two bodies interacting, neither contracted or enslaved: maybe belonging everywhere, to everyone. My first and only time – on the track – didn't reach the final, didn't even reach the heat that I feel now....

Run rabbit run.

A puzzle, that's not puzzling to Mirko. I, his companion, fucking his companion. An ever-ending tragedy, subversion, undercutting. Nothing, nothing to be done. It's history. He's dead, we all shall be, there is no mark to leave. Heavy, heavy; for me – it's heavy, though I don't often think of it. You don't need think – there it is, it's you, the silver cup you didn't win.

*

'What do you expect?' asks Florina, falling in step beside me, her hair streaked blonde and red, a grey pack dangled from an arm.... 'To give apologies? You enjoyed yourselves, I'm sure. Took nothing from your friend, maybe added paprika to his mix.

'Did he know? Stray sex – it's a wild card, played infinite times, it's always good, whoever holds it.

'Enjoyment? – it's hard to convince me you and she didn't get off on your transgressing....

'Consider! Those guys massacred on the Great Plains, the sepoys blown from cannon mouths – how the conquerors enjoyed the use of power!

'Apologise? Long after? Those guys, masters of empire? Well, that's another pill of enjoyment. self-satisfaction. You add the enjoyment of doing what you think is right to your enjoyment of being genocidal. Pleasure has more shades than pain, Uwe. Forget the reparations! There are none. Keep schtum! It's best not reveal yourself....'

'The world promoted Malcolm, I am suprised,' I say. 'He seemed all set to die despised – instead, he is heroic.'

I met Florina in his mausoleum – canned monks, the mass in D....

There's a panorama, like they made at Waterloo. An animated map, a battlefield with lights and bangs – for a quarter in the slot, brief flares and sounds; alarms. His little war.

*

Down on the plain, there's guns and tanks. It's a game. You don't see the drones, they take out everything. There's no defence. How do they get the guys to sit inside and be blown up?

'The side that got pushed out,' Florina says. 'And lost the scrubby land – they bought the drones. Now, they have won. Casualties – they matter, they show suffering – and it's the fuse for next time; when you buy more drones, your side that got pushed out may buy even more....'

'I might have guessed,' I say. 'Best be a soldier-sacrifice – you know you are a target; certain death, no loss of legs and arms. The worst is being innocent, civilian – there's accidents and famine ... massacres and lopping off of hands....'

'It's something humankind has always hoped to know – the when and why to die,' she says.

'Don't worry, Florina,' I say. 'I've done nothing. There's nothing to be done. I'm well placed, too. Friends and contacts everywhere.'

'Then you're sick,' she says. 'It's fear. There's nothing to fear – it happens to all of us. We can dream, invent – that means we're mortal. Only divinities just act.

'I think you're afraid of joining, of being who you are, or you could be.'

'I think that's right,' I say. 'You're absolutely right. A few years back, when we didn't know about where we were, the real cosmology, you'd say, it was logical to be afraid. Things went on – dangerous, of course – but manmade. Cold war, extinction. Then we saw there were worse dangers, we could fix the old ones – here's the new cast of challenges. And you're right – I'm not into all this modern stuff, and so there's fall-out. You look for safety, try to creep out to the edge, and naturally – you're odd, teetering makes you seem so – in the balance. If you aren't sick, you're suspicious.'

'It's not that,' Florina says. 'Now, you can do anything you like, but you must look for recognition. Bring it all out into the open. Get an audience.'

'I'm fascinated by Malcolm,' I tell her, trying to get her off her fixations. 'I thought he wasn't just a boss, but symbolised a way of being ... of being in control. Being raffish – it helped him to the top. They said – 'the truth's a ladder missing many rungs.' He used it like the stairway – stairway to heaven.'

I think it's self-evident. She shrugs.

*

'Help me, Uwe,' says Florina.

'Alternative lives?' I ask, to lighten up the discourse. 'I don't do that, Florina. If I do your drugs with you, I'll fall down in the hole.'

'Explanations,' says Florina. 'I may be the only one who's asked. They should be liberating. True freedom is knowing why you can't. What you can – is sailing in a leaky boat.'

'If you ask me for guidance, it puts me in the umpire's chair,' I say. 'That's not the way things are today. Women shall inherit what's left of the earth....' We laugh.

'None of that, Uwe,' says Florina. 'I have money. You don't. You walk – I take the bus. That establishes everything.'

'Two people, walking together, chatting – we shan't get far,' I say. 'Though it's been tried many many times.'

'Oh,' she says. 'I've had all that. I was once married, much in love, twin souls, a ten-year plan. I told him, the first night – 'I love you, Ilyash. But I don't do sex with men'.... He took it bad. There was a marathon of rhetoric. What a come-down! Was it all for that, our passions and our pains?'

'You were right,' I say. 'You were wronged. I'm not one who fiddlefaddles, saying that I see both sides.'

'In any case,' she says. 'Men and women don't like sex. It's like strong drink – the taste is off-putting, but the effect makes it worthwhile. Think of Babylon, the monuments – the men are goats or bisons – the women are in proportion, costly. They don't fit, the men and women not fitted together, never have been. The aesthetic for heteros is a disaster, and for gays – it's sentimental.'

'I'm not into that, Florina,' I say. 'On the road, a stranger isn't asked to comment, so I guess that shows you're right. It's violence and politics, like families where there's no money. Neither of us cares about all that – it'll go on till it stops. We investigate the species – why it began, how it will finish.'

'More or less,' she says, agreeing, I think.

'You're succinct,' I say. 'You leave out more than you cut through....'

'There's no time to work through, set things right, make a pile for someone to knock down,' she says. 'And, Uwe, don't bother with the dirty stuff. Malcolm! Albert! – your fixation on other people's fooling us and thinking for us. Forget him.'

'I shall,' I say.

'... if you can,' she says. 'You don't know what deal he cut with all those states – France, the Americans, the Russians. What is clear – they're on to you, Uwe. You're right to run – you'll never beat them – round every bend there's a new eye ... asking you to spy, betray, confess. 'What do you know, or think?' What do you believe?'

'Oh, lots,' I say, quite irritated.

'You are obsessed with Malcolm, how his life came to empower him and subdue us,' she says.

'Maybe it's that,' I say. 'I hadn't got there yet. I'm still involved with truth and credibility, history and metaphor, our genesis and our genetics ... eternal beginning and the pre-established limitations....'

'What might you be?' she asks. 'Nothing. You'll not come good – at anything. They make it so, and you can't know.'

'It's not my game,' I say. 'I don't play.'

'You must,' she says. 'Or end up in a hole. No one protects you. There are no secrets, everyone knows everything. But – you must run, must keep ahead. Think! That's your only projectile....'

'Yes,' I say. 'A cup of porridge.'

*

'How much money do you want to spend tonight, Florina?' I ask. 'My idea is – if little is spent on lodging, we shall be accommodated poorly. That's depressing. If you're rich, it's a falsity, and, it shows you think little of yourself and me ... dossing on the cheap....'

'Yes,' she says. 'I don't have just one forward gear, Uwe. I understand what humanity and money mean. I'm as intricate as you.'

So, we lie down together – under the stars, or – over them. Or ... in sight of enormous quantities of them. It's cold, we hug together, we count some stars, pick out some diagrams, we look for pictures in the sky. Surely in all these years, someone could, freehand, do some arabesques and scrolls.... '"in the time available for our brains..." she quotes ... '"immeasurable spaces, inarticulate nullities, reveal the enduring obsessive puzzling of the species...."'

'Us?' I say. 'The universe, obsessions – all meaning resides in our obsessions, unanswerable questions? All about us? What we mean, beyond the obvious of evolution, automatism ... us machines getting handier, kowtowing to fewer gods, believing more equations....'

'Perhaps it's language,' she says. 'The only carrier bag we have is language. Not spoken, not to anyone, but.... All we have and all there is....'

'Tomorrow, we'll remember Kepler and the cosmos....' I begin, but she already sleeps. We both sleep with Endymion.

*

We eat for free – gherkins, those *castraveţi*: cold vegan sausage. We don't hear a downside, no shouting, crying. Tranquillity. No tragedies.

'Not exactly free,' she says. 'I had to fuck the cook....'

'She didn't cook!' I say. 'Opened a jar and cut a length....'

'I'm a prostitute, Uwe,' she says. 'I work the mausoleum. Malcolm would appreciate me.... I have my work, like him ... I'm paid....'

'Like in Babylon...? A willing sacrifice?' I ask.

'The priestesses became part of the foundations when it all fell down,' she says.

'Malcolm got tired of his good times, became the boss of everyone – at last, said exactly what he thought,' I say. 'He couldn't keep it up – the booze, the orgies, high finance and basement politics. He told his truth – he knew everything, so he could boss us all. There's a lesson there.... He spied on everyone, and in the end the people trusted him! He did everything he thought of, wanted. He reached the top, or bottom. Chivvying us all.'

'You don't have good times, Uwe,' says Florina, 'That's why you overrate them. Him too.'

It isn't so, but not worth arguing.

'I stay here,' she says. 'Best if you do too. Wandering – you've not found anything.'

'It may not seem so,' I say, puffing myself up, 'But I devote my unqualified life to the wellbeing and assistance of all I come across. We know that doesn't work, many say it ought not, others that it should and doesn't. I confess – if there were other dimensions, if reality was not so one-dimensional.... I'd stay. And as it is....'

'Oh,' Florina says. 'You're right. What'd you do here?'

'Put it another way,' I say. 'Judging what we do and what we ought to do – I agree, we can't be judges of ourselves, nor of the laws we maybe follow. We don't make the laws – they appear through grimy glass, if they appear at all. And yet – who else can be the judge of our actions and our interpretation of the rules we follow, if not ourselves?'

'Well,' she asks, 'Which? Who's to judge you – you or someone else? And so what, anyway? The rules, the laws – who makes them? Useless to ask – they are inherited. I never did anything to be judged for. You – you contemplate evil. It's a lake, you don't know where to dive in – you're afraid of being eaten. That's why you're afraid of judgement.'

'I punish myself with useless thoughts, regrets,' I say, thinking of Mirko. 'You're right – it makes no difference. I didn't spy – that's probably a good, but then I didn't strive to find community, when Radu did....'

'You ran,' Florina says, and laughs. 'You're funny. Maybe you should stay.'

'Malcolm was intriguing,' I say. 'Full of tales, but in the end, pure dross. To be avoided, if you can.'

You must believe in something, someone. You don't need trust it, like it. Quite the contrary.

I trusted Malcolm, the bigot, who believed in nothing but himself. I thought it honesty. Why did I value honesty, anyway?

My story – starts here?

*

Time? Or life? The contours, the strategies to move around in either ... do they exist, do they apply? Or to find either, must you bustle? To be a success, even a successful fraud, you have to move around, know people, move from Bowery to Bronx, attend the vernissages, nearly drown in tempests, pay for operations, your, your mistresses and others' mistresses.

Which to pursue? Time?

A satrapy, like Bactria – always on the teeter, always on the edge. Thousands of years – here come the Greeks, who leave the colour of their eyes, their names. True and false. They're Greeks who aren't from Greece. Here come the nomads, mounted, armies like sandstorms – moving through, settling, Buddha and Christ, the Prophet ... the Scythians. Where did they come from, what happened to them? Nowhere. Nothing.

The place – desert, mountains, plains, rivers and rocks – everything thrown down like a handful of geographies on another scattered boxful of cinders and pyrites. Trying sometimes to be a country, usually a force – it takes and holds a shape.... It's a basket shaped by generations of dogs, all different in colour, temperament, dogs with litters, superfoetation, white, black and brown, hunting dogs and lapdogs, biting dogs and barking dogs. No offence, of course – it could be cats. But it's people – seductive and noble, scheming and loyal. Continuity and persistence, limitations, and the invisible clay of our imaginations. Two steps back, always an option.

Or life. While we're briefly here, history is the mountain, and some have a ladle they must use to level it, and of course the mountain's made of us, how we will be, as skeletons, twisted and porous, skinny and brittle and at the most to be inked on as the 'Great'. We'll level nothing, but we'll make another pile of bones, a platform where we stand, survey the mountain range of brothers' bones, and all we want is to be put on the pile we've made, and have another doughty set of bones laid on us, like a cloth of gold.

Love. That's what they say. Don't change the world – find love. Do good, or if you can't – be lovable. And if you can't be lovable, or loved, be 'sympathetic'. I think of Radu, Florina, strong powerful people, maybe a little paler in the shading that they say might deepen into love. There was some sentiment, for sure.

Being *sympa,* helping the wounded, taking off their clothes, and seeing there's a leg that's missing, or a hole in the trunk, like the one here that I have, with acid pus that eats your clothes, unless they're expensive or made of tin or leather....

I haven't got the stomach for a making of the history that anyway will make itself, and so – it's life.

Love.

Being yourself, not trying too hard, not trying harder than your nature, which besides, may not be lovable at all except to dragons, scorpions and unicorns.

'It means doing what I've always done, then,' I say, hopelessly, and Florina says, as she goes back to work,

'No, no. Don't despair, Uwe. It can't mean slummocking along like you have always done.'

'Love – it's very small,' I say. 'A speck.

'Other people, peoples, who weren't known before, or discounted – they seem to know where they are destined. Time – you don't necessarily want it – neither what's gone or what will come. Fear, Florina. That makes us seek some love – it's a necessity. It doesn't cure the fear, but makes us concentrate – upon ourselves ... our leisure and our food, our bodies and their decoration.

'We – the ones who thought we'd mastered time, and space, put them together, made history and the future – we're much smaller, more vulnerable today. Our time is not quite up, but contested as it hasn't been for centuries. Our world fought world wars, had empires, lost them. Now we have to fight for what we eat, along with everybody else.... Fighting dirty? Using power, soft, hard and overpowering, pushing our religion and our scepticism – will we win, or have we already lost, lost vital space, met lines of resistance, limitations, met our end or possibly the end of everything, or ... a smaller space, more vulnerable, more cruel...? Love is the answer that's no answer.

'It's tiny, Florina, maybe fifteen minutes and a shrug, a weekend or an afternoon. A consolation prize that can't console.... A jelly. Any religion trumps it....'

'Then you've lost both, Uwe,' Florina says. 'You lost the history, and can't find love ... or rather, you know you've been looking in the wrong place for history – in peripheries. and people who you can't love, and don't love you.'

'You come out worse than me, then, Florina,' I say.

'I don't think that consoles,' she says. 'And anyway you're no use to me.'

*

'I realise,' I say. 'I don't take account of accidents. Or most other things, that are ordinary, but complicated if you can't explain them, see them – or if you hear about them unreliably long long after ... Petrunya – always a feisty type – she shouted at the truck that backed into her, crushed her against the wall. Easier to move out of the way – but it wasn't in her nature.'

'And you, Uwe,' says Florina, 'All your walking, the jumping down from transport – if they take that leg off....'

'Oh,' I say. 'It won't affect my attractiveness – it'll be below the knee. And there's a waiting list – probably, there won't be time.'

'The people I come across,' she says – 'They have such tales! – duplicity, and treaties made above their head and kept a secret.

'So many people disappeared. You could make a country – no, a continent – of all of those, except ... you never hear from them, pure silence. Do the dead think of us, Uwe? I'm not sure the living do....'

'Thoughts are silent now, Florina,' I tell her. 'Once they might be audible, but silence is the modern way; the key – the "oilèd wards" remember? – soft and silent the key turns and shuts you away.'

*

Looking for life and love. The rusty compromise.

Malcolm had all that, and made history that smelled of nightsoil.

'You're interested in what no one else is,' says Florina. 'That gives you nobility and lasting fame – perhaps.'

*

They come to deport me. I don't know where to go. Do I belong somewhere, and what can that mean? Without documents, or too many of them, you're a dismounted nomad. No yak in sight.

Goodbye, Florina, goodbye Dogons ... 'goodbye' all the civilisations I set foot in, their stories, their laws ... in the air, you're lawless – except, if you go straight down – you're dead.

'This is a good place,' says the guy handcuffed to me, cop or brother. 'It needs people exactly like you are, or you could be.'

This is my recurring dream. Deportation for nothing I might have done. To stop me wandering and set me down somewhere unknown and strange, to start again. It's false, all this. You have to trek, and there's no frontier where they wait to greet you, give you a basket – jars of gherkins, vegan sausage, and a prayer requiring no belief, and no response.

'You're restless, Uwe,' says Florina. 'I'm not. You make me itch. Go away. I'll put you side by side here with Taras – he was restless; now he's found what to do.'

*

'That guy in Spain,' says Taras – 'He built cathedrals, none finished when he died. That's sad, but it signifies – he never ended. That's what I do, I build. I am inspired, a genius. I set up ladders – no one holds them, nothing to lean against – just up and up – into the canopy, into the clouds – and I climb up them. Mostly – the ladders fall, or some you go up so high you disappear. My ladder is the one where you go on climbing, always visible, always leaning on nothing, nothing at all.

'You build – the structures last for millennia, even when they slump down in the grass – you see them, ridges, bumps. Except – the structures that go on and on – castles, churches, bridges – either they're not necessary, or they fall down when it rains....'

'There's not much left,' I say. 'Not that you can make with random materials – from things that have already fallen, or will fall down soon....'

'I'd leave nothing that gathers people up, blows them in and out like leaves. So – theatres, pools, rinks and cycloramas – are out,' he says. 'Conference halls – those are the dregs....'

'The circus....' I start, hesitantly....

'Those dodgem tracks,' he ponders, 'Then there's stadia for gladiators, centrifugal drums, penguin landscapes.... Catwalks for models ... tunnels of love for ghost trains.... All vulnerable to change in fashion, or in sensibilities....'

'The name,' I say. 'Getting your name to stick to built environments ... that's tough.'

'Especially if I have to share with some hod-carrier like you, Uwe,' he says, quite kindly.

'Of course,' I say. 'There's foundations they don't know what for. Maybe they had your uncertainties. There's things like hypocausts. Hypogea. Shamans' listening posts. Geometries – sightlines that are the product – you don't put anything on top – the top's the sun, the sky....'

'Yes,' Taras says. 'Now you're into it! A ground plan – a plain, so extensive you would never cover it with stuff. Your invention, your imagination and vision is the plan, the plain ... and let some other poor idiot try to imagine a building that could be put on it. What principles, what functions...?'

'It's coarsely put,' I say. 'But that makes it more comprehensible. You and I, Taras, know what the product is, what it is to be. Will it be built? Probably not. What does it mean? It all depends. Some cities that seem a cylinder, a rock-face – they look as if they're made for everyone within. The pueblo. Equal protection, equality of citizenship. But it's not so. These places are – were – quite hierarchical. Religion turns mystery to secrecy – the unknown is not a monolith. It's gossip. There's always room for people who are qualified to say they know more about the unknown and unknowable than other guys – and they're the ones that anoint the kings and queens, and choose you, me, to be the sacrifice.... Set the work, allot the tasks, define the castes....'

'Yes, yes,' says Taras. 'So far, so banal. When did you realise you were a target for Intelligence, Uwe?'

'It would fit,' I say. 'Ambiguity abounds.... There's knowing, there's intending. and neither. A suspicion clings. But surely it's not so with me. I know nothing, am of profit to nobody at all.'

'Well, work it out,' says Taras. 'You talk incessantly. You have no judgement, no discretion, you tell everything to everyone. It isn't what you are, it's what you know and how it's told.'

I laugh, not much amused.

'These people that you quiz, Uwe,' he goes on, 'And talk to them about your doubts, convictions ... if you cast doubt on what there is, and say it could have gone quite differently ... surely you see? You are the rat that gnaws the central pillar at the root.'

'There's lots like me....' I start.

'That's so,' he says. 'But there's just one of you.'

'I dismiss all that. Let's work on our grid, the coordinates, the plan,' I say. 'And all the things we shall not build, but of a scale immense, materials hypothetical, made bland by previous use....'

'"Architecture, like music, is based upon a double mimesis,"' Yes!', says Taras, triumphantly – 'Architecture *realised.* It starts by disanthropomorphising, like it's been said. But as a project. unbuilt? Ruined? Buzzing and humming? Eliminate reality! Can we do that? That's why they're after you. Destroy reality – even an outbuilding, the crapper on the balcony. You plan the unbuilt – and so, you realise its unbuilt state. You make real what isn't there! That's immense! Something real that isn't there, but there it is, that's there but isn't – a challenge! It's revolution – terrorism, they call it now....'

'And you, Taras?' I say. 'You jogged me into this.'

'No, no,' he says. 'One sentence was enough from you! History has failed us, Uwe. The promise – broken irreparably. We're merely vipers, jackdaws. Take an example – class struggle. Build and destroy. Where has it gone? Into reality. Into books and into forgetfulness, derision, the unread and printed. Remember, "*Wer Wissenschaft und Kunst besitzt / Hat auch Religion*" ... "who possesses art and science Has religion too". Where did that end, Uwe?'

'It's a terrifying insight, Taras,' I say. 'History makes all our struggles and aspirations disappear into reality. So – we must abolish reality – but....'

'Not as a fantasy,' Taras says. 'But as a project.'

We stare at each other – all the misery of our unbounded, undirected lives is dissipated.

'It's just a slogan, though,' I say. 'It would bring hilarity – not at all what we intend. Or what we mean. Defining the unknown....'

'Potentially residing there....' he says. 'Us. Rent-free.'

We've known each other fifteen minutes, and in that time – have transformed all that we are, have been.

And yet.... And yet, our world is full of people who set their brains upon a liberating march – beyond reality, in maths and speculations of all kinds, where no real objects stand before them, no holes, no overhanging branches.... Have we discovered the familiar, the already-known?

'Yes,' says Taras, 'But I'm a builder too. And now – I've gone beyond the placing of a stone on stone....'

'We'll see,' I say.

Perhaps this too – is not quite me.... A speculative world where suicide and homicide in general can be avoided, consequences foreseen, forestalled, evaded totally ... but....

'Experience shows – it isn't so,' I say. 'The mathematics and the killings go on side by side, and hand in hand.'

'That's all irrelevant,' says Taras. 'The table of extinctions gives the odds. To me, extinction is a detail that will not concern. As Kepler says, the description explains the purpose. We shall make the voyage to the Andes, see what our forebears managed to set up – the diagrams, the landing fields....'

'I quite agree,' I say. 'Extinction comes to each unwelcome and inevitable. But the Andes ... no! No more! They were obsessed with when their time was up. We have become indifferent to all that. Therein, maybe, is the only freedom we have conquered. And besides; the mountains, the deserts, salt and sulphur, the alpacas – I was there, dear Taras....'

I remember the potato patch, the cold, the air you cannot catch and breathe....

From Malcolm's all-too-concreteness to Taras and abstraction, that seems thoroughly explored but always empty.... I have walked a circle. What does it enclose? I'm quite unsure.

*

We plod on, up the track. The lake, at the top, is flat, dark green obsidian. A centimetre deep, a surface atop a surface flat and proofed; quite lifeless, without currents. Not a ripple, though there is a wind. We don't taste, we speculate. Sour apples? A chartreuse? Or a green poison?

Immense, precisely carpentered into its shore – the lake. 'See,' Taras says. 'A calendar of all the time that's ever been, a diary of all the days to come, the portents, divinities, prevalences, high days and holidays; feasts, wars and betrayals....'

'A marvel, Taras, but it's not for us,' I say. 'This is finished, exhausted, false. Shallow – a skin.'

'I can tell you, Uwe, it's an object of my desire,' he says. 'Desire – is insatiable, they say. But if it's endless, maybe it can be transformed? Can extinction come through an excess of coming here? – see! How the lake is hard and sharp!'

'It's the repetition, then, Taras,' I tell him. 'The frequency of coming here, seeing the lake – the same, unchanging, like masturbation – you are repeated, find yourself, and yet – you're different... asserted and confirmed.'

'Yes,' he says. 'I'm its slave. It doesn't know. Is it the object of desire? My desire – or pleasure? Absence, or gratification? Both, maybe: the letting go, the being different and then – the coming home. Familiarity – and yet the lake is mystery.'

'You make it so,' I say. 'It's you, the mystery. Under the lake – there are coordinates – an outline of something quite unknown, unseen – that's the fulfilment of an architecture you know will never enter into a reality, never be a kennel, night-club, gas station. You know it, but you'll never witness it.'

'You have the addiction, Uwe,' Taras says. 'Of wandering, of discontent. It's beautiful, more radical than mine – a dependence complete and unacknowledged. Your slavery, your addiction, Uwe – does it change you?'

'No, not yet,' I say. 'The desire, the pleasure, repetition – that's the start. Addiction means you know there is an "after". A "without". I haven't reached either. They are there. In me.

My time. Like seed corn – potential, till you have consumed it....

'Maybe for you, you think the lake's outside, something you continue to connect with – remembrance and confirmation. The world is real, like the lake, but it's not always there. it need not be. For you – it is ungraspable. It can disappear – it's never here for you. It is a real hypothesis. You believe it, in its enormity, its duration. It's real, and here we are, standing before the lake. When we go down – it isn't there, it's not before you, hard and green, bottle-glass, the desert sand hoisted up ... sharp winds, sharp shards....'

'No, no,' he says. 'Volcanoes made this lake – a flake off this surface, obsidian set in a club, will cut you in a hundred ways. But it won't – that's you and it won't happen. The lake's an immensity, complete, a unity, pacific, untouched, untouchable....'

'It's your mind, in a picture, Taras. Yours and you, alive or dead,' I say.

'Oh,' he says. 'It's indifferent to me, alive or dead. Or, better – it doesn't need to make distinctions between life or death.'

'I envy you,' I say. 'I don't have this – this lake.'

'You understand my inspiration, though,' he says.

'To be a Kepler,' I say. 'A new science is required. You want to be the founder. Not "God is a mathematician", but "a mathematician is God"? With you, Taras, it's intimate, and there's no novelty. We started out to find a basis for our disbeliefs – now, you're the heretic who wants to plunge us into certainties about what is uncertain – abolishing reality means you replace it with your mimesis.... And that's the paradox that shows you've failed.'

'I look for something, Uwe; you seek a nothing where you'll find a stimulus,' he says.

We trek on down, it's cold. The air becomes more robust, our lungs swell out and hurt.

*

'I feel we're wronging someone. Something. Ourselves,' I say, when we are back, sitting by the road that goes round the capital, so fast – you know it was made many years ago, and can't be changed, however perilous it is. I go on,

'We're looking for what may not exist – we plan it should not – exist. And what of all the things we know go on, reported every evening in the news and then forgotten, trumped by atrocities a day before you couldn't believe they could be true, until a history lesson comes and...?'

'It all has happened, over, over....' Taras says. 'It is the species, Uwe. Species: lots are cannibals, lots have problems with too many kids surviving, all have problems with the food and wages. Alas, we realise – the place is not set up right for us.

'Our brains outgrew resources. They always have. Everywhere, I suspect. Impotence and suffering. That's our strongest point.

'You and I – we're not accountable. We don't owe explanations. Anything can happen to us – with no accounting; explanations are quite superfluous. Your Malcolm – he kept no accounts. He found the path to power and reputation by chance; he was unimpressed. Nonchalance, taking the hit, tolerating no shit from anyone....

'That's it. No plan, and no regrets. That's what you sought. And now you want the opposite, because you are a weak flower that grows down in the dark of maize-fields...'

*

'When do we start, Taras?' I ask.

'We've started,' he says.

'We saw the lake,' I say. A skin. Skin from no creature. A shape. Geometry. We saw and wondered – but did not see and grasp the grids, the staked-out deserts, the landing strips for aliens to set their craft.'

'There are no aliens, Uwe,' Taras says. 'You must just accept the differences. I'll sell another Rolex, and we'll fly again and see the lake and be inspired.'

'I thought – the architecture,' I say. 'We'd get lucky – the design – it might be built. An option, anyway.'

'I know about design,' says Taras. 'I can always pull one off. There's enough for me, but not for you. These are all sidelines, but you need them while you think about the big one.'

'That's so true,' I say.

*

I need advice. Florina? She's not there. Her mate, Saleha, says. 'Your philosopher Florina has gone. I don't do curlicues. You want advice? Forget, forget. That's all you can do.'

'Gone? How could Florina go? I had a squad, uncoordinated, but all could be deployed....' I say.

'Life is flowers, Uwe,' Saleha says. 'If you think you've got a sting – fly round, drink from each blossom, and then forget, like they'll forget....'

Forget. Forget being busy building, planning animals, all separate, jostling and shooting one another, starving the weak, neglecting the young – forget. Go back. Go nowhere. We don't have the power and knowledge of the mushrooms cabling the earth beneath us, we're little automata, tiny tools like spanners, screwdrivers – vulnerable and limited.... The trees, the mangroves – they know what they're for and throng around, quite leisurely, being themselves.... Talking together on bad days, not deferring to the boss, not tacking missiles to a launcher and pressing the red knob – doing the job intended. Sex when it matters, or is fun, without gifts, without disclaimers.... Forget. We all know how, it's easier than you think. Let the worms take us, the best joints, let the dingo dogs take what's left, bequeath the name, send it to the poor in poor countries, and on and on. Forget, expunge.

'My profession is forgetting,' Saleha says, coming close to me. 'I can't, I mustn't, do anything I do. So, as a second best, a strategy that stands on failure – I forget.'

'So,' I say. 'Everything you do is new. Is new to you, an invention? A discovery? We think those are the same – maybe it isn't so....

Besides, I think, most people don't know – don't think – that what they do they mustn't do. They don't know what they do – at all. What you are, what you were – it usually isn't made for doing what you do – not if you're a champion, or if you've dug up Brazil, bottled holy water or been a torturer, made things you don't know what they are with hundreds of others, who work all their waking lives at that ... or transferred capitals, or carved them with acanthus leaves....

'Certainly,' she says. 'It isn't so. What is "new"? If there was, really new – how would we do it, how would we know where to put it, if it was?'

'The people I know, Saleha, have all tried to find that out,' I say.

I think of Mirko – maybe he found it, the new; and now he's dead, what happens to it? Radu? He's new; being a Rom or being Roman – that is not. He's changed – in the village they all are. Saturnism: lead poisoning. They all are bowed by it, black and grey their skins; their eyes like agates sunk in coal. You wanted it, Radu – your place, your happiness, smart people who didn't strive excessively ... the Saturn of the golden age, the feast, the games ... instead, the god has a backside, grim and glum, that's what you get....

Florina – is the new a secret? Surely not ... it must be the most known, most explored. It isn't here, if it were, it would be something different. It's registered, and she's an original ... and yet ... she left, silent, all that talk she has, taken off somewhere.... If you want cash, sell TV cards in the market – people don't buy in the shop, the guy sells you the duds, you sell them on. The wages of deceit is hatred, but you know that from the start.

'I am not I,' says Saleha, decidedly.

'I am I,' I say, with equal force.

'Each resists,' she says. 'I'm sure. That's what matters – no fancy stories, no fascists; you know it. Resistance.'

*

'How come you ended up here?' I ask.

'I'm from Djerash,' she says.

'You mean you wish you hadn't left,' I say. 'No one would want to leave Djerash. But it's not so – your accent tells another tale...'

'We all speak in translation, Uwe,' says Saleha, 'Your accent gives no origin away. Does that mean you conceal it? Or have none?'

'I guess for you, it's Artemis,' I say. 'How can you renege on her? A homage it's impossible to cancel! The joyous hunt – that ends in rejoicing and a vegan mortadella.'

'Some places,' she continues, 'Have always been oases, in deserts we didn't make but were created such, right from the start. I find that reassures.'

'Stories are made for that,' I say. 'To reassure.'

'We can change their endings, and their meanings change with it,' she says. 'You can't change the opening, or no one listens. People, though: beginnings all different, ends the same. You, Uwe, never schooled and broken, still, always, a child, awaiting its first day, a primal scenario; wild desires and crimes foretold.... Can we, a society, afford you?'

'I'm not a catalyst,' I say.

'Well,' she says. 'Be careful. You're not a blowhard, tattooed with every chrism of a civilisation – boasting of your individuality, but identical, a photocopy, of millions like.... You're just a guy it's easy to eliminate.... Me? I'm an object of desire. I charge rent. I'm worth. You're becalmed – you have none of my horizons. I – can be interpreted. I'm a dream.'

It could be true – I'd wanted some advice; instead there's Saleha, faceless. Florina's gone. And Taras backtracks – his plan.... It so attracts – something unexplored that solves some puzzles, sets up a clean theory of aunity of forms, expressive structures ... and then he too is off, in full cry after something trivial – a guidebook, a documentary, some poems, travellers' reflections....

'You weren't in Syria, Saleha?' I ask. 'To hear the story told when all the places you have known fall down ... it's like becoming centuries old....'

'It's like being dead, and you are, mostly,' she says. 'You have to hope, in second-class countries, the armies are no good. Except, of course, the soldiers do everything they always have and aren't supposed to do. Wars last for fifteen minutes, or for fifteen years – the soldiers never ever go away.'

'And first-class countries?' I ask her. 'If there are?'

'Oh, anyone can be improved,' she says, 'with practice. But stay away, Uwe. I've told you all you need to know. If you enrol, do not desert. if you desert, wear your old clothes and limp – like you are doing now....'

'I've strong principles,' I say. 'You give me hope there's a way out....'

'No, no, my dear,' she says. 'You haven't understood. No hope, no exit. Start from that, and save yourself some fretting time.'

Mushrooms. It's a dangerous game – we have them every meal. Saleha knows all their networks.

'These little devils,' she says, lifting and peering – a tangled forkful of them, arms and legs, and probably some tails – 'They talk and plot together.'

I'm silent. 'Djerash – it's near the frontier,' Saleha says. 'You can go to Syria from there, or be leaving.'

'That sounds right,' I say.

'Florina's in Marseille,' Saleha goes on. 'The mausoleum was depressing. The canned chanting.... And all about a taradiddling. Great men! They pay well, sometimes they make you work for them. Sometimes they cheat you. It's all up to you.'

'Yes,' I say. 'I know. I know all about great men. I stick to principles – avoid enrolment, and great men. They take your youth. Old age – becomes a mystery, a paradise unreachable.'

'Well,' she says. 'What can you do in a life?'

'What can you do *with* a life? Is that it?' I ask.

'What is a person?' she says. 'That comes before.'

'That's been answered, Saleha,' I say. 'Suggestively, enigmatically. Do you have doubts? Doubts about where you stand?'

'No,' she says. 'But it's worth thinking about.'

'These aren't chanterelles,' I say, spearing some.

'They're called "sheep's-foot",' she says, waving a clump in the air, and downing them.

*

Later, I find a document. 'Saleha. 71 ks. 1m80; relatives deceased.'

It's true. That's her. She has some grey hairs, but no one wants to know. I don't have such a document, but it doesn't seem to add to what I am. Sex, work, nationality? They're important, in different degrees; I'll be criticised for underrating one or more. None seems much use in a document – they're used in identifying the dead or mute. Sex, work and nationality – all written with a finger in the sand.

She's a caryatid, solid, imposing. The others I'd known – Radu was a wisp, Babegul and Petrunya small and mobile. Mirko – dead. Malcolm – a dummy dressed in uniforms.

'I've been mistaken, Saleha,' I say. 'All my life. Mistakes, pratfalls. tumbles and bumbles.'

'And you're just starting,' Saleha says. 'Your latest is Taras. For you, he'll open up his world of absences – equations that don't equate, like rickety chairs ... algorithms that imprison populations, fission that doesn't, evolutions that go wrong – like making more giraffes.... It's how you're created, Uwe – you're jello. If you'd gone to school, you'd have been assigned an outline, a shape. As it is.... You're wrong. We have no history – we are romances, noise and throwing things and then oblivion. It's the mass that counts, Uwe. Look at Florina – she had a difficult life....'

'She never said....' I say.

'So, you would have to make it up.' Saleha says. 'A tale, a fiction.

'Florina was a sewer-child. The sewers there are beautiful, like a metro without the noise. The Romans built them – dry and airy. The problem is the people living in them. They sell you, like your family tried.

'Not individuals, Uwe. Big numbers matter, not walking the dog and hobbies.'

'It would be history,' I say. 'The mass. It's not my experience, and not a narrative that makes much sense.'

Saleha peels off her dirty knickers, sniffs them, replaces with a bright new pair.

'Well, there it is,' she says. 'Bodies are limited. The universe – there's no one out there to talk to, and the same's true for the sea. People are different, like ancient coins buried in a pot. You can study them all your life.

'Or – join the flow! People settled all their life, a house, a hut, a stretch of sidewalk – then sounds the trumpet! The clarion! Everybody on the move! Floods, wars, eruptions, plagues, expulsions! Join them, know yourself, and swim in tides of people....

'Down the hole, into the brig, down to Sewerville, up to the stars.... Your fellows are expecting you!'

*

'I have a plan, Saleha. There's settlements of people who've been displaced,' I say. 'Some like me. Just looking. Uighurs, Haitians, Malians, Afghans, Eritreans, Sudanese, Syrians ... a macedonia of peoples running, slouching, seeking. Slaves and slavers, manumitted, destitute and hopeful, people who cry for their country, people who've lost even its name.... Where do you look for what's no more? In documents, in blood, in memory – an origin, something that can understand you, accepts your existence...? I'll see how a bunch of people start and if they stay together....'

'Just go up the riverbed,' Saleha says. 'Up and up. Don't say you're bringing work or papers to be signed. You'll see them, I've been told, when you see the sails. They set up sails to catch the rain-clouds. There's no boats – they've had enough of those.... Just sails – our rain, of course....'

'I'll have time for my thoughts, and my regrets,' I say. 'I'll bring my wild parade up there, my *parade sauvage*, and have it link to theirs. I'll even write the music.'

'You'll hope it's anarchy,' she says. 'Not with chiefs and shamans – anarchy means you'll all get something, but not enough. Chiefs means you'll be in chokey or in uniform before you get to eat.'

'It's possible, of course, they'll have elected monsters,' I reflect. 'Remembering what's always been. Monsters and their drones, perched like Thors upon their thrones, with thunderbolts that never miss.... Remember the philosopher they bombed with tortoises....'

We laugh. She doesn't remember, and I forget the name. Seedy like Malcolm, generals with pee-stained pants. Did I once think he embodied all our natures, knew the tricks, the weaknesses, and still … and still, we'd have good times...?

We watch nature wither like an aspidistra, the plant of love broken in the turbulence.

Rom, Romanians, romantics – I'm not a Roman, I know that everything returns and nothing returns in its right shape. Poor Radu! Poor me, the spy who wasn't.... Does my hesitancy mean I don't get to choose? Not anything? China, or America ... the choice! Discipline? Or free weapons so you all get to fight it out...?

I see myself in Saleha's mirror – is that me, a grinning used-up old man, setting out and upward – a journey fatal, no return. What will I offer? Not even something I have spied. Nothing that's valuable, so someone would notice I've taken it away.

'I'm just something over 40,' I tell Saleha....

'And look older, much much older,' she says, tilting the mirror. 'Hooch and scams,' she says. 'It wears you down. If you'd wanted to be Malcolm, you'd have grasped the hook when it came dangling. Cranes have a hook to lift you up. You passed ... you've traded hair for wrinkles. A poor choice.'

What school of thought, of evolution, will they be following up there? Hunters and warriors? Or school and work? Philosophers used to fill in the difficulties with appeals to God

– He made the laws and cut you down for disobedience. He didn't last...!

Perhaps the displaced are squatters – not making choices, keeping the place quite clean....

*

I remember the ministry of education – the statue at the door, Laocoon and his sons, struggling with the snakes who struggle most of all, and outside on the parade ground – cadets at drill. It's metaphor, that Laocoon. Accents on ancient Greek, equations simultaneous ... those are problematic, divide the populations into smart and slow. Tough serpents, those. Philosophy brings hard choices, and examples made into statuary even harder and more drastic. Where did those snakes come from? What do they signify? A family reptile-farm gone critical – you see them all the way along route 66: 'crocs and fossils.' Buy one. Keep it in the bath. Remember everything, every trip....

'I'll need a lot of languages,' I tell Saleha, 'But I'm losing the one I'm born with.'

'That's not a problem,' says Saleha. 'Words are getting simpler, a sleeker language is emerging from the babel. It could be another tower, of course, but glass. See right through, as if it's not there. Like Taras says, it is a structure in your head. like all other structures, but it lacks materiality. It has familiarity, though.

'It looks like a tower – a tiny one, all yours. People whispering, of few words, all in the memory. They talk, you talk, you're all one. "Not available in your country", sometimes it says. Language – it must be the same everywhere, including insults.... So, if you don't grasp, just tap, and there'll be light. It's the battery, the connection. Waggle your hand, it'll come back.'

I go on, persevere, to help her – addressing the wrong God, I know....

It's a finger, yours, and writes 'you are weighed in the balance, but you don't tip the scale....' Light – reaches to heaven. You can keep language in your pocket, finger it; you have the finger of God, like they said – 'I feel Thy finger ... and find Thee....' Pocket interpreter full of bright lights. Remember to digitate! Word – that's it! The Word! The Word is Light! Search! there's a word for it, a picture, what you're looking for. Difficult stuff. and complications – what do they serve? Who's bothered with them?

Saleha's not bothered. Knows how to work it when it goes wrong, the checker fails....

'I leave you guys,' I say. 'Taras – will be waiting for me. I am his pal. You, Saleha....' I can't think why we're waiting for each other....

'Taras always needs a new apprentice,' Saleha says. 'Mostly he eats them – you were lucky, Uwe. You're smarter than he'll ever be. Forget him....'

*

Florina returns. 'Is that a kitten?' Saleha asks, quite sharp. 'Not here! Outside!'

'It's a child,' Florina says, laughing, laying it outstretched on the floor. 'Not mine. Property in persons – is not on.'

'It's your responsibility,' Salea says. 'And no messiahs here.'

It cries a lot. It's right to do so, but it is a pain.

'When he grows up,' Saleha says. 'He'll want to fuck you – that's what they say, Florina.'

'He'll need wait his turn,' Florina says. 'Then he'll be welcome,' and we laugh.

*

It's getting cramped here. Am I leaving for the sake of curiosity, or survival? Curiosity: is all that's left.

What do I need to take?

I take Mirko, for company, Malcolm for inspiration. Both have run their course – maybe, seeing that the upward path is stony, I should dump them – leave them – at the start. Death, friendship, early commitments and delusions – they stay with you, anyway. No need to hoist them on your back – they don't do good.

The path is steep. I see above the tall grey walls, a tiny window, a spy-hole, small as an eye. A stripy flag, and there'll be sentinels, no dragon, and no Siegfried. I've been here many times before – what is there to find? I've lived here, seen the groups coagulate, the castes, the classes, politicos and cops, the cafe with philosophers and then it's closed. No coffee, and the backyard stills start up.

They'll copy the town's mausoleum – another Malcolm here embalmed – perhaps a soldier, a Timur, a Tommy, a Napoleon, forgotten or embalmed in memory – the foreheads swelling and full of thoughts; the jaws – determination. they're the first to decompose.

I watch the eagles – Royals, Imperials – targeting the fledglings and the smaller birds. Is that the littlest of them, the *pomarin* – easy to shoot, and slower than the best...? Next for extinction, the most vulnerable.

*

I say, 'I turned back, Saleha. It was all too déjà vu. I can't imagine they will find another way – it's full in there, resources scarce – the warriors eat all the food ... they'll need to found another state – start off with cities, deal with the nomads, set up the feasts, the sacrifices....'

'Yes, yes,' Saleha says. 'Don't insist, Uwe. We planned to celebrate your going, drink to your memory, let off some fireworks, Roman candles probably....' And we laugh.

'I'll just pass through,' I say. 'There's jobs in spying wait for me. We all need some security, there's two sides to everything ... so they say ... serve them both, at once....'

'Oh,' Florina says, laughing and jgging up and down – 'How priestly you can sound, Uwe! You preach, lament, anathematise, and in the end, you wander on. You carry a long spoon, to sup with evil, since you don't carry a tureen.

'Drink some of this *ayahuasca*, fresh from the forest. The Amazonians left it here.... First time, it makes you puke; it crosses frontiers in the brain, and makes us all seem one and interchangeable. A primal scene, my dear.

'We share your endless curiosity. Go to! Your home is here; tomorrow you'll move on. And we're stuck here, the future sealed for us, while you....'

'It isn't all about me, not at all,' I say. 'I've put old Malcolm far behind – and all the other guys who've ended up in mausolea, put on show, cadavers on the slide.... Maybe you're right, Saleha – it's all about what a person is.... It seems quite trivial, when you travel round, but then again.... Quantities – they must have significance.... The masses, numbers – I recognise them all....'

'Real people – persons,' Florina says. 'Don't leave memoirs or memorials. That is the lesson, that is the true history. It matters to you, Uwe, but forget it, like Saleha says. It used to matter to us all – we all must learn. don't suffer for it.'

The drink is nauseous, but it's true – the world swells up and dwindles, all is revealed and then becomes a mystery, then naked as an egg again.... I puke and take another swig ... this time it's better, my head clears. Power. The universe is full of it, quite useless. The stars, red-hot. The guys here we call powerful – they're a joke. Stay clear of them – your life, your livelihood, is nothing to them ... not a crumb.

I'll stay here with Florina, with Saleha, then start off again – maybe go up the path to the new citadel, maybe at a truck-stop I can hitch a ride ... tomorrow morning....

I've found no mystery. Did I look for one?

About the author

John Fraser lives near Rome. Previously, he worked in England and Canada.

www.ingramcontent.com/pod-product-compliance
Lightning Source LLC
Chambersburg PA
CBHW020550310726
48979CB00008B/1165/J

* 9 7 8 1 9 1 4 9 3 8 2 4 5 *